Anawan's Belt

Anawan's Belt

A Novel

By Tom Lonergan

iUniverse, Inc.
New York   Bloomington

Anawan's Belt
A Novel

iUniverse books may be ordered through booksellers or by contacting:

iUniverse
1663 Liberty Drive
Bloomington, IN 47403
www.iuniverse.com
1-800-Authors (1-800-288-4677)

*Because of the dynamic nature of the Internet, any Web addresses or links contained in this book
may have changed since publication and may no longer be valid. The views expressed in this work
are solely those of the author and do not necessarily reflect the views of the publisher, and the
publisher hereby disclaims any responsibility for them.*

ISBN: 9781440143243 (pbk)
ISBN: 9781440143236 (ebk)

Printed in the United States of America

iUniverse rev. date: 5/22/2009

I

Once, the silence was so complete, a man could hear the whisper of a falling star. Benjamin Church, my cousin, told me this. By the time our father's ships had settled at anchor in Plymouth Bay, he'd said, pox and plague had emptied the coastal plain of nearly every Indian. Now our red brothers were again more numerous than us. Together, we'd survived, praying to our different gods, clinging with a shared, uncertain hold to the wild and unforgiving land.

I am Windracer, named by my boyhood friends among the Pokanoket for my shameless childhood boast that I could outrun the wind. The winter my parents died, Church had taken me with him to the village he'd founded on the shores of the wide bay of the Narragansett. He'd negotiated with Massasoit for the land. And with me working as his apprentice, he'd raised the first several houses, welcoming anyone seeking respite from the stern rule of our Plymouth elders.

I admired Church like no other man and emulated everything he did. I carried my musket loosely in my left hand, rather than in my right, ready to bring it to my shoulder and take aim as quickly as he. At my belt, I kept a hunting knife and tomahawk fashioned in the style of the Narragansett. And I wordlessly followed wherever he went.

Yesterday, our happy life was interrupted, however, by news that a young English boy had shot and killed a poaching Pokanoket on his father's farm.

It was Sunday, the first scorching day of summer. And within hours, a band of angry Indians had retaliated, murdering nearly a dozen of our English neighbors beneath the sleepy oaks outside their village meeting house in Swansea.

It was for that reason that I was on my way with my cousin and several others of our neighbors to Swansea where Philip himself, sachem of the Pokanoket, had gathered a menacing war party to besiege the unprotected village. Several miles behind us, the Plymouth militia was coming, we knew. There wasn't one of us who didn't have friends among the Pokanoket. Still the mood was vengeful. White men had been killed and mutilated, a tactic learned no doubt from us.

Beneath our feet were paths I'd trod many times. The Pokanoket Peninsula bordered our own land to the west. And except for the glimmering swath of blue cut from it by Mount Hope Bay, our forest formed an unbroken continuum with theirs. But familiar or not, today it was a terrible new world we entered. The air was suffocating, the tension heavy.

I had hunted this ground many times with my cousin, moving with the stealth of the game we stalked. But never before had my prey been man, red skinned or white. Never before had I chased quarry with the courage, recklessness or skill to do anything but run from me. For the first time in my life, I entered the forest fearing for my own life.

We'd been moving cautiously but swiftly south. From the position of the sun and the thinning of the low coastal pine, I'd guessed we were nearing the head of the Kickamuit River, the last stretch of fresh water on Matapoisset Neck. With the first of Swansea's chimneys coming into view, gunfire suddenly erupted a mile or so ahead. Wordlessly, Church dropped to one knee. With his hand he signaled me forward to his side, pointing to a small riverbank clearing ahead. Just as my eyes focused on the place Church indicated, just as I drew breath to shriek at the horror before me, I felt my cousin clamp his hand tight over my mouth.

"Pokanoket trophies," he whispered.

As I fought for breath, eight severed, scalped heads stared down on me from atop towering spiked poles set hard by the river in the muddy embankment. Beneath the scalped crowns of their skulls, the faces of the murdered Englishmen bore looks of the wild eyed terror they must have experienced at the instant of their deaths. I'd heard of such things, savageries committed during the far away wars of Europe, but never here, never by men I'd known throughout my life as friends.

"This is Philip's work," I breathed.

"Yes," Church answered quietly. "It's meant to scare us off."

If I looked carefully enough I was certain I'd recognize some of those tortured faces. But I dared not. They had been men once, same as me, robbed of their lives, their families. Now they were trophies of Philip's deceit.

"Come," my cousin whispered. "I will not allow those wretched souls to remain as they are."

Once again, I watched Church boldly stand and advance. Though the enemy could still be waiting in ambush for us, he didn't hesitate. The distant gunfire continued, a sign the Pokanoket braves who'd committed this atrocity had returned to burn the tiny village.

"Take these heads down and conceal them," he told me. "The men of Plymouth will make much of this spectacle. But it will do little to speed them forward."

Reaching high over his head, Church eased the first bloody skull from its impalement.

"For this, Philip will have his own head spiked on a bloodied pole," he groaned. "Soon enough."

For the next several minutes, we worked together in silence. There was not one other soul around, no other sound but the sporadic gunfire of Swansea. Even the birds of the forest had been quieted by the violence. We cloaked each head in shrouds of green pine needles and leaves, heaving each spiked pole into the river, erasing all evidence of the Pokanoket barbarity. Then we proceeded south, joining the rest of the colony's volunteers hurrying toward the western flank of the besieged village.

More than twice the size of our town, Swansea was comprised of three clusters of farms, perhaps eighteen to twenty of them, each surrounding a fortified garrison house to which the survivors of the massacre had fled. Separated by the narrow river from the attacking Pokanoket, the town's three crowded garrisons formed the Colony's outermost line of defense.

Foremost among these bristling fortress homes was the Miles garrison, located by a narrow bridge beyond which several of Philip's fighters had concealed themselves to snipe at the garrison's sentries. In the open ground before the house, one man lay dead already, his crumpled body unattended by the bridge. As Church and I swept past, crouched and running, I saw the poor farmer had been shot three times, his arm, back and shoulder torn open in a failed attempt to reach the safety of the garrison.

By the time we crossed the killing field, the main door to the garrison swung open and we tumbled inside among a crowd of dozens of armed men gathered from the rest of the colony. So closely were they packed together, it was difficult to spot a recognizable face. Even when my eyes adjusted to the shadowed space, I found it impossible to untangle the confusion of men. Many were hunters and farmers who carried flintlocks like us. Others were professional soldiers from Plymouth, helmeted men in breastplates carrying heavy European match lock muskets.

Later, with the arrival of Major Bradford and the trained militia of Plymouth, spirits inside the crowded garrison soared. Outside the gunfire continued. Musket balls tore into the heavily reinforced sides of the structure. But with the windows and doors shuttered, Bradford placed marksmen on the second floor to keep the enemy from crossing the river.

"Give the order, Major," one surly brute soon shouted from the middle of the crowded room. "My men will storm the bridge and send those heathen running."

Taking my arm, Church separated me from the swarthy monster who had hurried to greet Bradford.

"Keep yourself well removed from that one," my cousin cautioned me. "He honors no God of man. Murder and mayhem are his commerce."

"Who is he?" I asked watching an unruly crowd of cutthroats gather round him.

"Samuel Moseley," Church whispered. "He commands a force of thieves and pirates, villains paroled by the Plymouth fathers to join us in the fight

At that moment, Moseley looked up and caught me staring at him. Inclining his head toward an enormous Dutchman standing with him, the stout pirate captain whispered something. With his eyes still fixed on Church and me, Moseley then left the major and crossed the cluttered dirt floor to us.

"Benjamin Church," he growled. "I have heard much talk of you across this colony. They tell me you call these red swine brothers."

With his hand clamped firmly on his cutlass, he stepped closer to us.

"I have many brothers in this land," my cousin answered. "Both red and white."

And he squared his shoulders.

"I respect no man who fights hiding behind a tree." Moseley shouted loudly enough to be heard throughout the garrison.

Soon a crowd of Swansea men gathered close around us. I now recognized a few young farmers whom my cousin had taught to hunt and shoot.

"Ben is the best Indian fighter of us," one of them boasted.

"The best?" Moseley's booming laugh drew the large Dutchman to us. "And does he fight them hiding here in this place with women?"

My cousin was a man of varied moods. He was no coward in a fight. But often I'd seen him spend long hours over his bible after an argument. Watching him now, it was impossible to know which cousin it was standing with me. Was it the quiet man of measured temper, or the fury who once killed a mountain cat bare handed?

"Captain Moseley," Church astonished all of us with a wide grin, "ask this question of me tomorrow."

Reaching forward, he clamped Moseley's wrists in his, using his strength to pin the pirate's hands to his sides.

"Save your swagger, sir," he breathed. "You may need it when you face your first scalping knife."

II

As gunfire cracked through the long night, mothers and their squealing children huddled in the rooms above the cramped ground floor of the garrison. Beside me, scores of snoring men lay head to head, their cutlasses and muskets at their sides. For all of us, the dawn could not arrive soon enough. Against Moseley's wishes, a plan had been hatched for Church to assemble a group of men to rush the bridge at first light, dislodge the pesky snipers, and then lead the main army in a rout of the outlaw prince's force. With a stroke, the war could be ended, Philip in chains and on his way to Plymouth.

"Have you ever seen him?" I asked my cousin as we lay together in the suffocating gloom.

"Metacom?" Church spoke Philip's Pokanoket name.

Around us several others stirred in restless sleep.

"He's a man like any other," my cousin whispered. "No taller or more stout than you or me."

Outside, the gunfire had at last begun to quiet, leading me to hope the enemy was withdrawing from the terrifying shadows on the far side of the bridge.

"That is why our Pilgrim fathers do not fear him enough," he said. "They believe he is weak and that his army can be easily routed."

"But you do not?"

"You know those braves as I do," he reminded me. "They will stand and fight as well as any."

"Then why did you agree to lead the morning charge?"

"Because it's our only hope for peace. If the rebel king escapes from here, the war will spread. Every farm on the frontier, every woman and child will fall under Philip's war hatchet."

It was a heavy burden, bearing responsibility for a nation half a century removed from its first tenuous beachhead. Sleep was impossible and I counted anxious breaths until just before dawn when the signal was given for us to rise and leave the shelter of the garrison. Besides Church and myself, we had with us ten other fighters from Swansea, young, unmarried men like me, volunteers ready to protect the children of others.

As the first glimmer of light illuminated the bridge and our path to the opposite bank, we crept from the cover of the garrison's sentries and stole forward. Hardly more than shadows, not one of us dared even draw a breath. Together, we slipped past the body of the fallen farmer, onto the plank deck of the bridge, praying that our enemy had abandoned his positions on the far side.

The bridge at Miles garrison was no more than several yards across. Some days, I'd traversed it so quickly, my eyes so focused on the far bank, I hadn't even noticed the wide pine planks under my feet until they were past. This morning it seemed an eternity that I was on that bridge. I felt as though I were walking in a dream, my feet leaden, until a Pokanoket war shriek tore the heavy air.

In seconds, muskets flashed in the trees ahead and balls ripped the air around my head. Diving from the bridge to the cover of the far embankment, I heard another shriek. It came from behind me this time, not ahead, from one of our own men, not our enemy. And as I clawed the muddy embankment for cover, one of my anonymous comrades tumbled into the river behind me, killed by the Pokanoket volley.

"Daniel?" Church called out to me.

"I'm here." I could barely speak.

"This was a terrible mistake, my cousin."

The air filled with scores more musket balls as additional Pokanoket braves joined the ambush.

"They know we can't go forward or back," Church gasped. "They will soon come to finish us."

Against my leg, the dead fighter bounced on the sluggish river current.

"We have one chance," Church said. "Keep your head low and stay with me. We'll follow the river south until we're clear of their fire and then encircle them."

"Encircle?" My voice was thick with fear. "Why not cross the river below and retreat to the garrison?"

Church didn't answer.

"Stay close," he barked. "Move fast. Don't stop for anything."

In an instant, we were moving through the shallow water to our right. The air thundered with musket fire. But as the enemy shots continued to rip the wooden sides of the bridge behind us, our hopes brightened that they hadn't seen us slip away.

After several minutes of struggle, careful not to disturb the slender reeds that concealed us from our enemy, we at last moved beyond the Pokanoket line of fire. It was then my cousin turned and looked back toward the garrison. Following his eyes, I saw we were still visible from the windows on the second floor. I prayed our friends had seen us, that they would wait and watch, listening for our muskets to signal the springing of our trap. Then they would come to our aid. If not, my severed head could well end up fixed to a pole in Philip's camp that night.

Gathering our troop close around him, Church signaled it was time to leave the shelter of the embankment, to point ourselves away from the river into the forest to complete the encirclement of our ambushers. At the first step from the slippery river mud, we became the invaders, entering land all agreed was Philip's. War was begun. And the only hope for both our peoples was that it could be contained here on the Pokanoket Peninsula.

With my cousin in the lead, the rest of us had only to follow, relying on his sharp eyes to keep us clear of any braves who might be lingering on the enemy flank. We moved fast, uncertain how much longer the ambushers would be deceived into thinking we were still cowering in front of them. As long as their musket fire continued, it would be safe to advance. If the Indian guns quieted long enough for our enemy to realize we were not returning fire, our deception would be quickly discovered. The element of surprise would be lost and we'd be forced to stand and fight in the open.

Every second, every step forward, was critical. Every tree and rock gained secured our advance. The Indians we fought, the boys I'd run with as a child, were no stronger or more valorous than us. They carried the same weapons as we did, used the same tactics, even prayed for success to the same Christian God. It was Church alone who made the difference this day. And we followed him like children.

Soon the Pokanoket gunfire slowed. When it ceased altogether, Church gave us the signal to swing left again, behind Philip's position, closing the trap. I kept my head low, afraid of being seen, afraid also of seeing my enemy before me. Never before had I fired my musket against any man. My apprehension at using my weapon to kill was nearly as great as my fear of being killed.

At last my cousin halted us. Crouching on one knee, he signaled us to take cover behind a row of fallen oak. My position would be on the left flank of our hastily drawn formation. Church took his place at the far end, with the remaining Swansea volunteers spread between us in a firing line extending little more than thirty yards.

Cocking the hammer on my lock, sniffing the powder to be sure it was dry, I finally dared to peek around the tree I'd crouched behind. Immediately before me, a shirtless brave stood from cover, turned toward me, and as I took aim, I fired.

It was instinct that made me kill that day. I felt no hatred when I fired. I felt nothing in fact but the gentle resistance of the trigger, familiar as drawing breath. But when my shot tore through the eye socket of my target, when the Indian's head snapped back and he dropped instantly from view, I nearly wretched.

Again, however, instinct intervened and I ducked back for cover just as several enemy balls splintered the tree in front of me. Kneeling to reload, I heard tramping feet ahead. Assuming the Pokanoket had counterattacked, I hurried to ram powder and shot down the barrel of my musket.

Ignoring every instinct to run, I held my ground as the crash of feet drew closer. If I could deliver one more well aimed shot, if we all managed to stand together and fire one more volley when Bradford stormed the bridge, we might win the day. My hand shook as I powdered my lock, spilling several grains from the tip of my horn onto the ground at my feet. A shrill cry sounded as I rammed home a ball. And I managed to stand and raise my weapon just as a second Pokanoket rushed from the trees ahead.

The Indian was no more than fifty feet before me, running headlong through the underbrush when the air thundered with a second round of shot from Church and the others. The wild eyed native froze, my musket pointed square at his chest. And in the instant before I squeezed my trigger, our eyes met.

It was a moment unlike any I'd experienced. The Indian's eyes were neither fearful nor menacing. Instead they held such unexpected warmth that I found myself unable to fire. I knew those eyes. I'd seen them before. They belonged to no enemy, no man I knew. And in the instant I recognized them, I was rewarded with a smile I remembered from my childhood. It was a woman, a young Indian princess of the Pocasset. She'd been my playmate. Seeing her here, watching her vanish again into the forest so astonished me that I failed to see the first of Bradford's men burst through the trees ahead.

"Why didn't you fire?" one of them shouted.

"It was Wantonka," I murmured.

She'd been just a girl when I saw her last, no more than twelve. Now she was a woman, large eyed and long legged still, but supple and graceful as a goddess, the only person, man or woman, red or white, able to beat me in a foot race.

III

At our first volley, Moseley's pirates had rushed from the cover of the garrison to storm the bridge. At our second volley, those of the enemy left standing between our two forces had fled south. Before us, nearly a dozen Indians lay dead. The bridge had been secured, the garrison and the rest of the town relieved.

"We cannot linger here," Church beseeched the pirate captain. "Philip himself can't be more than a mile ahead."

But despite his protestations, my cousin could only watch as the pirate force scattered to pick among the dead.

"By the time they regroup," Church groused, "Philip will have found the means to escape the Peninsula."

Gathering our battle tested troop, my cousin and I were forced to lead the pursuit ourselves. None of the others who had stood with us stopped to question my judgment in letting Wantonka escape. Many knew her. Those who didn't realized the cost to all of us had the daughter of the Pocasset sachem, Weetamoo, been killed and the Pocasset themselves forced to rise with Philip against us. War was new to us, but not so new that any of us was prepared to slay a comely Indian princess.

Though Church's speed was no match for mine, his hunter's instincts enabled him to cover the uncertain forest floor more quickly than me. And once again, I found myself struggling to keep up as our band of volunteers raced the sun to halt our enemy's escape. Deeper and deeper we penetrated Philip's domain. On and on we rushed until my cousin halted us at last before a large outcropping of rock.

At first I was certain Church would signal us to keep well clear of the stone impediment, careful to avoid any ambushers Philip may have placed in hiding there. But without hesitation, our leader turned sharply toward the wall of granite and, crouching, signaled me to circle to its left while he hurried to the right. If someone were concealed before us, we would rush him.

I moved at once. From what I'd seen that morning, I was more confident than ever of my cousin's shrewdness. Any command he gave, I would follow without question. His quick thinking had gotten me this far. Despite my instincts to turn away from the menacing wall of stone, I knew that following his instructions was the best way to keep myself from being killed.

With a last glance at the top of the granite escarpment, scanning its craggy silhouette for the shape of an enemy shooter or the glint of the sun off the barrel of his musket, I raced to the left. Ducking limbs, crashing through walls of thorny brush, I made no attempt to conceal my purpose. Relying on speed and daring, I rounded the great rock and threw myself into the shadows behind it. To my astonishment, Church had arrived before me. Standing tall, his musket slung loose in his hand, he faced the same lithe goddess who had surprised me earlier at Miles' Bridge.

"Princess?" he called to her. "You left such a clear trail for us."

But Wantonka's bright smile was for me.

"I am sister to you." Her eyes lingered on mine. "To you both."

I was little more than a boy when I last saw her. Arousing little more than a child's love and playful curiosity, she'd been my friend. But now, when her eyes met mine I felt my skin burn.

"When Metacom left the Kickamuit," she said, "I ran from him."

"Tell us where he is," Church commanded.

"At the shore of the Bay. He will fight here no more but will take my mother in his bark across the water to the Great Swamp of the Pocasset."

"You will lead us," Church commanded her.

As my cousin and I flew across the forest floor, still miles ahead of our militia, Wantonka glided before us. Guiding us along several deer paths, she deftly plotted a course determined to confuse any of Philip's war parties. We were racing to snare Philip, not to be snared ourselves. Already we'd outpaced our friends from Swansea. We had but two muskets between us, two quick shots if we encountered trouble. Cunning and stealth were what protected us. And it gave me great pleasure to see Wantonka guide us with such confidence and daring. No white man but Benjamin would have trusted her to lead.

For that reason, no white men but he had the slightest chance of catching Philip.

The farther we went, however, the deeper we penetrated the peninsula without any sign of our enemy, the dimmer our prospects for success. But not until we caught our first glimpse of sunlight glinting off the wide bay of Mount Hope did we slow our pace.

"He's gone," Church growled. "There's no place left for him to be but there."

He pointed across the gently rolling surface of the water to Pocasset territory.

"Weetamoo," Wantonka breathed her mother's name. "She has talked of this day since Wamsutta died. Now she will avenge her husband by hiding his brother's warriors in her swamp."

She spoke of Alexander, Philip's older brother, Wantonka's father.

"We need men and boats," my cousin ordered.

And he turned to lead us back along the path we'd just traveled, north to intercept the sweating force of pirates, soldiers and militia commanded now by Samuel Moseley.

"You are a damned fool to have delayed, sir." My cousin's voice assaulted the pirate captain. "Order up boats now so we can pursue Philip under cover of darkness."

Moseley stood with his arms crossed.

"We will continue south, as planned," he ordered. "If Metacom has fled the peninsula, as you report, we will build a fort to ensure he doesn't return."

Church threw up his arms in frustration. For a moment I feared he'd strike the larger man. From the wild look in my cousin's eyes, I wondered if he feared the same himself.

"My responsibilities are to the people of Swansea," Moseley went on. "I will build a fort on this peninsula to protect them."

Slowly the fire quieted in my cousin's eyes. Straightening himself, he drew a long breath.

"Whether you build your fort or not," he was careful to measure his own words now, "Philip will not return here. He will move north and west to bring his fight to the Narragansett and the Nipmuc."

Moseley stood unmoved.

"Give me my volunteers at least," my cousin pleaded. "The men who stood with me at Miles' Bridge. Let us go after Philip while you build your fort."

"Very well." Perhaps sensing my cousin could not be deterred, Moseley reluctantly acceded to his wishes, providing him boats and two dozen skirmishers to lead across the bay. "But you are not to leave until morning."

That night, my cousin, Wantonka and I slept together among the rocks of the bay shore. At first, a gentle wind stirred, running against the retreating tide, sending tall waves crashing to shore around us. The day had been scorching hot and the rolling sea bathed us in cooling showers of salt spray that had us laughing like children.

It was a miracle of this New World, our home, that we could find such moments of playful solitude amid the savagery I'd seen. Later, when the wind had died and the tide turned, the silence was so complete that we could hear the war chants of the Pokanoket across the bay. Church had been right. Philip was waiting in the Pocasset swamp for us to attempt a crossing.

We built no fire that night, nor spoke a word between us. We lay side by side on a matting of fragrant pine needles, doing nothing to attract attention from the restive pirates nearby, keeping our own thoughts. I'd seen much in the past days. I'd stared on the mutilated corpses of Swazey's Corner. I'd watched a man fall dead at my own hand. So much had happened, so many terrible scenes of cruelty. Yet I could think of nothing but Wantonka. Her skin perfumed the night.

I had little idea what to make of the light she'd illuminated in me. Never had I felt such closeness, not since my mother died. Realizing these might well be the last peaceful moments I would know, I dared take Wantonka's hand in mine. And to myself, I swore I would never allow myself to be orphaned again. In the morning, I would cross the bay with Church. But I would return to this woman, my native princess. And she squeezed my hand so hard in hers, I was certain my thoughts had been her own.

IV

An hour before dawn we were roused by the splash of oars and the whispered salutes of two Bay boatmen summoned by Moseley from Portsmouth to carry us across the bay. Church wasted little time gathering his force and soon I was seated in one of our shallow craft, waiting as our boatmen pulled us from shore, watching Wantonka's now familiar shape slowly melt to nothing in the coming light.

We landed with the sun in our faces making perfect targets for the enemy whose shrieks and cries had disturbed our night. Though the shadowed forests lining the shore could well have concealed hundreds of Philip's braves, no one fired on us. And we left our boats to the same whispered commands and splashing of oars that had signaled our departure.

Pointing south, Church led us along the fringe of the Pocasset Swamp. Soon the sun rose scorching the air, making it difficult to breath. Many of the men began to grumble at our illusive enemy.

"The damnable heat and flies are all we'll have for this day's work."

Church silenced the complainer with a scowl.

"If it's Indians you want, keep talking," he said. "Soon enough you'll bring them down on us."

I knew my cousin had seen the same signs I had, heavily trod trails snaking through the forest, abandoned wigwams filled with cooking ware.

"There are Indians here aplenty," Church confirmed, not taking his eyes from the thick tangle of brush surrounding us. "Not too long and you'll have your hands full."

We had arrived at a newly cultivated field of peas overlooking the rocky shore of the Sakonnet River. At the center of the field, we stopped at a crude stone well to drink. As the volunteers worked to lower a wooden bucket into the cool shadows at the well's bottom, my cousin removed his cutlass and lay it on the ground beside his hat. Suddenly, two Indians appeared from the apron of trees at the far end of the field. One of our men raised his musket, but Church held the man's arm.

"We only want to talk," Church shouted.

But the Indians turned and ran. And as my cousin struggled to hold back our men, several broke ranks and raced into the open field in pursuit.

"Ambush!" my cousin hollered.

After scrambling across the rough ground from the well toward a low rail fence, several of our men had just stopped to fire at the retreating natives when the entire wall of trees in front of them exploded with musket fire. Seeing scores of muzzles flash at point blank range, I dropped to my knees expecting to be killed.

I closed my eyes and thought of Wantonka, of my lost parents and of running free as the wind. The air hissed, the ground thudded with the ambushers' deadly fire. But when I finally managed to open my eyes, I was stunned to see our entire company standing as before. Only their panicked shouts and the acrid gun smoke billowing around them hinted at the storm they'd weathered.

"Save your powder!" Church shouted. "If we empty our muskets they will charge and finish us with their hatchets."

Ignoring a second volley from the concealed warriors, he went from man to man, issuing orders to retreat to the cover of the rocks at the river's edge.

"Stay together and fall back."

We were just three dozen against scores of enemy guns.

"Remain behind with me," Church said as he knelt beside me. "Take careful aim but hold your fire. We will cover the retreat."

Before us the forest became eerily quiet. A rolling cloud of pale blue gun smoke was the only indication of the war party that had fired on us. It was impossible to tell if they had stopped to reload or were gathering to charge Benjamin and me. For several difficult minutes we watched and waited as our comrades clambered toward the river bank behind us. When Church saw that they'd arrived at last and taken cover amid the scattered rocks, he touched my shoulder and nodded it was time for us to join them.

I didn't hesitate. Crouching low and running faster than I thought my legs could carry me, I waited for the trees behind me to explode with enemy shots. In the open we were such easy targets and at every step I marveled that none of the enemy took advantage of the opportunity to fire on us. Daring a quick glance to my right, I saw the reason.

Not more than a quarter mile away, hundreds of warriors spilled from the forest, swarming along a distant ridge toward a flanking position on the riverbank. In minutes, the first of them advanced within range of us, sending musket balls ringing off the ruins of an old stone wall where Church and I dove for cover.

"There must be hundreds," one volunteer screamed.

"We're done for sure," another hollered.

"A boat will come for us," Church shouted to the somber faces peering from behind the scattered rocks. "They will hear the shots and come across."

Those of us still dressed in deerskin jackets stripped to our shirts to make ourselves identifiable from across the river. Perhaps my princess was standing there herself. Perhaps she'd shadowed our progress from the safety of the far bank. She would summon our boatmen to come to our rescue. And once we were saved and together, I vowed I'd never leave her side again.

Why Philip didn't rush forward and finish us was a credit to Church and the fear he inspired in every Pokaoket. Even with great odds in their favor, none of the enemy wanted to be the first to taste my cousin's steel.

"Cowardly redskins," one of the more sturdy of our number yelled from his shallow rock hollow. "If I could but get one clear shot ..."

But he never finished as a hail of shot tore the hat from his head and had all our faces pressed into the sand.

"Gather stone," Church ordered. "Extend the wall to our left or we'll be flanked."

Keeping myself as close to the ground as I could, I struggled to free a boulder from the tight hold of the sand. Prying it loose at last. I managed to roll it ahead of me toward our unprotected flank. Perhaps twice the size of my hat and head, the precious stone rang with well aimed shots, forcing me to keep my face pressed tight to the damp earth as I struggled to heave it before me.

Inch by inch, I worked, as the others grunted and groaned with their own heavy loads. And after an agony of sweat soaked work, we came together at last, heaving, lifting, pushing our granite cargo in place, creating a few precious feet of solid wall behind which we could safely gather more stones.

"We'll have a fine little fortress," Church shouted above the steady scream of ricocheting shot, "but precious little powder to defend it."

Once we had sufficient cover for our troop to gather, my cousin ordered three of our men to fire their muskets in succession, our signal to the boatmen on the opposite side of the river that we were in trouble. Then we would wait, conserving what remaining powder we had for any of our enemy who dared rush us, hoping that some among the boatmen of the bay were brave enough to risk the hail of shot Philip's shooters were certain to fire at them.

Soon a sloop appeared, sailing toward us from Aquidnet Island. Slowly it came, drawn by an on-shore breeze that would make our escape difficult. Several of our men curled in panic, so paralyzed with fear they were unable to fight. All knew of the horrors inflicted on the men of Swansea by these Pokanoket warriors. Were the Indians to guess the situation of our powder, we faced the same hideous fate.

Some men prayed aloud as the sloop drew closer, calling on the God who had nurtured us in this land to help us now. But when the boat arrived within a hundred yards of us, the enemy turned such hot fire on it that the skipper was forced to turn sharply away.

"You there!" Church roared above the steady thunder of the Indian muskets. "Loose that canoe at your stern."

He pointed out a narrow bark lashed to the sloop's gunwale.

"Draw close again and push it to us!"

"I cannot," the boatman cried from his hiding place behind the cover of a bulkhead. "I'll be killed for certain."

"My God man!" one of the others yelled. "You can't leave us. We're nearly out of powder."

"Fool!" My cousin grabbed the man by his collar. "Don't let our enemy hear you."

My cousin's eyes were fierce.

"If you don't dare help us," he screamed across the water, "then leave or I will shoot you dead myself."

If ever blind rage could save the day, I prayed it was now.

"We should make a plan to run for it," one of our panicked comrades pleaded.

"No," Church growled. "If any man abandons this post, I will kill him myself. Fear me more than those cowardly Indians," he spat. "Then we will prevail."

Seeing the timid boatman draw further from shore, the Indians doubled their fire, filling the air with the whisper of speeding shot. For hours we lay trembling beneath a fiery afternoon sun and a deadly storm of enemy fire.

"Look about you, my friends." By now Church had moderated his tone. "Except for the fact that I lost my hat and cutlass yonder."

He pointed to the well in the middle of the pea field where we had stopped to drink. There lay his cherished hat and sword, abandoned during our scamper to the cover of these rocks.

"Except for them not one of us is scathed." he said. "Save your powder for those that choose to die rushing us. And I swear I will bring us all to safety, my hat and cutlass included."

It was an unlikely boast. But it was clear to all that Church believed it.

"Consider this," he shouted. "There must be three hundred of them, by my count, and but twenty of us. They fill the air with their Godless whoops and cries. They assault these stones with shot. And yet they don't dare to come for us. God is watching over us," he loudly exclaimed. "We are his elect this day and he will protect us from this heathen bunch."

Though my cousin did his best to buoy our spirits, I was certain, however, that each of the others shared the same dark thoughts of death as me. Through the long afternoon, I imagined each man must have in his mind images of home, parents and friends, those most dear. As for me, I had no one, save my cousin and Wantonka. The sweet Indian princess flitted through my panicked visions like an angel from my cousin's protective God, commanding me with a remembered smile to be at ease. And at once I knew my cousin had been right. I would survive. I would see Wantonka again. Her vision assured me.

During that fearful standoff, I learned a lesson I hoped would serve me whether I lived but a few minutes more or for decades after. As some of our fellow fighters groveled in the sand between Church and me, I stood eye to eye with death. And with the falling of the burning sun and the lengthening of the cooling shadows from the forest, I slowly lost my fear of it. If my end were at hand, let me earn a glorious death. For the first time, I dared look across our hiding place and toward my cousin. After hours of trembling, my resolve was firm and I felt man enough to meet gaze.

V

"They come," Church said, his dark eyes flashing.

And with a steady hand, he pointed to the darkening outline of Aquidnet Island where a second sloop had put out on the silver surface of the bay.

"Captain Roger Goulding," one of the others shouted.

"I know him," my cousin answered, watching the brave boatman's steady progress. "He is a man for business. He won't leave us here."

True to Church's prediction, Goulding boldly sailed toward us. And over the course of the next several minutes, he maneuvered his vessel into range amid a storm of Indian shot.

"I will float a buoy with my canoe tied to it," he shouted as balls shredded his canvas and splintered the sides of his boat.

Crouching low, moving fast, he managed to slide the slender bark to us. Since the canoe carried but two, our evacuation proceeded at a dangerously slow pace. In their excitement to strike the lumbering craft, however, the Pokanoket shooters fired wildly, their balls landing wide and high of their mark.

Two by two, our comrades scrambled from their hiding places into the canoe. With each trip our group dwindled as Benjamin and I remained behind with the best of our shooters to provide cover for the others. So great was the risk in the dangerous escape that the hopelessly panicked ones of us had to be forced from the ground and dragged out of hiding.

With luck and grit, however, all were moved to safety but Church and me. When it came our turn and I watched my cousin for the signal to stand and run to the river, I was astonished to see him leave the shelter of the rocks and walk slowly into the field of fire toward the stone well where he'd abandoned his prized cutlass. By now, most of our powder was gone. I had but one shot remaining to cover him.

"Cousin," I beseeched.

"I'm for my cutlass and hat," he answered amid a shower of enemy fire. "I will not leave them for those swine to take."

With Church taunting them, the Pokanoket began firing even more wildly than before. Knowing my cousin could outfight any of them, they held their ground, loading and firing their weapons as fast as they could manage. Muskets cracked with a drummer's brisk tattoo. Balls tore the air and thumped into the ground well short of the foolhardy Englishman. But Philip's best warriors were in so great a hurry to slay the bold white man that none took time to measure his powder or aim his weapon carefully.

Striding briskly to the center of the field, Church stooped beside the well, scooped a handful of precious water to his mouth and then swiped his treasured hat and cutlass from the ground. Turning back at last, he quickly drew the reckless enemy fire to the canoe where I was crouched. Shot splattered the water around us as my cousin stepped over the side and began paddling.

"What powder have you?" he shouted from the stern.

"Little," I gasped.

"Load all of it into my musket," he growled. "I will not leave this place without sending at least one of those scoundrels to explain himself to the Almighty."

With none to threaten them, the Pokanoket ambushers began to stream from the forest toward the river. Seeing the embankment soon fill with shrieking warriors, I bent to my task. When I was done, when I'd rammed home what little powder remained, I watched my cousin put aside his paddle and take the musket from me. We were but halfway to the sloop. The others waiting there implored us to hurry. Their shouts could barely be heard above the relentless crack of enemy firearms.

"That one there will pay the price for this day."

My cousin closed one eye, rested his cheek against the stock and took a last long breath.

"Philip," he breathed. "The rogue."

He squeezed the trigger. The lock released. The flint sparked. And the muzzle flashed. But there was too little powder to send the ball farther than the end of the barrel where it fell harmlessly into the water.

"Damnation." Church raised the musket high over his head. And for an instant it looked as though he'd beat our canoe to splinters in frustration.

From their hiding places behind the stout oak sides of the sloop our comrades shouted hurrah as, first myself, and then my cousin clambered aboard. Without rising from the deck, Captain Goulding pulled a rope, filling the tattered remnants of his canvas with a fading evening breeze.

And as we watched in breathless quiet above the railing, the riverbank and the last Indian volleys slowly fell behind. When a final spent musket ball bounced harmlessly on our deck, Church stood and went directly to our captain whom he clasped in a fierce embrace. Never had I seen two men of our colony exchange more than a formal handshake. In a place where even a welcoming smile was unusual, my cousin's display of appreciation was as inspired as his bravery. Soon each of us followed, standing one by one on uncertain feet, crossing the rolling deck to embrace our bewildered savior. And as I clasped Goulding to me, I felt his anxious heart still beating beneath his sweat soaked shirt.

"Thank you," I whispered realizing it was my heart, not his, that I felt.

It was dark by the time we finally landed at Aquidnet Island. We were safe, but miles from where I'd left Wantonka. I longed to be with her, to melt into her warm eyes. But it was far too dark and we were far too spent to travel. So we camped for the night, weary and despondent. Philip was free. The war would spread and, despite our efforts, the colonies would burn with his rebellion.

For the moment, however, war was distant. Tonight was a night stolen from death, a respite not one of us would have dared believe we'd enjoy. None celebrated our escape, however. None spoke at all of what we felt. There was no need to put any of it into words. Some had acted bravely. A few had panicked. And Church had led us with foolhardy courage. Knowing this, we shared a final, hurried prayer of thanks among ourselves and settled into our blankets. And the next morning, though anxious to return to our command, to Wantonka, I accompanied Benjamin for one last farewell to the man who'd saved us from a Pokanoket scalping knife.

When we found him, the worthy boatman was hard at the task of stitching his rent canvas. Standing to greet us, he seemed to have grown a foot. So cramped and bent had we been during the ordeal of our escape the previous night that only now could we take full measure of each other.

"My cousin and I will be forever grateful," Church saluted him.

"Any man would have done as much," the leathery salt water man replied.

As large as Goulding seemed now that he stood before me, his sloop seemed to have shrunk in length and beam beneath him. Such a delicate splinter could never have accommodated its lanky captain and his desperate cargo. So anxious had we been to save ourselves, we must have lain one on top of the other, unaware how crowded we were.

"We will meet again," my cousin told him. "I intend to return with a larger force and make another crossing."

But the other man shook his head.

"You have not heard?" he asked. "Your Pilgrim commander Bradford has commanded his troops to abandon the Peninsula and return to Plymouth. You have been ordered to return yourself," he told my cousin. "They will have you take command of the militia."

Once more I saw the anger flare in my cousin's eyes. Though I was pleased to learn Moseley and his pirates no longer threatened Wantonka or the other friendly natives of the peninsula, I could feel his fury at the lost initiative. And we both raced south, anxious to attend our separate business.

While Church craved to return to harm's way, I longed to remove my princess from it. The scene which greeted us on our arrival at Sakonnet, however, was shockingly different from when we'd departed just two days before. Though signs were plentiful of the presence of our occupying army, stripped and flattened ground, abandoned fires and scattered camp debris, the only souls to greet us were the handful of men left behind to complete construction of the unneeded stockade Moseley had ordered.

What was most troubling was the absence of the friendly Indians who had abandoned Philip to remain in peace. Dozens of them had been present to greet Moseley's arrival. Now not one red skinned one of them, man, woman or child, remained.

"Taken as prisoners to the Colony," one of the builders told us. "By the pirate captain."

"All of them?" I hadn't felt such panic since my escape from the Pocasset Swamp. The image of Wantonka bound and led by a rope like a dog by one of Moseley's foul pirates was suffocating. "Even the young princess?"

The others would not look at me.

"Was the girl taken?" Church roared.

"Same as the rest," one of the builders responded at last.

Never before had my legs felt such desire to be moving. Every nerve and muscle screamed to be off in pursuit of Wantonka.

"Go at once," said my cousin who knew me better than any.

And I didn't wait to draw another idle breath before my feet propelled me east along the path taken by the army. Moseley had at least a day's lead on me. But I calculated his pace, slowed by his train of Pokanoket and Sakonnet prisoners, would be at least half mine. Since a swift Indian runner could cover the path from the Miles garrison to Fort Hill in Plymouth in little more than a day, I intended to reach there by nightfall, in time to overtake the pirate captain before he sold my princess into slavery.

The path was level and firm beneath my moccasins, worn nearly two feet deep into the sandy forest floor by generations of native runners no different from me. Red and white, we were the ones born to the land. Philip, Church, Wantonka, myself. In these rugged forests there were no differences among us. Each was worth what he earned.

Despite the searing heat, I still wore the white shirt that would identify me as an Englishman to any anxious farmer I might encounter. Stopping only once to quench my thirst at a cooling spring along the path, I let loyalty and love drive me harder and faster. I had little idea how to pursue my quest. But from my cousin I'd learned intensity of purpose. Nothing short of death would stop me.

It was nearly sunset when I at last glimpsed the ragged outline of Plymouth's outermost stockade. The first shadows of night were creeping from the forests. In the old Pilgrim village on the coast, meeting house bells were sounding curfew as the officer of the guard readied his men to close the gates of the stockade.

"I am Daniel of Tiverton," I shouted. "I have come to inquire about a troop of soldiers and their Wampanoag prisoners."

The guard's flickering torch swung around toward me, illuminating a sight of unspeakable horror. In the center of the stockade, behind the officer and the open gate, hung the shirtless body of an Indian man. The agonies of suffocation had distorted the poor wretch's face. Only a sign hung from his grotesquely elongated neck identified him.

TRAITOR, it read.

"There are no prisoners here," the officer said. "Inquire at the governor's house. But you will want to wait until morning. Anyone found out this night is likely to end up like that one." He nodded toward the hanged Indian. "Caught stealing eggs at Careswell."

But I didn't wait for the grinning officer to finish. Turning, I plunged downhill toward the coast. Careful to avoid the scattered clusters of rugged beamed houses, I skirted the village, pointing myself north for Marshfield, the home of Governor Winslow.

Blacker even than the risks I faced traveling alone at night was the prospect of bringing my inquiry to the Governor himself. Winslow was a man both my cousin and I loathed. Descended from the generation of Pilgrim founders who had depended on Massasoit, for their survival, Winslow had done much to undo the peace that had existed between our peoples for more than half a century. Unscrupulous, even illegal, activities had enabled the soldier governor to amass significant land holdings at the expense of his Pokanoket neighbors.

In January, I'd accompanied my cousin to the governor's formidable home overlooking the wide salt water marshes where the Green River wound its way into the sea. With us, we'd brought a Christian Indian, John Sassamon, who had been a good friend to us both. Sassamon, who was later murdered, had carried dire warnings of Philip's pending uprising.

Though the articulate native had studied at Harvard College and later taught me at John Elliot's school at Nemasket, Sassamon was dismissed from the governor's presence after the briefest of visits. The friendly Indian's suspicious death shortly afterward had left Church and me convinced that our governor had had more than a little to do with causing this war. Only the most desperate of petitions could have driven me to him this night. And I filled my mind with visions of Wantonka as I knocked at his massive front door.

Though lights burned bright behind his uncontained windows, the governor had withdrawn his latch string for the night.

"Daniel Church," I responded to the challenge from within. "Cousin to Benjamin Church of Tiverton. Returned this night from hot action against Metacom in the Pocasset Swamp."

Foremost, Winslow was a military man. And his door flew open at the promise of news of our campaign on the Pokanoket Peninsula.

"Give me your news, boy."

In contrast to his martial training, the governor was a slender, bookish man. Beneath a graying mane of curly red hair, his mouth and eyes still held the boyish softness that had led many before me to underestimate his steely resolve. Dressed in his nightshirt but still wearing his muddied boots, he stood blocking my entry with his cutlass.

"We were ambushed yesterday in Pocasset." I quivered at the recollection. "We were but thirty men against three hundred."

"Don't exaggerate," Winslow growled. "I've heard rumors running through this colony that Philip has amassed an army of thousands. We are but twenty thousand in all New England. I can't have you panic folks with your tall tales."

"It's true," I managed. "But that's not why I've come."

Winslow stared past me into the night, his mind a dozen miles away.

"A group of loyal natives has been taken prisoner by Captain Moseley," I informed him.

"There are no loyal natives," he barked. "Whether they be Wampanoag, Nipmuc, Narragansett. If some are for this war, they all are for it."

Unable to keep my legs from holding me up any longer, I collapsed to the stone door step at the governor's feet.

"Those heathen of whom you inquire were taken directly to Boston where they will be shipped to the Spanish colony in Cadiz."

"No!" I tried to stand, but slipped back down. "There is a girl among them."

But at the thought of Wantonka, my words failed me entirely. For a moment, I feared the stern old warrior would slam his door on me. I tried to rouse myself once more to the task, but couldn't. Then the governor put his hand on my shoulder.

"You've indeed had a hard fight," he said to me. "Stay the night here. And in the morning there will be a sloop leaving for Boston."

His hand squeezed tight.

"I assume it's your misguided notion to save this Indian girl by marrying her," he whispered. "Very well, if you will act before this mischief escalates I will send you with a pardon for her."

It was as if I were in a dream. I heard his words but could only murmur dumbly, my tongue swollen from lack of water, as Winslow's servants carried me inside the shadowed manse.

VI

The next morning, Winslow kept his promise, instructing his footman to escort me to Plymouth where I took passage aboard a sloop bound for Boston. Amid coiled rope and sodden barrels of salted cod, I took my place in the stern as the amiable Quaker skipper and his son bore me with them north, past Nantasket shoals, through the scattered inner islands of the great bay of the Massachusetts, and into Boston harbor.

It was my first visit to the teeming Puritan town. Clinging to the edge of the sea at the foot of three steep hills, the Bay Colony capital was little more than a foul smelling tangle of shingled homes and beamed warehouses connected by a warren of muddy cow paths. Before it, dozens of vessels, from sleek coast runners like ours to wide beamed, square rigged behemoths, vied to maneuver through the narrow main channel beneath the menacing cannon at Fort Point.

Already the beacon was lighted atop the foremost of the town's three high hills. And the bells at King's Chapel were sounding over the water. But activity at the harbor's edge was undiminished. As barrels of molasses, rum, tobacco and gun powder arrived on the busy wharves, crates of fish, hemp, linens and iron goods, as well as stacks of freshly cut lumber, departed. So great was the bustle that our captain was forced to wait at anchor in the main channel for a berth to open on the choked quay.

Before us a ghastly tarred frigate blocked our way. A hundred yards from its menacing black prow, several long boats bristling with armed men had just pulled from the Long Wharf at the foot of King Street. With a wave of his iron pike, the soldier in the bow of the foremost craft signaled to someone on the deck of the ghostly black frigate. Behind him, dozens of wretched souls, Indians bound in ropes and chains, were crowded on the floorboards between the rowers.

"Wantonka," I cried.

Frantically I searched their down-turned faces for my princess.

"Be still," our captain whispered. "Those slaves are for the *Seaflower*."

He indicated the dark outline of the frigate.

"In my bag I carry a pardon for one of them," I told him. "Must I stand helpless as she's taken from here?"

"They are bound for the Indies," he said. "But that ship will not be leaving soon."

Again he pointed, to the ship's rigging this time where ropes and halyards hung empty of sails.

"Her canvas is off for re-stitching, I'd guess," he said. "There's still plenty of time for you to take your business to the governor."

At that instant, as if God himself had willed it, my eyes settled on hers. Wantonka showed no surprise or fear. Clutching a small boy to her side she nodded her head one time as our boat was at last waved forward to the empty berth just vacated by her long boat.

Without waiting for the bow lines to be flung to the dock boy, I was over the railing and racing up cobble stoned King Street to the governor's manse. The faces of the citizens I met on the crowded walkways, gaunt and bent to their commerce, were unlike any I'd encountered back home. In Plymouth I knew farmers and builders, Pilgrims like Church, with clear eyed enthusiasm for the land and its bounty. In contrast, these Puritan soldiers of industry passed with their eyes turned within, laboring over their thoughts with pious determination.

At the top of King Street one of them directed me to an enormous town house newly roofed and sided with white cedar shakes. Measuring at least forty feet from base to cupola, the governor's quarters dwarfed every other structure in the port. Commanding a wide view of the waterfront and the crowded harbor, the tall building was the boldest achievement I'd known man to have fashioned. Outside, dozens of merchants wearing wide brimmed black hats shouted and railed in the inscrutable language of trade. Inside, sat the governor himself, overseeing the frenetic commerce of his town from a simple, unadorned writing table.

Unlike the sun scorched, foul smelling streets outside, the governor's chambers were cool and fragrant with the earthy smell of fresh cut wood paneling. The governor was working alone by candlelight, the great hall so quiet I was certain he could hear my panting breaths as I closed the door behind me. With a dark look, he raised his eyes from his work and motioned me to him.

"Young man." He spoke with a softness that belied his stern face. "You appear to have come a great distance to see me."

For the first time I took stock of my own appearance. My shirt was torn and soaked in perspiration. My pants were muddied from the ground I'd clung to at the Pocasset Swamp fight. And my moccasins were stained with tar from the deck of the sloop which brought me here.

"From the Pokanoket Peninsula," I told him.

"Indeed?" He dropped his quill and stood at once. "What news have you?"

Governor Leverett was a small man with raven hair covering the collar of his ox-hide coat. He kept a mustache and a spot of a beard beneath his tightly drawn mouth.

"I have come for one of Captain Moseley's prisoners." Speaking the pirate's name caused a chill to shiver through me. "I come with the compliments of my cousin Benjamin Church and a pardon from Governor Winslow."

"And who is this celebrated prisoner?" he asked.

"A Pocasset princess. Daughter of Weetamoo. Granddaughter of the sachem Awashonks." I swallowed hard. "She helped us track Metacom and I intend to marry her."

Behind me the door opened casting a sudden shaft of light across the long room, revealing the shadows of several newly arrived men. Returning to his chair, the governor waved them to his side.

"Well," he told me as he reached for his quill and a blank sheet of parchment. "If she has served us as you say, then it appears you will have your red bride, after all."

His smile lingered as he scratched several lines across the crisp new parchment. While he wrote, I stole a glance at the others who had joined us. Despite the summer heat, they were dressed in the heavy cloth shawls of Puritan elders. Unlike the governor, however, each wore his hair clipped close in the fashion of Cromwell's Roundheads.

"Take this to the boatswain at the wharf." Governor Leverett stood and handed me the freshly sealed document. "Pay him for the girl and he will fetch her."

"Pay him?" I felt the eyes of the others on me. "But I have no means."

The governor squinted through the growing shadows.

"She was sold," he pronounced. "A contract was entered into with the owner of the *Seaflower*."

He eyed me closely.

"You must buy her back," he pronounced.

I couldn't breath.

"Certainly you understand," he continued. "She is the property of our Commonweald. The money she and the other wretches bring will help finance our defense against Philip and his rebels. I am giving you the opportunity to buy her back at the same price for which she was sold. You cannot ask more of this office."

He straightened.

"The *Seaflower* sails in two days," he announced. "Perhaps in that time you can find a lender to provide you with currency."

With little idea where next to turn, I retraced my steps to the waterfront. Perhaps my cousin could have helped me, but it was impossible for me to go to him and return before the *Seaflower* sailed. Dodging the clattering hooves of a passing wagon team, I arrived at the Long Wharf to see that even my friend the Quaker boatman had already departed for home, his sloop passing the great rock promontory beneath Fort Point under full sail.

I didn't know one other soul in the town. Night was descending. And the only person I felt connection with was imprisoned within the cavernous black hulk resting at anchor no more than one hundred yards from where the harbor water lapped the muddy ground at my feet. Rather than forlorn, however, I was outraged, at Leverett, at Winslow, but most of all at Moseley. He'd known of my friendship with Wantonka. He'd waited until I was safely removed to take his vengeance on her and the other friendly Indians.

In anger, I picked up a stone and flung it, watching it splash harmlessly in the water several dozen yards from shore. I picked up a second and then a third, feeling my rage build, hurling each stone farther than the one before. The waterfront was quiet now. The last of the citizens had disappeared in anticipation of the first night watch policing the curfew along the Battery March. I picked up a fourth stone and a fifth. Let them arrest me, I thought. I had no where else to go.

My journey had ended in such failure, frustration so tormented me that when I released the last stone, it flew from my fingers with such force that it sailed well beyond the others. Disappearing against the night sky it landed with a sharp crack against the hated prison ship, bounding with a clatter that echoed through the streets behind me. But incredibly, no one stirred aboard the *Seaflower*. No light was lighted. No martial voice shouted a challenge. And in that instant of deathly quiet, I stripped off my shirt and moccasins, hiding them with my musket before plunging, knife in hand, into the chill harbor.

Growing up on the wind lashed shores of Mount Hope Bay, I'd learned from my cousin to be a strong swimmer. And despite the pull of the uncertain harbor tides, I was able to reach the dark frigate in minutes. Lingering in the water long enough to assure myself all was still quiet on the deck above me, I pulled myself up the coarse anchor line, hoisting myself hand over hand until, with a lunge, I was able to grasp the ship's railing.

Hanging by my hands, my feet touching the whispering tides below, I gathered myself. In the distance, a crier sounded his bell. The shrill clang sounded once and then was lost in the numbing quiet. Drawing a final breath, my knife blade clenched in my teeth like the pirates I was stalking, I pulled myself up and over the railing, landing on my feet before the towering shape of the enormous Dutchman who had stood with Moseley at the Miles garrison in Swansea. His broad shoulders and scowling face were illuminated by the light of a single flaring torch. He held his knife in his hand. At his feet lay the stone I had flung from shore, untouched, waiting for me to retrieve it.

"I knew you would come," he said, his accent heavy through his tangled beard and broken teeth.

I was no match for this giant. After fighting, running, swimming hard, my situation was hopeless. Still, I set my quivering legs, lowered my shoulders and gripped the handle of my knife tight in my fist.

"Now you will fight me?" The Dutchman astonished me with a booming laugh. "I have seen you fight, English. I don't need to see it again. The girl will go with you now."

I gripped the handle of my knife even more tightly as water from my body puddled the deck between us.

"I have nothing to pay you with," I stammered.

"Pay?" Again a smile creased his craggy face. "I don't wish for you to pay for her. I have won far more on my wager than she is worth."

Expecting a deceit, I glanced from side to side to be certain we were alone.

"The others wagered you wouldn't come for the redskin woman," he said.

"You took her to test me?"

"Not me, English. I told you. I saw you fight. I knew it from your eyes that you would come for her. Now go." He sheathed his knife. "And take the boy she keeps with her." He looked over the railing into the dark water. "Though I don't know if he can swim."

I was not about to hesitate. If Wantonka had a boy with her, he would join us. If he couldn't swim, we would carry him on our backs. The pirate bent to open the cabin door behind him and Wantonka stepped from the shadows. She came to me with the same look of certainty I'd seen earlier in the long boat. Like the giant who'd released her, she'd known I'd come for her. And when I squeezed her to me, my dripping arms around her middle, I knew, as they knew, there was nothing else I could have done.

"Go now," the large Dutchman barked.

When at last I managed to pull my face from Wantonka's sweet smelling hair, I saw an Indian boy looking up at me through fierce dark eyes. And without giving me an instant longer to study his face, the boy stepped forward, took Wantonka's hand and pulled her with him to the railing. Immediately, he was gone, over the side, splashing into the darkness below. And with a beckoning glance at me, my princess dove after him.

"We will meet again, English," the pirate whispered as he hoisted me in his great arms and tossed me as easily as I'd tossed those stones into the black night.

Never had I so welcomed the water's cold embrace. Plunging to its depths, I felt myself pass into a new life, carried by tides and currents away with my angel. When I finally kicked to the surface, I saw her silhouetted against the great lamplit counting houses of the Merchants Row. She swam as though she were suspended in air, her slender arms carving graceful arcs in the black night.

Straining to look ahead and behind me, I heard the boy cry out.

"Wantonka," he rasped. "Hurry."

Now I saw him, already on shore, lighted by the torches lining King Street. A better swimmer than either of us, he'd covered the distance to the harbor's edge while I'd fought my way to its surface.

After reaching shore and making a hurried search among the shadows, I managed to find my shirt, my musket and the deer skin pouch in which I carried my powder, shot and valuable letters of passage. I needed to move cautiously, keeping Wantonka and the boy out of sight of the town, circling the three hills of the Massachusetts to the unsettled west side of the peninsula where I hoped to find a boat to bring us across the river.

I was an Englishman with letters of pardon signed by two governors. But due to circumstances of a war neither my princess nor I had wanted, I was forced to sneak like a criminal past the sleeping homes of my own people. If we were discovered, my princess and her charge would certainly be delivered back to the custody of the slave ship.

We moved in silence, not daring even to whisper. Hour after hour, we struggled through tangled oak and pine, over slippery stone outcroppings, keeping the lapping river close as the bells from King's Chapel tolled behind the hills. It wasn't until the first silver threads of light illuminated the sky behind us that we broke through to a long, smooth stretch of shore.

At once, Wantonka stepped to the water's edge and dropped to her knees. At first, I thought she was thirsty and intended to drink. But soon I saw her lift her eyes to the graying sky and move her lips in a whispered prayer of deliverance. Again I didn't know which God she spoke to, the God of my people or hers. For several minutes, the boy and I waited in anxious silence for her to finish.

"Princess," I whispered. "We can't stay here much longer."

But she didn't move. She simply extended her arms and laid her hands, palms flat on the river's surface.

"We must keep moving," I begged, glancing up and down the muddy riverbank for signs of pursuit.

"No," she breathed, her hands still resting lightly on the gently flowing current. "If we keep running we will be lost. We must stop and listen."

Again I tried protesting. And again she refused.

"Sit here by me," she commanded. "Hear the voice of the river."

Closing her eyes, she lowered her face to the sea grass growing at her side. Turning her head slowly back and forth, she caressed her cheeks and forehead with the slender fingers of green. Soon the boy and I joined her, sinking to our knees in the muck, waiting, listening.

"For too many days," she spoke with her face flush in the wavering leaves of grass, "my ears have been filled with the voices of men. Red men. White men. They make a confused sound that blocks the voices of the land and water."

Once more I tried to speak, but she covered my mouth with her damp fingers.

"Shhh," she whispered.

And so I was compelled to oblige her, waiting by her side, listening, not for the sounds of the water, but for the dreaded sounds of men pursuing us. Hers were beliefs so far different from mine, I could only wonder at them. I could no longer argue against them. Only time could prove their worth.

Finally, after several minutes more had passed, Wantonka stood. Gathering several young reeds which she cinched beneath her beaded belt, she then led the way along the riverbank, hurrying beneath the shadowed hills, leading us back in the direction of the rising sun. We had been walking all night and had managed only to circle the peninsula, returning within a mile of *Seaflower's* anchorage. We had found no means to cross the river and were forced to attempt passage through the fortified gate at Roxbury Neck.

A land crossing by way of the neck was doubly dangerous. Not only did we risk capture by Leverett's sentries, but as long as we were exposed to view during the half mile crossing of the sandy strand, we were at the mercy of any citizen with a weapon. Until we reached the cover of Roxbury Woods, we were at risk both to musket fire and pursuing horsemen.

The boy, whose name I learned was Oneka, was Mohegan, sired by a bastard son of Uncas, friend to the English. Oneka had been orphaned when his father had been killed in an earlier fight with the Pokanoket. Not more than ten or twelve, the boy was watchful and stealthy, sneaking ahead and to the flank to scout for trouble while Wantonka and I followed.

When we reached the steamy swamp that fringed Boston's Common, Oneka signaled us to come forward. With a dove's mourning call, he beckoned us to a hidden pond where frogs the size of infant humans swam. It seemed such a sacred place, even in my rush to leave the peninsula I was compelled to stop. These were creatures unlike any I'd seen. And so far removed was this special place of theirs, it was impossible to believe we were surrounded by conflict.

Once again Wantonka stopped to gather grasses for the bouquet at her belt, preparing herself, I guessed, for the ordeal ahead. The guarded gate lay before us, its stockade walls bristling with sharpened poles that towered above us. My chances of passing the sentries with my companions seemed so slim, I slung my loaded musket at my side, prepared for the first time to fire on one of my countrymen if I had to.

Fortunately for us, however, the guards at Roxbury Neck were more concerned by what intruders lay beyond their gates than by those of us looking to exit from within. Their anxious eyes were fixed on the distant hills where Philip was rumored to be gathering an army of ten thousand. They had little interest in anyone, red or white, foolish enough to risk venturing beyond their defenses.

We were just passing the last of the sentries, just stepping onto the unprotected strand beyond the stockade gate when I craned my neck to steal a look at the platform where the sergeant of the guard was stationed. Instead of the cold eyes of the watchful soldier, however, I gazed upon the wild-eyed death mask of an executed Indian, his head impaled on an iron spike.

Before I could gather myself to turn away and take another step I realized the boy had stopped in front of me. Transfixed by the same horrific sight, he seemed to study every detail of the swollen, blackened shape above us. Did he recognize the tortured face, I wondered? Was it someone he loved, or loathed? I dared not ask. I needed to deliver us from this tragic place, not linger before its horrors.

With a whispered word, I coaxed the boy forward, comforted to see Wantonka had not noticed the guardsmen's hideous trophy. And yet throughout our long march across the narrow strand, the image was fixed in my mind. Days earlier, I'd laid with my face pressed flat in beach such as this, surrounded by Philip's army, fearing it would be my head that would end up a trophy of theirs. Now I realized the Pokanoket's was savagery learned from us.

Never had I felt such relief as when I led my new little family from the exposed beach and into the whispering forests of Roxbury Hills. But it wasn't until I saw Wantonka drop to her knees and hug the boy, that I realized how great her own anxiety had been. Seeing her turn her grateful eyes to me I recalled Governor Winslow's insistence that I marry this Indian woman in order to save her. But at that instant I knew that any union proscribed by God or man was meaningless before the bond that held us now. It wasn't through marriage that I'd saved her. Rather it was in saving her that we had been forever joined

VII

Although the children of Taunton were at play in the ripening fields surrounding their meeting house, tension among their parents was great. Philip was said to be everywhere. Every animal cry or stirring in the forest was thought to be one of his murderous war parties. False alarms were sounded daily, sending families racing for the shelter of the nearest garrison. By the time Wantonka, the boy and I arrived at the Plymouth colony village, every adult of the town was haggard and hollow eyed from lack of sleep.

With all of Taunton glaring warily at our arrival, therefore, I chose to build our camp on the outskirts of the town. From one of the settlers I learned my cousin had traveled to Rhode Island where some of the Quakers of Aquidnet Island were said to have just returned from a last attempt at reconciliation with Philip. With little choice, therefore, but to wait here for him, the princess, Oneka and I lay down to rest for the first time in two days.

Beside the pine canopied clearing where we set our blankets, a swift stream carried fresh water to the fields of the town. It was there we bathed and washed our clothes. As the boy slept, Wantonka and I undressed together, allowing our nakedness to be the first shared gift of our new union. Not touching, not even daring to look at one another lest it break the mood, we bent together and splashed ourselves, giggling like we'd once done as children.

Surrendering at last to fatigue, I dressed and lay beside Wantonka, falling

35

into a sleep so peaceful and deep that I failed to hear the clatter of Philip's approaching war party. It was Oneka who alerted us. Creeping to our sides, he pulled us forcefully apart, signaling us to follow him at once. Gathering our things, we scrambled on hands and knees over the matted pine needles, plunging together into the leafy underbrush as the first warrior strode into view. Only exhaustion from his long march from Pocasset could explain the brave's failure to see us. And in an instant, he was joined by others, scores of them, filling the forest around us. Again my heart beat so loudly I was certain one of the enemy would hear it. Closer they came, more and more of them until we were surrounded by hundreds, gaunt and weary, passing like ghosts from hell.

For several long minutes we knelt together waiting for the rebel army to pass. Once Wantonka clutched my arm. With a nod to her left, she drew my attention to the stooped, wild haired figure of a woman.

"My mother," she whispered. "Weetamoo."

At the woman's side strode the body guard Philip had entrusted her to, Nimrod, another of the Pokanoket war captains. Later, I saw one or two of the braves I'd known as boys, many of the same Indians who had ambushed my cousin and me in the Pocasset Swamp. They had journeyed far from their fields of corn and peas. The size of their group had frightened away all the game in their path. Now, exhausted and half starved, they were perhaps even more dangerous than before. And we waited long after they departed, long after the last rustling leaves and cracking twigs could be heard before we dared stand from our hiding place.

"They march to Rehoboth," Wantonka whispered. "We must go there to warn them."

In order to avoid the menacing Indian army we took the long route to warn the people of Rehoboth, a narrow path pointing north toward the Woodcock garrison. We ran together more than three miles in the imperfect light of the moon before breaking sharply to the west and the long ten mile leg to the town.

On a good day, I could cover the distance in just over an hour. But with the slower pace forced by the darkness and my wearying companions, it took longer. Even so, it was barely two hours after we'd been wakened by Oneka that we came upon the first of Rehoboth's inhabitants, three hunters sneaking in the predawn twilight to their hiding stations along the deer path we followed.

At the pace the enemy army had been moving, I estimated we'd have only an hour before they passed in the vicinity of the town. After informing the hunters of the threat, I led Wantonka and Oneka to the manse of Reverend Noah Newman who I knew had gathered around him a strong fighting force when word of Philip's mischief was first received. Wasting little time, the determined Pilgrim minister hurried from his home the instant he heard of the approaching Indians. After sounding the alarm for his men to assemble, he then informed me of the recent arrival of a swift force of fifty Mohegan led by one of Uncas's sons.

"Together," he said, "our English and Mohegan brothers might well be able to capture Philip and end this madness."

Dispatched at once, Mohegan scouts quickly reported hearing sounds of trees being felled at Nipachuck Swamp several miles to the west. Convinced Philip was setting his camp there, Newman and the Mohegan captain chose to march at once. With his back to the swamp and flanked by two allied forces, our enemy would at last be forced to stand and fight. If we moved quickly and with stealth we could choose our hiding places and do to Philip what he and his ambushers had nearly done to my cousin and me in the Pocasset Swamp.

Crowded by the densely wooded land, we advanced in a column no wider than two or three abreast. Wantonka, Oneka and I followed the main body of the English while the Mohegan maintained their quick pace more than a half mile ahead. The skin on my arms and the backs of my hands was perfumed still with my darling's fragrance and I stole frequent breaths to reassure myself of the miracle of closeness we'd shared just hours earlier. The sun was nearly risen. My head was bent, my princess's hand in mine, safe in the protection of the English rear guard when the first muskets sounded ahead.

"The Mohegan are engaged," the shout came down the line.

But as quickly as they came the sounds of fighting ceased, only to be replaced by the clatter of helmets, breastplates and cutlasses as the entire column tried to break ranks and hurry forward. Then the musket fire resumed with an intensity many times what it had been as Newman and his officers struggled to harness their heavily armed force.

From the steady crack of muskets, I imagined the Mohegan fighters were tangled with the main body of Philip's army. When Newman at last restored order and arrived at the front, his phalanx bristling with long pikes and match locks, the Pokanoket faced a fight no Indian captain would choose. With his back to the swamp and the murderous English closed ranks formations in his face, Philip would be forced to watch his band cut to bits by sure firing Mohegan flintlocks on his flanks.

For many minutes, the English officers maneuvered, creating several tightly packed squares of pikemen and musketeers able to cover a front nearly half a mile across. By the time we found cover in an orchard that flanked a shallow hill, Wantonka, Oneka and I were forced to peer through rolling clouds of dense, blue gray gun smoke to follow the action. Even the boy had difficulty distinguishing his Mohegan brothers from the enemy. Only the white shirts and glinting armor of the tightly packed English were recognizable.

For nearly an hour more it continued, the shrieking and crying of men against the thunder of their terrible weapons. The sun climbed in yet another burning summer sky as I watched tears well in my princess's eyes. Before us lay the worst of all sights. Not only were we powerless to stop the slaughter of red by white, but Wantonka, granddaughter of Massasoit himself, was made to witness the tragedy of Indian against Indian.

With a dark look of his own, Oneka stood and crossed the clearing to where a spring appeared from between two large rocks to feed the wild orchard. Kneeling, the boy took a long drink. His shirtless back was bent like one of his tribe's strong bows, his knotted spine nearly bursting through his tan skin. His was the doomed generation, I was thinking. His was the strong back which in time would bend and break from the agonies the prideful missteps of his fathers and mine would bring.

Suddenly, the boy stiffened. Flattening himself on the ground before the rocks, he motioned to his right. Soon Wantonka was pointing. And after a breathless interval I saw movement in the thickets a hundred yards beyond our hiding place. In the distance, the gunfire had diminished greatly leading me to think clever Philip and some of his warriors had once more managed an escape.

Wantonka swept a knife from beneath her shirt. I crouched low, my musket raised. From his advanced position, Oneka had a better view of whomever approached. I could only wait, watching as he cautiously peered from inside the walls of his rock hiding place, waiting for a sign from him indicating whether we faced friend or foe.

The movement in the thickets drew closer. I strained to see beyond the blanket of foliage that hid us when the boy abruptly stood. Revealing himself to the others, he stepped boldly forward to meet them. Still, I kept my musket at the ready. It wasn't until Wantonka stood that I relaxed my grip on the long barrel.

"Pokanoket," she said as she strode forward to join the boy.

I was reaching for her arm to stop her when a ragged lot of Indian women and children spilled into our clearing. With them was Weetamoo, her eyes fierce beneath the tangled mess of leaves and twigs that had caught in her hair. Standing tall, she marched straight toward me, drawing the others with her like dried leaves on a brisk wind.

"It is you, Daniel," she said reaching her hand back and striking me hard across my cheek. "You bring yourself much shame this day."

With my cheek burning and my eyes filling with tears, I felt like a child before her.

"Nimrod is killed," she said as the others collapsed to the ground at her feet. "Metacom lies wounded at the swamp's edge. Only the greed of the Mohegan in stripping the bodies of our dead have halted the English attack."

She had just reached her hand back to strike me once more when Wantonka caught her wrist.

"I saw you in the forest," the sachem growled at my princess. "I saw you lying with this English and told no one. Now you bring these dogs to hunt us down."

Weetamoo pulled to free her hand but Wantonka held firm.

"The shame is yours," Wantonka said.

The last of the distant musket fire had ended. Still my princess shouted, her strong words forcing the already frightened women and children to cower from us.

"What path have you set for our people?" Wantonka shook the sachem's arm in anger. "And what of these good souls who cling to you now? Christians, they are, most of them. Like the English you fight. Who will save them now?"

Never had I seen her so enflamed.

"Protect them yourself," the old sachem spat. "Otherwise the English will hunt them too."

Wantonka's scowl darkened.

"I will tell you what will happen to them," she told her mother. "I will tell you of the pirate captain who will take them as he took us when you and Philip fled across the bay. Before he sold us to the ghost ship that rode the waves beneath the high hills of the Massachusetts ..." she paused for another shuddering breath, "he took one of our women, a Sakonnet who prayed to the Christian God."

Again Wantonka drew a difficult breath.

"The pirate captain laughed when he heard her prayers," she rasped.

Her eyes were wild, staring blindly into the sun bathed distance.

"Then he gave her to his dogs," she whispered. "And on each of the days after, as he led us tied by the throats to the black ship, he boasted to everyone of this."

Wantonka drew herself up until she stood taller than the graying sachem.

"His dogs pulled our woman to pieces," she said. "While you and Metacom hid in the forests. Now Philip lies dying by the Nipachuck Swamp. And you blame us for this? Go now! If you cannot watch over these people any better than you did that woman leave them to us."

At that, Weetamoo summoned two of her accompanying warriors to her side.

"I have no time to waste here," she told the helpless people at her feet. "I must hurry to our brothers of the Narragansett."

Turning, she next glared at Oneka.

"Now that the Mohegan have joined the English in their fight, my cousin Canonchet will be ready to bloody his tomahawk."

"And these women and children?" I finally found my voice. "What of them?"

By now nearly a hundred had stumbled into our clearing.

"You help them, Daniel," Weetamoo barked at me. "You fix the wrong you did this day."

Then she and her warrior band were off amid the cries of the wretched souls she'd orphaned.

"What will we do?" Oneka asked.

"The same as she." Wantonka pointed to the trail taken by her mother.

"We will take these people to the far side of this hill where we will remain out of sight of the English. We will rest there, feed them from the game of the forest. And when they're ready, we will travel south. To the Narragansett," she pronounced. "The people Roger Williams befriended. They will help us."

What a group we were. Wantonka, princess of the Sakonnet. Oneka, bastard grandson of Uncas. Daniel, orphaned son of the English. And scores of Pokanoket and Pocasset refugees. But with the Mohegan likely in pursuit of Philip north and west up the Blackstone Valley, and Newman's force retuning east to Rehoboth, it was the only way to keep our new charges from a pirate slave ship. In the meantime, given the situation we found ourselves where the cry of a single child could bring disaster on us, we had no choice but to find ourselves a hiding place until it was safe to move.

VIII

There next occurred for me the most pleasant interlude of my life. Not only was I husband to my new wife, father to Oneka, I was also king to an entire people. While war raged around us, my little community was, for the time, safe. Besides the children who were a constant source of spirit and hope, it was the elderly Indians who proved most valuable, men and women who imparted such knowledge critical for our survival, I doubt we could have long endured without them.

After a first restive day and night spent in watchful silence at our camp overlooking the river, earnest activity was begun to feed our starving troop. Stout poles were cut for use by the old men and young women in spearing river trout and bass while the old women scoured the hillside for edible greens, fruits and berries. Meantime Wantonka taught the young children to fashion simple rabbit snares from sticks lashed together with lengths of sinewy vine. And with the musket I'd carried with me since my cousin and I left home, the boy and I tracked game too large for Wantonka's snares.

At night, we huddled together by our fires, listening to the elders tell tales from a simpler time. Of particular interest to me were stories of the Narragansett, the proud and powerful people we were soon to visit. But one night, long after the sun had set and we had fed and bedded most of our flock, Wantonkla and I listened to a tale of a time even more terrible than this, of a lost tribe that once ruled the lands west of the Narragansett.

"Pequod," the old man whispered. "More powerful than the Mohegan and the Narragansett, more powerful even than the Wampanoag before the great plagues."

From my cousin I knew a little of this, of a tribe who once controlled the immense wampum for beaver exchange that dominated the economy of the colonies a generation before mine. So powerful had European demand for beaver pelt made the Pequod that even the English had feared them.

"It was Uncas of the Mohegan who first made mischief with the Pequod," he said, "telling the English fathers lies about them."

He cast a careful glance toward the sleeping boy.

"Even the heart of Miantonomi, sachem of the Narragansett, was turned," he told us. "And soon a great army was gathered. One thousand soldiers of the English and the braves of Uncas and Minatonomi marched to the castle of the Pequod. There was a great fight."

His voice quivered, but his English remained strong.

"Many fell," he said. "More than many."

I was stunned to see the glint of tears in his eyes.

"I was a boy," he told us. "I saw them."

Then he stood and without another word, he left us.

"Do you know this story?" Wantonka quietly asked me.

I told her I did not.

"After a hard fight, the English filled the Pequod castle with their soldiers. They lighted fires in the wigwams where the women and children hid." She took a long breath. "A great wind rose up. Soon everything was burning. And the English made a circle around the fires, shooting any Pequod who dared run from them."

Annihilation. It was a word my cousin had taught me, from the terrible wars of Europe.

"The Mohegan took the Pequod land," my princess breathed. "Uncas became a very big sachem. Now he sends his sons to fight again with the English to slay all my people, as the Pequod."

That night, the forest had a new voice. In addition to the screech of the night owl, the bark of a dog and the cry of the wild cat, I heard the voices of the land's lost souls. They had been people same as me, condemned to ashes. And for the first time, I recognized their dying whispers in the gentle zephyrs that stirred in the trees around us.

"Do not forget," they pleaded. "Do not let anyone forget."

For much of my life, the Indian way had never seemed far different from my own. Though my cousin and I built our house and laid out our fields with

English permanence, we hunted as the red man, dressed as the red man, even spoke much of the native language of the Wampanoag. For that reason, I felt very much at home among my flock. Seeing only Indians, I soon thought of myself as one of them and was astonished whenever I caught my reflection in the smooth waters at the river's edge, or saw the moon glow silver on my arm as it lay across Wantonka's shadowed shape.

Having no contact with the world at war and no interest in naming or counting the days, I had only the incremental shortening of the sun's cycle with which to measure the passage of time. It was for that reason that the appearance of the first russet leaves of fall arrived with shocking suddenness. Soon the cold rains of October would force us to seek shelter among the Narragansett. And a new plan was made to cross the river and move our flock with deliberateness in the dense pine cover of the western bank.

Though it was to be a journey of less than twenty miles, the feebleness of our very young and very old required that we extend it over many days. We would move like an army, with advance scouts setting up new encampments ahead of the main body of our people. Provisions would be carried, parties of hunters and gatherers sent out for game, fruits and berries. And there would be a rear guard of strong young women who would break camp and police our path for stragglers.

Despite our efforts at stealth, however, it became clear on our second day out of camp that we were being watched. Since no English would dare allow such a large body of natives, even harmless women and children, to pass unchallenged, it was obvious that the unseen eyes in the forest were Indian. And since every mile we journeyed drew us closer to the Narragansett, I was certain it was Canonchet himself, the Narragansett sachem, who'd ordered his braves to track our path.

At every rustling leaf and cracking twig Oneka would glance at me and nod, a signal that his instincts were the same as mine. Any game large enough to make the sounds we heard was sure to have long since run to deep cover before the clatter of our troop. If we were right, if it were Canonchet who watched us, we could only hope that his intentions were friendly and that he wasn't leading us to ambush.

Keeping my concerns to myself, I led my tribe more deeply into Narragansett territory. At night as I lay with Wantonka, listening to the coughing whispers beyond our teepee, I prayed that my efforts would be rewarded, that my attempt to save these people had not put my own family at risk. In trying to soothe my troubled heart to sleep, I thought back to happier days months earlier. Then there had been no war, no need to fear surprise or treachery. Then my cousin and I had contented ourselves with hewing and shaping the beams for our home.

But as idyllic as things had been, mine had been a life without Wantonka. And every time my spirits darkened at our prospects, I had only to recall it had taken adversity to deliver us to one another. In that way, I found comfort enough to sleep each night and strength to go forward each new day.

Although we made every effort to avoid the settlement he'd founded at Providence landing, Roger Williams still managed to find us before we'd penetrated too deeply into Narragansett territory.

"Fear not," the elderly man of peace greeted the boy and me. "I come as a friend."

We had been following a narrow tributary of the river south, just rounded a bend amid a dense cluster of willow, when he appeared standing before us.

"I have come from Canonchet who knows of your presence here." Stepping through a curtain of hanging branches, he studied my assembling army of refugees. "What have you brought us?"

"Weetamoo abandoned them at Nipachuck." Wantonka stepped boldly forward. "The English would have sold them all as slaves."

Williams rubbed his clean shaved chin.

"I am Wantonka. Granddaughter to Massasoit. I myself have seen their black ship and its cargo of Wampanoag."

Turning, Williams made a signal to the trees behind him where a party of armed Indians suddenly appeared.

"Canonchet has sent these men to guide you along the secret paths through the Great Swamp to his castle," Williams told us. "I will camp with you tonight by the river. Then you will leave with them in the morning."

Several of the braves I recognized as having traveled with Weetamoo when she'd fled from my family of orphans.

"You are welcome to travel with me," Williams then said to me. "I return east to Mount Hope Bay."

"I cannot," I stammered. "This is my wife." I took Wantonka's hand. "This is my son." I pulled the boy to me. "And these are my people."

"God smile on you," was all the Quaker said. "On you all."

That night we sat with him over the last cooking fire of our journey. Williams was pensive during the practiced preparations for feeding our flock. Even the Pocasset warriors who had accompanied him seemed respectful of the skilled cooperation that had developed among us.

"What I see here is what I've been told once existed throughout the colonies," the Quaker elder said at last. "Not so long ago."

Though slight of stature and slender of build, he spoke with quiet force, his eyes still burning with the righteous fervor that had defied the leaders of both New England colonies.

"It was just forty years past that seventeen great sailing ships appeared at anchor off the shoals of Nantasket," he related. "On these ships arrived enough English to increase the population of the colonies by five times. Puritans, they were, bound for Boston and Charles Town. And once they stepped ashore nothing was the same again."

He took a long breath as two of Weetamoo's warriors settled at his side. One of the Pocasset lighted a corn cob pipe and passed it with a bow to Wantonka. With a bow of her own, my princess drew the first smoke, letting it curl in the air before her face and then returning the pipe to its owner.

"By then, the Pilgrims of Plymouth had lost their way," Williams told us. "Their spiritual leader in Leiden had died. Land was being settled many times more quickly than before. They feared the intrusion of their Puritan neighbors in Boston would swallow them and their beliefs."

"I myself landed in one of those great Puritan waves," he said. "The talk in England was of an enlightened New World where none of the injustices of the Old World would be tolerated. There was more land than a man could imagine."

Spreading his thin arms wide, our guest drew smiles from his Pocasset neighbors.

"Water sweet as wine. Earth so rich it could be planted without being turned. And a native population eager to be welcomed to God's grace."

The smiles lingered on the faces of the two braves. As they passed the pipe between them, I wondered what of Williams' narrative they understood, what of England?

"But the truth of what a man says is in his deeds, not his words." Williams glanced with fondness at the others gathered by their own bright fires as the late summer chill closed over our camp. "It did not take long for me to realize that, despite their lofty Christian ambitions, these Puritan elders were as intolerant and intractable as any of those we'd left behind in England."

Reaching for the pipe as it passed once more before him, the Providence Quaker took a long breath, exhaling the sweet smelling smoke into the air between us.

"I disagreed with all of them." He coughed. "Puritans and Pilgrims. And in time I was banished from both colonies. That is how I came to settle among the Narragansett. My claims against these hard men in Plymouth and in Boston were many. But foremost of them was the taking of land from the natives."

This time, he drew longer from the pipe when it passed. It astonished me how much at ease his presence made the Pocasset warriors. Weeks before, it had been these same painted warriors who had tried to take my scalp. Now we faced each other in humble silence as the elderly objectionist spoke.

"Regardless who we thought we were," he continued, "or what God we bowed our heads to, this land belonged to its native people. Every acre settled must be purchased legally. No swindle or coercion."

He refused the pipe when it passed this time, stroking his rounded chin instead.

"It was those beliefs that had me banished, first from Boston, and then from Plymouth. Within five years of my arrival here, I was sent into the wilderness and settled among the Narragansett. They've been my trusted friends and I theirs for forty years."

He drew a tired breath. For a moment, I expected him to rise and excuse himself to settle in his blankets for the night. It had been decades since Roger Williams had first sprung nimbly into these forests. He was nearly three times my age, a fading light. That's why his spirited resumption of his late night narrative startled me so.

"Times have changed," he said leaning closer, letting the firelight bathe his craggy face. "I have seen things in these past weeks that trouble me deeply."

"Among the Narragansett?" I finally asked.

"They speak of peace," he said. "And yet they prepare for war."

"Weetamoo," my princess growled. "She has poisoned the heart of Canonchet."

Williams nodded.

"Weetamoo has made things difficult for everyone," he said. "Even though she has married Quinipan, another Narragansett sachem, her presence here has put the tribe at risk. Governor Winslow has demanded Canonchet return her to Plymouth. By refusing to do so, he appears to be siding with the rebellion."

"What does Canonchet say of this?" Wantonka asked.

It was the most important question of all. With an army of two thousand warriors at his command, the Narragansett sachem could easily tip the balance of power to Philip.

"He says nothing," Williams answered. "He keeps Weetamoo in his protection and prepares for war. He gathers his people, food and powder to his fortified camp in the Great Swamp."

"But certainly the English would never dare attack him there."

I was thinking of the overcautious pursuit of Philip, the hesitant English advance down the Pokanoket Peninsula. Even the opportunity gained at Nipachuck by the daring of the Mohegan was lost to English caution.

"You have been here in the forest many weeks," Williams reminded us. "You have missed much."

By now the first of the two Pocasset braves had settled back on the ground and was snoring. Soon the second brave joined him, leaving Roger Williams free to speak more openly to Wantonka and me.

"There have been terrible defeats in the west," he confided to us. "After he escaped from here, Philip joined the Nipmuc at Menemeset. Soon the war reached the edge of the frontier. At Brookfield more than one hundred English were killed. Fifty-nine soldiers were said to have been buried in a single grave. There was a full day of mourning in Boston."

He was whispering now, his face shadowed, his eyes still bright in the light of the dying fire.

"People are panicked," he breathed, "so much so that in their desperation they might strike the Narragansett before Canonchet has the opportunity to grow stronger."

"For what purpose?" I asked recalling the old Indian telling of the shameless massacre of the Pequod.

"Annihilation." It was Wantonka who surprised us, the difficult English word seeming too large and terrible to have been formed by her sweet lips.

Around us, the whispering voices had quieted. It was oddly dark. The cook fires which often lasted until dawn were all but out. The coals of a few cast an eerie glow on the faces of those sleeping closest to them. As I watched, the ghostly light dimmed further, and one by one, the faces vanished, the darkness drawing closer than on any previous night. Perhaps it was the chill end of summer dampness that had cooled the fires. Or perhaps it was a sign, encroaching night covering the faces of the sleeping natives a symbol of the conflict that soon would darken the faces of an entire people.

The next morning, Roger Williams left us. As he promised, the small band of warriors who had accompanied him remained behind to escort us the rest of the way to Canonchet's castle in the Great Swamp.

IX

Canonchet's castle was the most fearsome defensive structure I'd ever seen. Set on several acres of dry ground, an island really, in the midst of an immense and impassable swamp, the capital of the Narragansett nation was surrounded by a bristling stockade. Fashioned somewhat in the style of English forts, sharpened logs set deep in the earth and lashed tightly together with stout leather straps, the Indian fortress nonetheless had a wild, irregular look to it.

Using neither the circle nor the square for a model, the Narragansett had let the contours of their ground determine the shape of the structure and the odd angles of its walls. Coming upon it along the narrow, meandering path on which our guides led us, the castle appeared to be nothing more than a tangle of sharply pointed logs dropped in a pile from the heavens. One of the battlements stuck out from the sloping ground at such a low angle that an attacking army would have been impaled had it tried storming it directly. The only entrance was a crude log bridge thrown across a murky stretch of water.

The bright orange hue of the freshly turned earth and the silver and blond gashes in the newly cut wood indicated much of what I saw was new. Inside, the crowding together of scores of wigwams and the purposeful yet unhurried industry of hundreds of Indians, men and women, spoke of a powerful imperative newly settled on these people.

"The last stand of the Narragansett," I heard Wantonka whisper.

This was dangerous ground for all of us. Not only was a lone white man looked upon with contempt by the Narragansett, but even more so were the Pokanoket and Pocasset refugees. Long enemies of their powerful neighbors, the people of the Wampanoag confederation were considered unworthy by the sons and daughters of Miantomono. Now Philip's recklessness had forced even more discomfort on them. As a result, there would be no warm welcome for the people abandoned by their own rebel sachem.

Still, the respect held for Roger Williams was considerable. At his word, we were to be granted a grudging place behind the castle's walls. And soon my tribe melted into the warren of teepees, absorbed into the streams of anonymous natives preparing for an English attack.

Food gathered from the summer harvest was buried in secret hiding places. If the fortress fell and Canonchet was forced to flee with his tribe into the wilderness, provisions enough for them to survive the winter would be waiting, safe from English torches. Dried corn was sealed in barrels which were then stacked within each wigwam to protect its occupants from musket fire.

Despite the intense activity, however, my presence and that of my wife did not go unnoticed by the princely sachem. Before we'd managed to find a quiet piece of ground on which to spread our blankets, Weetamoo herself came to summon us to him.

It was with a changed look that Wantonka's mother regarded me this time.

"You have managed the impossible," she said in school learned English. "Let us hope the souls you recovered and brought in from the forest don't die here in this swamp."

With a brusque nod to Wantonka, she turned and led us to the far end of the castle. Oneka followed at a distance, his vigilant eyes scanning the ground to either side of us for signs of Narragansett mischief. But for once his watchfulness seemed unnecessary as we were in perhaps the safest place in New England. The frontier was dangerous for everyone, red and white. And the larger settlements of Plymouth and Boston were teeming with panicked English. But here among the painted warriors of my enemy, even I was safe.

"You are welcome here," Canonchet told me when I found him.

He was tall, solidly built, ten or more years older than me, dressed in the white shirt and long pants favored by the English. Except for his swarthy skin and a solitary hawk feather in his knotted hair, he was no different from any of his white neighbors.

"Thank you," I answered him. "But I wish only to remain the night. Then I will return with my wife and this boy to our home in Sakonnet."

At first the sachem seemed confused by my reference to Wantonka as my wife. He glared at her and she at him until he grunted once and gave a sharp nod of his head.

"No," he told us. "You stay. You both stay."

He squatted on his heels before us, motioning us to do the same.

"I make no fight with the English," he said, "because it is a fight we cannot win. But if war is forced on us, we will fight and die as Narragansett."

He gazed calmly at me.

"I was taught by Roger Williams of the English," he said. "I have read much and know the long ago stories of your people. They are powerful stories of warriors who lived many lifetimes past. The Narragansett have no long ago stories, only what is told by old to young."

He paused again, considering his words.

"You will stay with us, English." He abruptly stood. "You will see all that passes here and you will tell our story. Not an English story," he shouted. "A Narragansett story."

And he turned as abruptly as he'd stood, leaving me to consider my new role, historian to the Narragansett.

"I see your eyes," Wantonka later told me. "Canonchet has filled your head with troubled thoughts."

I nodded. "He truly believes the English will attack."

"He only knows what all my people know."

Taking my hand, she led me to an empty corner of the camp where no one could hear us.

"The God of the English sees only the color of the red man's skin, not what is in our hearts." Her voice was quiet, steady. "Philip has angered the English God. Now they must punish the Narragansett. Because there is no one else."

I remembered Governor Winslow's words. "There are no loyal natives. If some are for this war, they all are for it."

For the next several weeks, Wantonka and I mingled with the growing numbers of frightened Narragansett. As the days shortened and grew colder, more and more natives took shelter with us. Gathering for winter was a necessity for these people of the forest. This year, it took on greater importance as Canonchet prepared for invasion, not only of cold, but of fire and steel.

If the sachem knew when to expect attack, he never said. I imagined the overly cautious whites did not themselves yet know what Wantonka knew, that unprovoked attack against the powerful Narragansett was inevitable. As she, Oneka and I crowded into a wigwam with several other families, war preparations continued. By the time the first flurries of late November lashed the willow and cypress, and the night cold skimmed the waters of the swamp with ice, the fortress had been strengthened in every way

Except for concealed escape routes cut into the stockade at several strategic places and the massive oak gate at the castle's main entrance, only one section in the encircling wall of sharpened poles remained oddly incomplete. A gap in the towering wooden palisades extending more than a dozen feet across was blocked by a single felled oak. Of substantial girth, this log would still do little to block an enemy assault if it were discovered. With all the work in progress, the army of workers preparing their sacred ground for defense, it astonished me that not one person had attended to the critical breach.

From my meeting with Canonchet, I knew he was not the fool many English thought he was. A gap in his defenses could only have been planned. And with a careful eye, I studied the ground facing the breach, seeing nothing that would hint at the sachem's strategy.

"There's nothing but open ground between that hole in the wall and the heart of the encampment," I told Oneka one morning.

We'd been hauling rocks from the freshly turned earth at the base of the stockade to be stored in barrels with which we'd encircled our little corner of the wigwam. When the fighting began, we'd take shelter there. It would be our castle keep.

"Killing ground," the boy answered.

I stopped what I was doing to ask him what he meant.

"The English will come there," he told me pointing to the opening in the wall. "And they will die here."

He inclined his head toward the wide apron of unprotected ground on which we stood.

"Canonchet wants the invaders to attack here?" I glanced beyond the fortress walls to the impenetrable swamp. "But how will they cross the water?"

And as soon as I asked the question, I received my answer as a dried leaf dropped from its stubborn hold of a lone oak and settled on the frozen surface of the swamp.

"Ice," Oneka said.

In another week, the swamp would be frozen thick enough to bear a man's weight. Canonchet had planned for this all along, a flank attack across the ice. He would use the unfinished section of the stockade to draw the English here. He would conceal his braves in the fortified wigwams ringing the open ground where the boy and I stood. Thinking they'd found a chink in the Narragansett defenses, the attackers would rush the breach, spilling into the killing field before the shooters hidden in the harmless looking wigwams. That's when Canonchet would spring his trap.

The first volleys from the concealed warriors would tear through the lead ranks of the English army. Hearing gunfire, others would press the attack from outside, crowding the breach, creating enough chaos within to allow the ambushers to reload and deliver more shot. Slowly, methodically, a small group of defenders could chew through the entire attacking army, picking targets as they came, twenty or so at a time, into the killing field before them.

"Thermopylae," I said.

Oneka nodded, although it was impossible for me to believe he knew the story from ancient Greece.

"Three hundred Spartans stopped an army of thousands," I told him. "The pass at Thermopylae forced the Persians to advance on such a narrow front the superior Greek warriors were able to patiently cut them to pieces."

The sun was bright. The hard December chill had melted in its warming light. Still, I shivered at the thought of my cousin and those others, friends, neighbors, bleeding their lives into this unforgiving ground.

Just then a lone figure appeared from the cover of the wigwams lining the far side of the killing field. At his welcoming wave, I recognized one of the elderly Pokanoket who had followed us from Nipachuck, the old man who'd entertained us with his stories of the Narragansett and Pequod. Remaining in the open, he continued waving, beckoning the boy and me to join him.

"Come see," he managed through his toothless gums.

Knowing him to be earnest and trustworthy, we followed him, winding through the densely packed wigwams of the main camp. By now I was no longer a curiosity to these people. And they bumped and jostled me as if I were invisible.

"Look," the old man gummed as he pointed to a large excavation in an empty corner of the fortress.

"Wampum," he told me.

Halting us at the edge of a wide ditch extending more than thirty yards from the base of the stockade, he indicated several young braves unearthing dozens of stout, carefully sealed barrels. With unexpected agility, he then leapt into the hole, landing astride one of the newly exposed barrels. None of the other braves stopped his work as the old man took a knife from his belt and worked it in the iron rim that sealed the barrel's lid.

With considerable effort, digging and prying with his knife, the toothless old warrior at last managed to snap the rusted band, releasing the lid and spilling dozens of polished beads at his feet. Now one of the braves turned from his work at the far end of the pitch casting an indifferent look as the old man stood transfixed before the sparkling treasure. So brightly did the colored beads shine, it was as if the Narragansett diggers had uncovered the hiding place of every star from the night sky.

"Wampum." The aged Pokanoket spoke into the overflowing barrel. "Buried by Miantonomo after the days of the Pequod."

At his insistence, Oneka and I helped him raise the barrel from its place in the ground, careful not to spill any more of its contents.

"Our people made these from the shells and stones of the sea," he breathed. "We gave them to the English for these." He pulled a shovel from the piled earth. "And for muskets and powder."

I was astonished that the English would trade items of such value for nothing more than polished stones.

"For beaver," he told us. "Once the across-the-water English wore the skin of the beaver on their heads."

Losing his balance, the old man fell against the barrel dislodging more of the sparkling lode like drops of frozen spring water on the ground at my feet. Again I was struck by the colorful rainbow patterns caused by the sunlight striking the remarkable beads.

"The far away English are many," he continued. "And we dried many skins until our beaver vanished toward the setting sun."

He stood with his hands on the barrel top, staring deep inside for his long ago story of the brief economic Eden which European demand for beaver pelts once caused to exist here. My parents had told me stories of the rise and ruin of their own fortunes because of it.

"When the beaver vanished to the west," he told us, "the Narragansett made wampum for the English to trade with the Pequod and Mohegan for the pelts they took from the rivers of the Connecticut. But one day the far away English took the beaver from their heads and never put them back. Then the Pequod were driven from their castle. And Miantomono buried these barrels in this place to keep the Narragansett from ever again following the twisted path of the English."

"So why do you dig them now?" I asked.

"For our wigwams. Miantonomo's wampum will buy no more Pequod beaver. But it will stop the shots of English muskets."

Once we heard the old man's story, once we understood the value of his cargo, then and now, Oneka and I put our backs to it. And together we managed to haul the barrel through the camp to our wigwam where we placed it to one side of the entry place. When the English attacked, when we took cover here, we'd roll the barrel full of valueless treasure behind us, concealing it behind the wigwam's deerskin flaps in hopes it would protect us.

Gathering around us, Wantonka and the other women of our wigwam stood transfixed before the glittering barrel of light. Several times, one or another of them would reach out her hand, fluttering her fingers in the rainbow light reflected from the beads, hesitating like a child about to steal a sweet before pulling back and leaving the prize untouched. It was exquisite being witness to the very private moment when these people were reunited with their forgotten treasure, a treasure granted value and then made suddenly valueless by the whims of our absent English lords and ladies across the sea.

Unwilling to leave us and his recovered prize, the old man stayed with us that night, taking his meal with us and draping one of our blankets across his bony shoulders as a sudden squall lashed our shelter with snow and ice. Watching him, I saw the firelight illuminate an elaborately stitched belt that encircled his narrow waist. I'd seen the belt before and many times had wanted to ask him its significance. As the air grew colder, as the swamp water froze more thickly, as the time for battle drew near, I finally summoned the courage to inquire.

"Here is the story of my people," he answered me, unknotting the leather tie and slipping the precious belt from his waist. "Take and read of my father's father, and his father's father."

Careful to keep clear of the flames of our cook fire, he passed the ancient relic to me. Though faded and worn, the intricate patterns of thread stitched into the time stiffened deerskin intrigued me.

"I cannot die here in this place," he confided. "I must first pass this to my son."

At one end of the sacred belt, the woven threads were more coarse and faded, the patterns more crudely formed. But as I moved my eyes along its length, I discovered the stitching grew tighter, the threads finer, the patterns more sophisticated and recognizable. It appeared from the progression of shapes, animals and men, that each succeeding generation had told its story with greater care than the one before.

With a gnarled finger, the old man pointed me to the farthest end of the belt and the least faded of all the patterns.

"Anawan." He smiled proudly as his finger settled on a finely detailed likeness of a star shower. "My son," he gummed. "The sky was falling on the night he came to us."

His fingers trembled as he again took the precious belt in his hands.

"He's with Philip" I told him. I had recognized the name of one of the rebel's fiercest lieutenants.

The old man nodded.

"He would not take the story belt from me at Nipachuck. He said he would not wear it until the last of my story was written. But how can that be if my story ends in this place?"

He was crying now, this man who had seen so much, brought low by the thought of never seeing his son again.

"You will not die here," I tried to comfort him.

Wiping his cheek, he shook his head.

"Many will die here," he said. "I will die here. But you, English. Neither the Narragansett or your own people will wish you dead. You will live and you will bring this belt to Anawan." "Promise me." He held me with his claw fingers. "Swear."

And with no idea how I would ever deliver on my promise, I did as he asked.

"I will," I whispered as Wantonka smiled on us. "I swear."

X

Late that night, the English attacked. With visions from the old man's treasured belt swirling through my dreams, the first thunderous musket volleys tore the quiet. As Canonchet had planned, the sounds of battle came from the area where the Narragansett stockade was breached.

"We must run," Wantonka whispered.

Quickly I grabbed my musket and guided my family beneath the deerskin flap of our wigwam and into frigid predawn gloom. Around us was a frenzy of activity. As armed men raced toward the sounds of fighting, women and children struggled in the opposite direction toward the escape routes hidden beneath the castle walls.

Careful to avoid attracting attention to myself, I led Wantonka and Oneka to safety. Waiting until we were through the walls and clear of the camp, across the frozen surface of the swamp, I finally stopped.

"My cousin will be with the English attackers," I shouted. "I must go to him."

Hesitating long enough to receive a reassuring nod from Wantonka, I then turned and hurried back inside the castle. Snow stung my face as dawn began to cast its glow. After fighting my way through crowds of native women fleeing with their children, crossing through the rapidly emptying camp, I arrived at last at the killing field where the boy and I had stood just the day before. Ahead of me, scores of musket flashes illuminated rolling clouds of smoke and snow. Men shouted in English and warriors whooped and shrieked as the thin December light slowly revealed the hellish scene.

As Canonchet had planned, the attackers had rushed headlong into his trap. With the ground beneath their feet already littered with dead and dying, the English had boldly reformed their ranks, dozens more streaming through the stockade opening behind them. On and on they came as merciless Narragansett defenders poured shot on them from three sides. As long as their powder lasted, the Indian shooters seemed well positioned to withstand wave after wave of the English assault.

In vain, I peered through the acrid smoke clouds looking for my cousin. But as anxious as I was to see him, I prayed I wouldn't, not in this place, not before this murderous fire. It seemed hopeless for them all. And, powerless to intercede, I groaned aloud each time I saw a white soldier fall. But I knew these English. They had come to this land from a place of far greater savagery. They were propelled by forces darker and stronger than ten thousand Narragansett. They would keep reforming and advancing with cold resolve.

For several long minutes, the English assault remained stalled. Then suddenly, the Indian fire slackened. I saw Canonchet racing between the wigwams shouting to his warriors. But more and more of their muskets grew silent from lack of precious powder. And as the clouds of gun smoke thinned, I was at last able to view the battlefield more clearly.

Before the regrouped attackers, Canonchet had placed his best shooters in a tumbled pole barn. Serving as a blockhouse, the ramshackle structure stood square in the face of the English, holding their advance while Indian flankers firing from fortified wigwams positioned on each side of the breach tore their ranks with shot.

But as precarious as the English position was, as many of their men had fallen, it was the Narragansett whose dead and wounded mounted terribly. By now perhaps fifty Indian bodies were piled at each flank. With their tightly massed ranks of heavier match lock muskets, the disciplined English officers waited until their enemy showed himself before ordering devastating rounds, each of which cleared the ground of standing enemy.

I saw Samuel Moseley hold his men in place with remarkable daring. With more than a dozen muskets aimed at him, he held his position, directing fire amid a storm of shot. At the center of Moseley's square stood the enormous Dutch pirate who had freed Wantonka. At least a head taller than the rest, he made a tempting target for the Narragansett shooters. Though dozens of shots splintered the stockade behind him, however, he remained untouched. In their excitement to slay the white giant, the defenders fired without taking careful aim, wasting still more valuable powder.

Behind the English front, in the choked swamp beyond the breach, Governor Winslow could be seen driving another column of his force on the run into the battle. Remaining well out of range himself, the stubborn leader waved his cutlass signaling his storming column to force its way through Moseley's stalled position. Ignorant of the fortified pole barn in their path, however, the eager attackers rushed headlong into a withering volley. Shot tore through flesh and splintered bone as nearly a dozen officers fell shrieking.

Stunned to a halt by the loss of their leaders, the soldiers of the attacking column gave their enemy precious time to reload. And in the agonizing instant of silence that followed, I stupidly thought that the horrors of the slaughter had so affected the survivors on both sides that they had been compelled to cease. The attackers would back away. The defenders would bring aid to the fallen. I had never before witnessed so brutal a spectacle and in my ignorance believed it could not resume.

But it did.

With the wild eyed rage of cornered animals, the English force rose up and rushed the Narragansett blockhouse. At their front I saw my cousin. His head had just turned toward me, his eyes had just looked in mine, when he was struck by a second volley from the blockhouse. The spark of recognition between us was quick as a musket flash. Then he was on his knees clutching his thigh. That was all it took for me to release fear's grip and I was up, my legs speeding me to his side.

Now muskets on both sides took aim at me. Dressed in deerskin, running hard at the attackers' broken ranks, I could have been Indian or white. And as fast as I covered the open ground, I knew I could never outrun a well aimed shot. Balls tore the ground around me. But, speeding, I was a difficult target and arrived unharmed at Church's side just as the English storming column rushed headlong through the tumbled walls of the pole barn scattering Narragansett before them.

"You?" It was all my cousin could manage through his panting breaths.

Reaching under my deerskin jacket, I pulled at my shirt tearing off a strip of cloth long enough to bind his streaming wound.

"Wantonka and I were brought here after Nipachuck," I explained as I wound the cloth tourniquet tight around his leg.

Again shots thudded into the hard earth around us.

"They're firing from behind us," Church gasped.

Turning I saw that Canonchet had moved a force into the swamp behind Winslow's position.

"Our fortunes are reversed," Church said as I helped him to his feet. "Now it is they who attack us inside their own citadel."

I saw at once what he meant. Canonchet had made a dangerous gamble.

By leading so large a force into the field, he'd abandoned the fortress to his enemy. If Winslow saw the same thing and ordered his soldiers forward, the Narragansett castle would be his. By now, however, several of Moseley's pirates had begun torching the empty wigwams surrounding the killing field, destroying what valuable cover and food stores they'd provide.

"You must help me to the governor," Church cried. "He must stop this action and save the castle for ourselves."

Here was the man who had protected me from so much, who had faced danger with a daring I emulated. To see him like this, bearing his weight against me as I struggled toward the stockade, was humbling. But the battle had turned away at last. On distant elevated ground, I could see Narragansett warriors engaged in a running fight, darting from tree to tree as they fired on the English rear guard. We were out of range and out of danger. Our only concern now was the slow progress we made on the uneven path leading to the breach in the wall. So soaked in blood was the ground at our feet that several times we slipped, falling to our knees, covering ourselves in the gore of our fallen neighbors.

The fires were growing behind us when two men from Tiverton arrived at last and relieved me of my load. Taking Church by both arms, they hurried him out of the fort and straight to the low hill from which Winslow commanded his men.

"You must lead the army into the fort and stop the soldiers from firing the wigwams," Church implored the general. "Darkness will arrive soon. We're more than twenty miles from the nearest white settlement. We need food for our army and shelter for our wounded from the snow and cold."

The governor drew his officers close to confirm their agreement. Then he led his horse clear of my wounded cousin and began his descent of the hill. He'd just issued the order to enter the castle when Moseley appeared from inside the stockade.

"Where are you going?" The pirate caught the reins of the governor's horse in a great, bloodied fist.

"Church tells us the fort has been cleared and that we should shelter the army there for the night."

"Church lies," Moseley roared. "He will see you killed before this day is finished."

By now loss of blood had my cousin slumped unconscious against the men of Tiverton. Flames were visible above the walls of the stockade. Inside, Moseley's killers were incinerating Narragansett women and children. Outside, there was no one with the stomach to stop them.

"If you move to enter that castle," Moseley said raising his musket toward the governor, "I will shoot your horse dead from under you."

Not easily cowed, Winslow seemed ready to have the insubordinate officer removed when another man stepped forward to agree with him. An argument then ensued during which Church continued to bleed. With little choice but to save my cousin, I was forced to leave Moseley to his vile enterprise.

With the help of one of the surgeons attending to Winslow's staff, I managed to move Church away from the horses, further up the hill to the shelter of some rocks. Together we ripped away the torn and bloodied pant leg from his thigh, cleaned his wound with a splash of water from the surgeon's pouch, and after releasing the tourniquet's tight grip, we bound it snug in fresh bandages.

By now Church's face was nearly the color of the freshly fallen snow. But with his heart still beating under the surgeon's blanket, he was lifted from the ground and taken to a litter for carriage back across the frigid swamp to Bull's garrison in Wickford. As Church had said, it would be a journey of more than twenty miles. Those less fortunate of the wounded who would not enjoy the comfort of transport might well die along the way. But with the Narragansett castle now fully enveloped in Moseley's fiery retribution, there was no alternative.

As the sounds of musket fire drifted further to the west, I thought of Wantonka, praying she'd had the good sense to keep moving. Putting as much distance between herself and the vengeful English was the only way to save herself. If my princess bothered to return for me, she'd be killed at once.

Beyond the crest of the hill, I watched a group of soldiers advance on a lone Narragansett. Kneeling before them, the outnumbered Indian had folded his musket in his arms across his chest as a sign of surrender. Yet no sooner did the whites have him surrounded than one raised his musket and killed the poor wretch.

For the next long hour, sporadic gunfire continued inside the burning castle as more of the Narragansett met similar fates. With my cousin tended to and safely on his way home, I decided that my allegiance to this murderous English army was ended. But before I sneaked away after my princess, I entered the castle one last time to discover what fate had befallen the poor old man.

On both sides of the bloody killing field the dead lay in heaps, both red and white. Among them, scores of English looters picked their way, stealing what little remained unburned. Beyond these pirates, fires raged in every corner silhouetting their shameful deeds. No one seemed to care if any Narragansett were still alive. Their cries and shrieks were lost in the pitiless roar of the flames.

With the village now in ruins, it was almost impossible to find my way to the wigwam where I'd last seen the old man. Once there had been order here, even among the meandering dirt tracks at the center of the camp. Now everything was charred and flattened. Occasionally a recognizable shape appeared, the body of a child perhaps, its dead arms clutching still the flames that licked the ground around it. For the most part, however, blackened bodies were indistinguishable from smoldering lodge poles and scorched earth.

Several times I stopped to wretch. The battle was over. Death had taken more than its due, leaving me unharmed. And yet I couldn't have felt worse if I'd sustained a dozen wounds.

I was about to give up, to move to the farthest corner of the stockade, to the place where I was certain I'd led Wantonka to safety. I was ready to follow her and the wide bloody track along which Canonchet had dragged his dying wounded. But it was then I spied the old man's treasure pile gleaming amid the ruins. The wampum barrel had burned away and the polished stones, though blanketed with soot, glowed like a solitary tear amid the continuum of fire and ash.

It was impossible to know if the old man were among the dozens of crumpled, burned bodies scattered on the ground around it. Thinking I would never learn his fate or that of his family's cherished story belt, I decided to cross the smoldering ground to retrieve at least a bit of the desecrated treasure. If I were to carry with me the story of a people extinguished by the horrors of this day, what better symbol of its fall than these fire scorched beads?

Kicking aside the still glowing ashes, I knelt on the hot earth beside the wampum pile. With my knife, I swept aside the layer of soot and burned stone that covered the top, revealing the unblemished jewels beneath. Careful to keep from burning my fingers, I lifted one of the largest pieces. Watching scores of smaller stones cascade into the place left open by the one I'd taken, I caught a glimpse of colored fabric.

Again with my knife blade, I swept away more polished pieces, revealing a greater treasure than I could have imagined, the old man's story belt, hidden no doubt by its owner where it would not be burned. Before he'd died he'd left it for me. If I had not returned here, it might well have been lost for good.

With the unburned belt in my hand, I studied the ground around me, the faces of the Narragansett corpses made unrecognizable by the pirate's fire. One of them, I was certain, was the ancient warrior, father of Anawan, murdered by Moseley's criminals. Yet even in death, his worth had been far greater than theirs. The belt I held confirmed it. Returning it to his son would give the worthy Indian immortality.

Once outside the walls of the stockade, I found the scene nearly as chilling as the one I'd left inside. Before me, the snow ran red where two wide, bloody paths diverged in the Great Swamp. Along one, the English carried their wounded and dead, scores, perhaps hundreds of them, over the frigid track east to Bull's. And on the other, pointing north to the Blackstone River, Canonchet led his broken tribe. Weeks earlier I had come the same way leading the refugees of Nipachuck. I couldn't imagine how many of them had survived the fight this day. I could think only of Wantonka as I left my people, my land and my cousin behind to follow the path of the Narragansett.

XI

At Misnock, near the Nipachuck Swamp where Uncas and Reverend Newman battled Philip early in the summer, Canonchet had made his camp. That was where I found Wantonka and Oneka, tending to the army of wounded whose bloody trail I'd followed there. Fortunately, the weather proved to be as mild as any winter weather I'd experienced. The land was clear of snow, making it easy for the Narragansett to dig for ground nuts and impossible for their enemy to track them. Though war had exacted a terrible toll on the mighty Narragansett, Canonchet's people were hardly broken. Despite hundreds of wounded, the sachem still had with him an army many times larger. And as I helped Wantonka prepare oak leaf dressings for the hideous wounds of the fallen, vengeful warriors gathered in angry groups to plan their retribution.

But more than rage and vengeance, I saw something else in the eyes of those desperate men that winter. The Narragansett had faced the largest colonial army ever assembled. They had met the English bravely on their own terms and yet been badly beaten. There would be no more victories for these men, their eyes told me. They were the living dead, determined, even anxious to fight, but knowing in their hearts they were doomed.

Several weeks into the new year, Canonchet again called me to him. Word had spread among the Narragansett of the Pokanoket story belt I carried with me. And though I worked hard to heal his wounded and shield the treasured belt from the suspicious eyes of his people, the sachem had grown distrustful of me.

"This belt you have," he barked when I appeared before him. "You must bring it to me."

Like the others, this fight had changed him. The somber and reflective leader whom I'd met a month before now burned with loathing.

"They say you took it from one of our dead," he spat.

"From one of the Pokanoket," I told him. "An old man who traveled with me to your village."

The sachem inclined his head to one side, as if by viewing me from a different angle he might better understand.

"I swore to him I'd carry his belt to his son." I formed my words with difficulty.

"Who is this man?" Canonchet shouted.

We were surrounded by several others. Weetamoo and her husband Quinipan stood with younger men I guessed were Narragansett war captains.

"The father of Anawan," I managed.

"Anawan?" The name was repeated by every person present.

"He is Philip's war captain," Canonchet told me, his tone quieting. "They are with the Nipmuc at Menemesset. It is many miles from here."

I said nothing. The thought of pursuing my quest deeper into the wilderness was daunting. I knew there were scattered English settlements in the west. But most had already been abandoned because of the war.

"This is good," Canonchet announced at last. "I will bring my army there to join the Nipmuc. And you will carry the belt of Anawan to him."

"I am to be your prisoner?" I stammered.

"You are prisoner not to me," he concluded, "but to your word."

By early February, the ground was still unexpectedly clear of snow. It was then that Canonchet's scouts reported seeing the last of the English army leave Rhode Island and withdraw to Plymouth. As he'd assured me, the Narragansett sachem had no desire to return his surviving warriors to the scene of their defeat. Instead, he pointed his people north along the Blackstone River toward the castle of the Nipmuc.

Now the English had gotten for themselves exactly what they'd feared most. Their unprovoked attack against the Narragansett had forced Canonchet to join the rebellion, doubling the size of Philip's army, giving him the chance he'd wanted to drive the whites from his land and into the sea.

With many of the Narragansett wounded still unable to walk, Wantonka and I joined the teams of horse drawn litters that carried them. As we traveled at the rear of Canonchet's long line of march I watched Oneka, his eyes fixed on the horizon over his left shoulder. There his people lived, the Mohegan, allies to the English.

Day after day, I studied the boy, certain that if I relaxed my watch he'd vanish into the forest that bordered the river. I had no idea whether Canonchet would extend his threat to someone so young, whether he would send his scouts to track and kill Oneka. Yet even if he didn't, even if the boy managed to slip safely away, I would feel his loss. Like me, however, Oneka was too bound to Wantonka to leave. And together we journeyed deeper into the wilderness, more than ever a family, annealed by our shared ordeal.

After nearly a week of travel, we were camped by a frozen lake when musket fire erupted in the distance. In what would be the first of several skirmishes between Narragansett and Nipmuc scouts, the Nipmuc probed what they believed was a traitorous army allied with the English. For days, we waited as the weather worsened. Harsh winds drove the now unrelenting snow in drifts too tall for a man to walk through.

Only by fashioning crude rackets for our feet from the cut ends of pine boughs could we move to gather firewood and to tend to the growing number of starving and infirm. There was no game to hunt, no digging for ground nuts. What little food we'd carried from Misnock had long since been consumed. If Canonchet could not convince Monoco, Muttawmp and the other Nipmuc sachems that he came as a friend and ally, if he could not gain invitation to Menemesset's rich stores of food from the Nipmuc harvest, his army would starve. Both the Narragansett and my new family were close to extinction when Wantonka stood from our fire, lashed rackets to her feet and bid Oneka and me to follow her.

From fire to fire we went, circulating among groups of freezing warriors, gathering the few hideous trophies they'd managed to carry from the battle at the Great Swamp. Too weak from the cold and fatigue, too desperate from lack of food and shelter to argue, the weary braves were soon persuaded by the forceful words of my princess to part with the frozen scalps of their English killed. And after hours struggling through the deep snow, we carried several of them to Canonchet's tent.

"Take these," Wantonka told the startled sachem. "Bring them to Monoco. Show him you are enemy to the English. Do this now before more of your people die."

By early the next morning, Wantonka's plan succeeded and we were rescued from our snowbound encampment by a Nipmuc war party. Leading us through drifts, some of which towered over Oneka's head, our new allies brought us to the Wachuset Hills and the first of what I would learn were three camps of the Menemesset village. The weather had again turned mild. The sun shone in a clear sky and melting snow rained from the pine bows overhead as I watched Monoco and his great war chief Muttawmp greet Canonchet. Behind the Nipmuc leaders, more than a thousand natives stood cloaked in blankets and furs. It was the largest gathering of natives I'd ever seen. Even Wantonka seemed stunned by the spectacle of so many of her people gathered in one place.

"But Metacom is not here," she whispered.

Although it was nearly impossible for me to be sure from the great numbers of anonymous dark faces that stood around me, I saw none of the warriors I knew from my first encounter with the Pokanoket. Still, if the English were to know of this great gathering of Narragansett and Nipmuc, panic would sweep the colonies.

For the next few days, Wantonka, Oneka and I traveled among the three Memenesset camps helping to find lodging for the Narragansett infirm. Already the war had produced others like me, English caught up by the great gathering of Indians, white prisoners working as slaves for their red masters. One of them, a man named Robert Pepper, had been a prisoner at Menemesset since summer.

Because we were in the protection of Canonchet, and because all seemed to know we had little chance of survival were we to run from them, Wantonka, Oneka and I were granted a fair amount of freedom among the Nipmuc. That's why our first night at Menemesset we were able to sit with Pepper at the wigwam of Sagamore Sam, the Nipmuc sachem who was his master. In the wide plain outside our village, Sagamore Sam, Monoco and Muttawmp led their huge army of braves in a war dance. Indians shrieked and pounded the ground as we whispered together in the flickering light of their roaring fire.

"It's another attack they're planning," Pepper told us that night. He was unwashed, unshaved, his clothes in tatters as was the blanket he'd wrapped himself in. "Lancaster, I'd guess."

I recognized the name of the frontier settlement. The minister there, Reverend John Rowlandson, a respected soldier and man of God, was certain to put up a fight.

"With all the western towns abandoned," he told us, "it's time for them to turn east. Concord. Medfield. Sudbury."

Pepper was from Hadley. After a terrible massacre at Deerfield, he'd been part of an expedition sent in September to evacuate the outermost English garrisons at Northfield.

"We were thirty-six mounted men and an ox drawn wagon," he said. "Commanded by Captain Beers of Watertown."

Having left their horses to ford Sawmill Brook, they were ambushed by Pocumtuck and Nashaway.

"Monoco hid them behind an embankment and caught our line exposed," he continued. "I was last in line. Ahead of me my friends were crying and falling. It was a terrible slaughter, so I threw down my musket and hid in a gorge overgrown with thistle."

There were three of them. From their hiding places, they'd watched as Captain Beers managed a difficult retreat to a near hill.

"The musket fire lasted all morning," he said with a shudder. "When it was done, the Indians came back looking for us with the bloody scalps of our mates hanging from their belts."

Pepper was the only one Monoco found. After torturing the poor man trying to find the hiding places of the others, the warriors took him prisoner.

"They threw a rope around my neck and dragged me here," he told us. "I've been in this terrible place since."

He then asked me for news of the war and was astonished to hear of the English attack on the Narragansett at the Great Swamp.

"This is not a fight we're likely to win," he moaned as the shrieking outside our wigwam intensified. "Not with an Indian army this size. Not if we keep up the way we've been."

Pale and gaunt from lack of food, Pepper struggled on with the story of the battle Roger Williams had informed me of the night we'd spent together with our army of Pokanoket refugees in the Blackstone Valley.

"Along the muddy brook that runs south of Deerfield, it was," he told us. "One week after I was captured, Monoco joined us up with Muttawmp and his braves."

Together, the Indian war captains had retraced the path Pepper had taken days earlier with the doomed Beers party.

"It was the troop evacuating Deerfield they were after," he went on, "pointed toward Hadley, same as us."

As they'd done at the Beer's ambush, the Nipmuc waited in hiding at a place where the brook would likely stall the English line of march.

"They tied me to a tree." He brought a soiled hand to his face, pulling at his tangled beard. "Put cloth in my mouth so I couldn't shout a warning. And left me to watch."

His head was bent, his long hair covering his face, when a tear dropped onto the blanket that lay beneath us.

"Our boys stopped and stacked their arms so they could take refreshment from some wild grapes that grew along the stream. It was like the Indians knew they would," he said. "They watched and waited until Captain Lathrop let his men get too far from their guns. Then they shot them down. Scores of them. Unarmed and unable to fight back."

He reached under the knotted fall of his hair and wiped his cheek.

"But Captain Moseley was nearby," he continued. "And I wept as I saw him bring his troop along on the hurry-up."

I felt Wantonka stiffen when Pepper looked up at last, his uncut hair spilling away from his streaming cheeks.

"They made a day of it," he said. "Both sides. Until that muddy brook ran red."

He took a racking breath, coughing and weazing in the smoke filled wigwam.

"The next day," he stammered. "Monoco and Muttawmp marched us past Hadley. And those painted devils let out whoops for every English man they'd killed. More than a hundred, I counted."

"Don't let me die here," he pleaded. "Take me with you when you go."

But leaving was something none of us could consider. Red and white, we were all prisoners to the weather and the war.

"Why didn't they kill me?" he moaned. "Why am I here and all those others dead?"

"You are hostage," Wantonka answered him. "If Philip wins this war, everything will be changed for the Nipmuc. If Philip loses, the Nipmuc will trade you and the other whites for peace. Philip will be hanged. But for the Nipmuc everything will be the same as before. Because of you."

In the meantime, the combined Nipmuc and Narragansett armies would rampage through the settlements, driving as many English from the land as possible before the fighting ceased. It was cruel logic forced on the western settlers by the illogic of Winslow and the other Pilgrim fathers. From their action against the Narragansett in the east, hundreds of western whites would die.

"Why is Metacom not here?" Oneka suddenly asked.

"He's gone to the land of the Mohawk," Pepper told us.

The Mohawk were the most feared warriors of all. None of the New England tribes would dare to face them, few would dare even follow the western trail through the mountains to their land.

"If Metacom gets them to join his fight," the boy said flatly, "the English will lose."

By dawn, the great warrior army was gone. Even with scores left to manage and protect the camp, Menemessett assumed a ghostly quiet. While the thoughts of the red men and women were for the well being of their sons and brothers gone to fight, I felt numbing gloom for the unknowing whites of Lancaster and the horrors they were soon to suffer.

As yet another snow squall blanketed our camp, the war fires of the previous night continued to smolder, blackening the freshly fallen snow. This was Hell. I could taste it in the acrid, smoke filled air. We were no longer in the company of men, but fallen angels who, by choice or desperation, had taken Evil as their currency

"Who are these people?" I asked aloud as Wantonka and I circled the near empty camp.

"The Nipmuc are sons of Massasoit," she answered. "Brothers to Philip in blood."

My princess then went on to tell me of the astonishing link that existed between the warring Indians of the east and west.

"When Massasoit grew old," she whispered, "he left his sons Philip and Alexander to lead the Pokanoket. Then he came here where the Quabaug and the other Nipmuc tribes named him sachem."

Leaving the smoldering council fires behind, we followed the snow covered path along the frozen river.

"Massasoit made the peace with the English when he was young," she told me that morning. "But as he grew old, he worried for his sons. Some believe he made this alliance knowing war would come."

XII

By mid-February, the weather had warmed sufficiently for steady, cold rain to fill our days. With the ground still frozen underneath, water ran in torrents through our camp forcing the evacuation of many wigwams. Conditions were paralyzingly crowded as few ventured outside the smoke filled lodges. It was then the war party returned from the east, far fewer than had left, looking even more gaunt and weary than the sorry ones who'd stayed behind.

There were no celebrations this time, although many belts were hung with scalps. Instead the faces of the surviving braves showed new desperation. With them, the Narragansett and Nipmuc fighters brought several prisoners. One was a woman with two young children and a dying infant in her arms. Her name, I learned, was Mary Rowlandson, wife of the Lancaster minister. She'd lost two brothers and a son in the massacre. And she was dragged to the middle of our camp, her despairing eyes fixed on her failing infant, as her two children, a boy and girl, were taken from her.

"Weetamoo will make her slave," Wantonka informed me. "The children will be led to the upper camp and kept from her."

Never had I felt such sorrow at the plight of another. The tragedy of the entire frontier was written on her shadowed face. But for her concern for her children, I was certain Mary Rowlandson would have begged her captors to let her die. Hope had been extinguished. God had abandoned her among the most heartless of his creatures.

"We must help her," Wantonka said.

At once, she dispatched Oneka to follow the two Rowlandson children to see where they were taken, to communicate some hopeful news to them, if possible, and monitor their condition. I was to remain alone as Wantonka took herself to Weetamoo's wigwam, welcome or not, to care for the mother and her dying child.

For several days, the camp remained quiet. With the weather too inhospitable for dispatching additional war parties, most of the Indians were forced to remain under cover by the fires in their lodges. Wantonka, meanwhile, struggled through the rain and snow between our wetu and the wigwam of her mother. Each morning she left me to care for Mrs. Rowlandson and her failing child, returning each night with pitiable descriptions of the white woman's plight.

Unknown to me at the time of her arrival, Mary Rowlandson had been wounded at the Lancaster fight, a musket ball passing through her side and into the body of the infant she'd been shielding. Though Wantonka was able to apply poultices that extracted the older woman's infection, the baby, Sarah, remained mortally ill. Throughout the day, Wantonka sat with the moaning infant in her lap, feeling the child's tiny heartbeat slow as her anguished mother lay beside her.

On the sixth day, the ordeal ended. Sarah died in the arms of my wife. Few among our captors seemed to take notice of the tragedy. Weetamoo herself railed at Wantonka over Mrs. Rowlandson's refusal to be parted from her infant daughter's corpse. But one man, a Narragansett, brought to the bereaved mother a bible he'd taken in the Lancaster raid. A Praying Indian himself perhaps, the thoughtful warrior might well have known the comfort derived from the words inside. And, as my wife described to me, Mrs. Rowlandson opened the great book at once to read.

"Though we were scattered from one end of the earth to the other, yet the Lord would gather us together and turn those curses upon our enemies."

Educated as a Christian herself, Wantonka had marveled at the calm that settled over Mrs. Rowlandson after that. With the bible clasped in the arms that once held Sarah, she waited through each day for the word Oneka would bring her of her other children. The resourceful Mohegan boy had followed each child, befriending the child's new master enough so that he could visit daily.

By bringing food to the Rowlandson boy and girl, keeping alert to their welfare, and informing their mother of their well being, he did more to aid their survival than any other. From Wantonka, he had learned to love both red and white. To both, therefore, he was a trusted friend.

By the end of the month, Nipmuc scouts reported a large Puritan army, soldiers and cavalry, marching toward Menemesset. The weather, though rainy still, was sufficiently mild for Monoco and Canonchet to order the breaking of camp and evacuation to the north. Word had also been circulating among the warrior force that Philip was returning from the west. By moving their army up the valley of the Connecticut, the two sachems hoped to intercept their rebel leader at a village where the Mohawk Trail crossed the broad river.

With a small party of braves sent south to confuse and delay the English, our march began. Young and old, women and infirm, were merged into the ranks of the warriors. Some of the elderly were carried on the backs of their children as the purposeful, if disorderly, retreat proceeded.

As unpleasant as our condition was, however, as painful as it was to put more distance between myself and my kinsmen, I found it impressive how well managed the march proceeded. The Nipmuc especially knew the land so well and worked together so effectively, that I was certain their speed far outpaced any English pursuit.

Still the chaotic transfer of so many across such difficult terrain meant the few English prisoners among us were so widely dispersed that Oneka was required to scurry the length and breath of the line of march to keep watch over the Rowlandson children. His remarkable diligence and the ceaseless encouragement of Wantonka, I was certain, was all that kept poor Mrs. Rowlanson going. Many times, I saw her collapse to her knees in tears. And each time, either my princess or the Mohegan boy found a way to encourage her forward.

And yet, as Wantonka's attentiveness to her mother's slave persisted, Weetamoo herself became more cruel. Once we were both forced to intercede as the Pocasset sachem threatened to beat her prisoner with a log. Tension was high throughout the Indian army. But no one evidenced the strain more than Weetamoo. Each day, her behavior became more unusual.

Lately, Weetamoo had taken to dressing in the finery looted from the English women murdered at Lancaster. As our march progressed, she could frequently be seen by her husband's side wearing stolen jewels on her wrists, in her ears and around her neck, the gold and silver necklaces sometimes piled to her chin.

Weetamoo had also taken to powdering her hair and painting her face in the fashion of the English ladies who were her enemy. Carrying herself among our refugee army like any white queen, she frequently drew sharp glances from Mary Rowlandson. Once I heard the English prisoner exclaim at the

Indian woman's pretensions. But the more Mrs. Rowlandson scowled and protested, the more her pretentious mistress mistreated her.

For weeks we journeyed over the cold, inhospitable ground, at times struggling in driving rains through knee deep snow, our bellies so empty they'd stopped growling. So close were we to starvation, so weary and lethargic, that we'd stopped caring about food at all and had to make considerable effort to stop and search for it.

It was during that hideous march that I developed true respect for the native way. The ground was frozen, the trees barren, the lakes and ponds covered with ice. And yet, with the guidance of our captors, we clawed and dug for sufficient sustenance to continue our journey. We tore bark from the trees, cut the ice to fish and scratched the hard earth for edible roots and ground nuts. So successful was the army at nurturing itself from the land that, in the weeks we traveled, not one person, elderly, infirm, or child, perished from hunger.

By the end of the third week, we arrived at the Bacquog River, the largest of the eastern tributaries of the Connecticut River. With the persistent rains and warming temperatures, the early winter melt had made the angry current almost impassable. But once more, the natives found a way. With care and diligence, Monoco and Canonchet settled their people on the river bank while their warriors felled trees and crafted sturdy wooden rafts.

With straw beneath their feet to keep the frigid river water from soaking them, the Nipmuc and the Narragansett men ferried their women and children to the northern bank. The crossing took three days. Once the first braves were landed, they erected wigwams that grew in numbers as more and more crossed the churning river. Wantonka and I followed with Mary Rowlandson who appeared deathly fearful of the water. At first I thought she was afraid of falling off the raft and drowning. But when we arrived on the far bank I realized it was her children she'd been concerned for. There Oneka greeted Mary Rowlandson with the news that both her daughter and her son had crossed safely before her. Only then did the anxious mother relax the grip fear had held her in. And she hugged Oneka to her as if he were her own.

For the rest of that day and all through the next, the young Nipmuc men continued working to carry their people across. Their clothes were soaked and frozen to their bodies. But still they labored, using poles to wrestle their unruly craft through the swift current. During that time, I saw at least one raft dashed to pieces on the rocks submerged just beneath the river's churning surface. I didn't know if anyone was lost, but I heard no cries or complaints. Whether the Indians' ordeal was brought on by the folly of the English or themselves, not one in our enormous party cursed his plight.

During the first night, Wantonka and I camped with those remaining on the south bank of the Bacquag. On the second night, after crossing the river, we found ourselves in an overcrowded but comfortable wigwam on the north bank with Mrs. Rowlandson and Robert Pepper. It had been weeks since I last saw the captured soldier. As was the case with the rest of us, his skin had grown more sallow, his cheeks more hollow. Sitting by our fire, his dark eyes stared blankly at the ground. He seemed so weary and dazed, I thought at first he didn't know us or his surroundings. Rocking slowly back and forth, clutching his knees to his chest, he was murmuring to himself when he suddenly lifted his eyes to mine.

"I know this land," he shuddered. "I have been here before."

Wantonka quickly stood to gather the poor wretch's blanket more tightly around his shoulders.

"With Captain Beers," he said. "This was our line of march. These swine are returning me to Northfield."

I watched Pepper chew, wondering what food he'd managed to find to fill his mouth.

"Yonder," he raised a filthy finger toward the west, "is the river of the Connecticut."

He turned and spat toward the fire. One of the burning logs hissed as a blood red gob of spit struck it. I turned to Pepper, saw him chewing still, realizing it was the inside of his mouth the man was tearing with his teeth.

"Not many whites have come this far and lived to tell it," he croaked. "To have done it twice scares me."

He raised his head, glaring with wild eyes at Wantonka and me.

"Some say God himself has no eyes for what happens in this place," he said. "It's the Devil who watches us now."

By the middle of the next morning, it became clear that Pepper was right about our destination. With everyone safely across the river, our troop was roused and marching with the winter sun at our backs, moving north and west along the path which, according to Pepper, the doomed Northfield rescue mission had followed six month earlier. Behind us, a party of warriors set fire to the abandoned wigwams to keep any pursuing English force from taking shelter there. Ahead of us, the terrain grew more difficult.

For days we followed a meandering course, circling miles out of our way to avoid the treacherous slopes of several snow covered mountains that stood in our path. Besides the nearness of my princess, the only thought that buoyed me during that time was the hope that every step taken by this ghostly Indian army ensured a longer peace for the English settlements behind us. Perhaps this migration west marked the end. Perhaps the fight was finished and in the spring those few of us surviving whites would be ransomed to the English to secure the peace.

It wasn't until we crested the last craggy ridge overlooking the broad plain of the Connecticut Valley that I saw how wrong I'd been. Standing with the setting sun in my eyes, my wife's hand in mine, I beheld the terrible spectacle of a second Indian force nearly as large as ours awaiting our arrival.

"Metacom has returned from the land of the Mohawk," Wantonka told me as shouts went up from hundreds of warriors on both banks of the wide river.

Once more I was reminded of Pepper's words. God had no eyes for this place. These shrieking devils confirmed it.

This time, the Pokanoket provided canoes for our crossing. Still, it took two difficult days to remove everyone to the distant bank. Enormous blocks of ice and fallen trees littered the swollen river, creating hazards that tore open the sides of more than one of the natives' delicate bark craft. As great care was required to avoid these obstacles, each crossing trip consumed more than an hour.

When it was our turn, Wantonka and I were once again allowed to accompany Mrs. Rowlandson. Although Oneka had already reported the safe crossing of the two English children, their mother seemed more troubled than at any other time during her captivity. After struggling briefly with the two Pokanoket braves who were to paddle us across, she burst into tears as she was pushed into the bottom of the canoe that was to carry us.

"Why do you cry?" one of the warriors asked.

Although I didn't recognize him from my time at Mount Hope Bay, I was certain he knew who we were.

"They will kill me," Mrs. Rowlandson sobbed.

"No," the brave promised. "None will hurt you."

Taking his place in the bow, he waited as a second Pokanoket warrior pushed us from the river and climbed into the stern. Reaching into the deerskin pouch that hung at his belt, he then provided the poor woman a handful of cornmeal.

"Philip will have you come to him this day," he informed her, somberly watching as the starving English woman struggled to chew the dried meal.

His words and the paltry handful of meal had a sudden calming effect on Mrs. Rowlandson. She dried her tears at once and took her place in the bottom of the narrow canoe, murmuring a passage from her bible as she chewed.

"By the Rivers of the Babylon, I wept," she whispered.

For the next hour, the two braves fought the swirling river current. As they paddled, one in the bow and the other in the stern, the three of us laid on top of one another, our clothes soaked with freezing water splashed from each strong stroke of the paddles.

Under my blanket and shirt, I still carried the sacred belt for Anawan. I wondered if Philip knew of this and would he welcome us as well. As the canoe drew closer to shore, I scanned the faces crowding the river bank ahead. I wasn't sure I'd seen Philip before. So many natives had passed through my life as a result of my cousin's strong relations with their sachems it was impossible for me to know if the Pokanoket sachem had been among them. Of the warriors I saw that day, I recognized only those we'd traveled with.

With the arrival of each canoe, the men of Philip's army converged on their Nipmuc and Narragansett brothers, laughing and shouting, sharing stories with the mock bravado of the doomed. It was clear from their thinned ranks and the overly boisterous welcome they gave that things had not gone well for the rebel leader among the Mohawk.

"There was a great battle," Oneka later informed me. "The Mohawk killed many Pokanoket."

Among this army of warriors, the boy had become invisible. He was able to go everywhere and hear everything. Nothing appeared to bother him, neither hunger nor fatigue. He flew from place to place, an anonymous little bird among these dangerous men, bringing us bits of news from all over our new encampment.

"Philip murdered two Mohawk," he soon reported. "He told the Mohawk captains it was the English of Albany who killed their braves. But one of the Mohawk had escaped Philip's ambush and told his captains of it."

Often stone faced in the presence of others, Oneka spoke with sudden animation when he was alone with Wantonka and me.

"The Mohawk attacked Philip at Schagticoke." His eyes were wide, his hands cutting the air between us as he spoke. "Many Pokanoket scalps were taken."

Glancing from side to side to be certain he wasn't heard by any others, Oneka leaned close.

"Philip ran while Anawan and the other strong ones kept the Mohawk from chasing him," he whispered. "Now he is here before Monoco and Canonchet, a war captain with only half an army."

It was just as my cousin had told me. When things looked bad, Philip would run. Only Anawan and the other war captains kept the Pokanoket in the field when their leader's deceits were discovered. But it wasn't until we were summoned to the council fires of the Nipmuc and Narragansett sachems that I finally got my chance to measure the man for myself.

Keeping my prized story belt concealed beneath my blanket, I followed Canonchet's emissary to the great lodge newly erected at the center of the camp. At my side, Wantonka proudly strode among the curious braves who had gathered to see Weetamoo's daughter, the white man's squaw. With her head held high, her eyes fixed on the lodge before us, Wantonka gave no sign she even noticed their angry faces. She was royalty, heir to a queen. She cared little for the opinions of these surly, filthy braves.

Inside the lodge, the Indian leaders glared at us from the elaborately stitched blanket that covered the ground on which they sat. I recognized Canonchet, Quinipan and Monoco. Behind them stood Sagamore Sam and the other Nipmuc and Narragansett war captains. Weetamoo was there as well. Bedecked in silks and jewels and other stolen finery, she stood at once and distanced herself from her daughter.

Only two men present were unknown to me. One, an inconsequential looking man of medium build, weak chin, and nervous, darting eyes, sat with the other sachems. Assuming him to be Philip, I glanced instead at the tall man who stood directly behind him. Other than the Pokanoket sachem, this warrior chief was the oldest man present. At least two decades senior to me, he stood a head above everyone gathered there.

At a signal from Canonchet, the tall brave stepped from behind the council of sachems and came directly to me.

"Anawan," Wantonka breathed.

Standing with his arms folded, he waited as I opened my blanket and lifted my shirt to reveal the belt entrusted to me by the Pokanoket old man murdered at the Great Swamp.

"Ahhh," Anawan moaned, taking the treasure from me.

Towering over us, he looked ready to topple, a great oak that had lost its rooting. A solitary tear dropped down his weathered cheek. But with his back to the others, the great warrior's hurt was visible only to Wantonka and me. It wasn't until he'd composed himself that he nodded sternly to me and returned to his place among the war captains.

"Your deeds have earned you a place here," Canonchet told me. "As keeper of Anawan's belt."

To his right, Philip fidgeted beneath his blanket, still refusing to meet my eyes.

"Now," the Narragansett sachem went on, "as keeper of the stories of my people, you will tell this council of the fighting in the Great Swamp."

At first, I was so stunned by his request, I couldn't speak. These were the most dangerous men in the colonies, feared throughout New England. I was but one man, one of the English they so fervently despised, made to stand before them now and tell the tale of barbarity against the Narragansett. But arranged before me on their colorful floor mats, staring at me with the respectful curiosity of children, they seemed so harmless. Even Canonchet gazed up at me with such open faced wonderment, I nearly forgot that mine was a story he not only knew, but had suffered through.

"There were more than a thousand English," I began. "They came across the ice at dawn."

At my side I felt Wantonka take my hand.

"They attacked at the place Canonchet had planned, an opening in his castle's walls where his warriors were waiting."

Now even Philip's eyes were fixed on me.

"They came ten or twelve abreast into an open field surrounded by Narragansett. Musket balls tore them like leaves of grass. But no sooner did one line of soldiers fall than another stormed into the castle to stand in its place."

"Name them," Canonchet barked.

"Governor Winslow led the army," I said.

Philip turned to whisper something to Anawan. But the big Indian stood with his family's story belt in his hand, his eyes on me.

"My cousin, Benjamin Church," I stammered. "And Captain Moseley."

This last name drew scowls and grumbling from them.

"They are stubborn, vengeful men," I told them. "The more that fell, the harder they fought. Every volley of their matchlock muskets killed a score of Narragansett."

I went slowly, not wanting to offend, but feeling a growing responsibility to them to tell their story fairly.

"Canonchet ran among his warriors urging them to keep a steady fire. But their powder was running low. Soon the bodies of the fallen were piled high. And the English continued coming through the breach until there were more inside the Narragansett castle than outside."

Even Weetamoo seemed transfixed. She stood behind the men, hanging on every word I spoke. It was then I noticed her resemblance to Wantonka. Never had I seen it so clearly. Though her eyes were wild, her hair a tangle, there was something suddenly familiar about the roundness of her chin, her mouth and the rise of her cheeks. Caught in the light of the council fire, her skin illuminated with the same welcoming glow I'd come to love in my princess, Weetamoo seemed human, almost beautiful.

"Canonchet was forced to move his fighters to the swamp where they could attack the English rear still outside the castle," I continued. "Winslow and my cousin Benjamin Church stood to face the Narragansett counterattack. But Captain Moseley remained inside the stockade where his men set fire to the wigwams."

Again the council members grumbled.

"My braves wasted all their powder trying to kill this Moseley," Canonchet shouted.

"In September, we bloodied the waters of the Muddy Brook," Sagamore

Sam growled. "Nearly one hundred English fell that day. But we could not kill this white devil."

I had seen it myself. The murderous pirate seemed to defy death.

"There were many dead inside the Narragansett castle," I told them. "The paths taken by both armies, one to the east and the other to the west, ran red with the blood of the dying. White and red."

I did not tell my own story, of finding the burned bodies and recovering Anawan's belt from its hiding place in the barrel of wampum. I had not been invited here to celebrate my own deeds or to share my very private moment with anyone but Anawan himself.

"Daniel," Canonchet said at last. "You have spoken true."

He looked from one to another of the war chiefs seated beside him.

"It has been decided you are to return with me to the land of the Narragansett," he pronounced. "We need seed corn to plant to feed our people. You will come with me to the place where it is hidden. It will be the last part of the story of my people. When the seed corn is found and returned here, the Narragansett will be no more. Our corn and our people will feed the new nation of red brothers we have made in this place."

I thought of the panic that would fill Plymouth and Rhode Island when they learned Canonchet had returned east.

"The English will kill you," I told him.

"Yes," he said flatly. "It will be the last of my story also."

Signaling me to go at last, he watched as Anawan left his place among the war captains to follow me. Once outside the wigwam, the tall war captain spoke briefly to Wantonka in their native tongue. Turning to me, he then cinched the story belt around his waist.

"We are as the flowers of spring," he told me, "and the leaves of summer. We will all die soon. Because of you, I will wear the story belt of my family until that day. Then I will carry it to you."

"But why?"

"My father has made you keeper of the belt," he said. "When I am gone and my children are gone, it is you who will have it."

I tried to protest, but Wantonka interrupted me, speaking once more to Anawan in the common language of the Wampanoag.

"What did you say to him?" I asked her when Anawan had left us to return to the council lodge.

"I told him it was done," she whispered taking my hand to lead me back to our own wigwam. "I told him you would take the belt, but only if he carried it to you on the day this war ends."

XIII

With an army of one thousand warriors accompanying him, Canonchet made it clear he intended more than the gathering of seed corn. After journeying nearly two weeks, we had arrived at last on the outer edge of Plymouth colony. Five days before, the equinox had passed. The weather was crisp and dry, the sun warmed ground raising the first green sprouts of spring.

Canonchet had stopped his force by the falls of the Blackstone where braves, both Narragansett and Nipmuc, had gathered outside the sachem's brightly colored wigwam to prepare their weapons and blacken their faces for battle.

"The English come," Oneka informed me.

It was weeks before planting season. But I still could not imagine the colony mustering a force strong enough to match the one Canonchet had brought to fight them.

"They will need an army as large as the one at the Great Swamp," I said.

Ignorant of the devastation Canonchet was about to bring them, the fighting men needed here would be with their families now, attending services in meeting houses from Providence to Boston. It was Sunday. Even in captivity I'd kept track of the passage of the days, careful to make my weekly prayers to the Almighty whose help my people desperately needed now.

Wantonka, Oneka and I were made to stay with the squaws. But with every brave eager to rush off to the coming battle and no one left to watch us, we were able to slip away and follow them at a distance. Less than a mile from our camp, we arrived at the top of the falls and an escarpment of rocks that gave us a good view of both banks of the river where Canonchet set his trap.

It was a terrible vision, the vengeful survivors of the massacre at the Great Swamp lying in wait to exact their retribution. I prayed my cousin wasn't in the party Canonchet expected. I was able to help him once. But now the odds so greatly favored the Indians that no white man was likely to survive this day.

The action began with the very distant crack of muskets. Canonchet, I'd assumed had employed the same trickery used on Church and me in the ambush at the Pocasset Swamp. Pretending to be surprised by the English, a small party of Indians placed well down river would run from the approaching soldiers, luring the whites into the native ambush.

The sun was high. The swollen river tumbled against the rocks with a roar that all but obscured the approaching musket fire. Next to me, Wantonka knelt beside the boy. With their eyes fixed on the shallow pool at the base of the falls, their faces reflected an odd calmness. It was a look I'd seen before. With danger near, they maintained the same stone faced determination I'd seen among the Narragansett after the massacre of the Great Swamp.

Suddenly, the river bank was filled with soldiers. And just as suddenly, the trees before them exploded with musket fire. With fewer than a hundred men facing nearly five hundred muskets, the English commander quickly ordered a retreat across the pool to the far bank of the river. But no sooner had his men accomplished this maneuver, carrying their wounded with them out of range of the ambushers, than they were assaulted by a second force on the opposite shore.

Now the English were surrounded, outnumbered ten to one, standing shoulder to shoulder in a ring at the very edge of the river. Before them and behind them, Canonchet's fighters were arrayed ten deep in places, delivering a withering fire that relentlessly tore the English ranks.

For two long hours, it continued. One by one, the English fell, each dying soldier blessedly relieved of the shame I felt and of the loneliness and terror still to be endured by the thinning ranks of his surviving brothers. Closer and closer the Indian ambushers drew. And then, with fewer muskets to deter them, they dropped on the last of the white soldiers with terrible fury, beating them to the ground with their bloodied war hatchets until none was left alive.

I was beyond feeling, so numbed by what I'd seen that I was indifferent even to the sight of Canonchet's braves mutilating the bodies of the fallen whites. My only contribution here was as witness to the atrocity. And I remained where I knelt until the very end.

When Canonchet returned his fighters to our camp, he would discover our absence. Whether he chose to come searching for us or not, I no longer cared. I was so shamed by my inability to stop the slaughter that I still couldn't move from my place above the falls.

Below me, the river's waters licked at the boots of the scalped English dead. Canonchet's fighters had removed their own fallen, leaving the bodies of their enemy for the animals of the forest. Many were naked, stripped of their weapons, their clothes and their valuables. Dozens of the twisted torsos were headless, the Indians taking retribution even on the lifeless forms of their enemy.

I had come with the natives to this place. I'd watched them prepare their enormous force for battle. I'd stood by as they blackened their faces and set their trap. And I'd done nothing to help. On my conscience, I carried the loss of each Englishman and would wait here through the night for their killers to return for me. If they did not, if I were to continue to live, I would carry my shame and news of this massacre to Providence. I had saved no lives here. But with luck I might be able to save the next poor souls who stood before Canonchet's bloodied scalping knives.

Without a word of question, Wantonka and the boy remained beside me. Perhaps they'd realized what I hadn't, that this battlefield was the last place Canonchet would think to look for us. His mutilation of the English corpses had had one purpose, to so terrorize the white intruders in his land that they would run from him. He hadn't learned the lesson of the Great Swamp, that English resolve was only hardened by events such as these.

Even I was beginning to feel my determination stiffen. Until now I'd been a reluctant participant in this fight, caring only for myself and my family. But during the long evening and night that followed, as the ghosts of the battle prowled the ground around me, I made up my mind to find my cousin and join with him in tracking Canonchet.

Whether the unprovoked attack at the Great Swamp had caused it or not, the Narragansett sachem had been transformed into an inhuman monster. He had to be tracked and killed like the animal he'd become. I knew his plan and could help my cousin mount a force to do the job. Perhaps that had been Canonchet's desire all along. Perhaps the last part of his story was not just mine to witness, but to orchestrate.

At dawn we left the falls and, passing wide of the ground where the dead English lay, we followed the river south to Providence. As difficult as it was to imagine Canonchet turning against Roger Williams, his friend and benefactor, I had seen much to convince me that the Quaker city where the great man resided would burn. Sensing his own death was near, the Narragansett war chief would exact the dearest price his life would bring. With dozens of unfortified English homes in his path, he would put aside his regard for Williams and bring his army there at once.

Since Narragansett scouts were likely close behind us and frightened English farmers ahead, we moved swiftly but carefully. Oneka was certain he'd seen several loyal Praying Indians among the English fighters at the falls. For that reason we had to consider the fact that one or two of them may have escaped ahead of us with news of the massacre.

"I saw one Cape Indian black his face with powder," he'd told us. "He stood among the Nipmuc and the Narragansett as they stole from the bodies of the English."

If, by this ruse, any of the Praying Indians had managed to flee the ambush, the entire countryside would be alerted. Dressed the way we were, a white man and two Indians, my family and I could easily be mistaken for our enemy and killed by the panicked English we'd come to warn.

Holding to the high ground that overlooked the river, avoiding the shorter lowland route a reinforcing English army might take, we covered the difficult terrain with the caution of a native war party. Separated by nearly a hundred yards, the boy and I moved ahead as flanking scouts with Wantonka following between us and behind. This way, using hand signals and bird calls to assure one another the path ahead was clear, we moved unnoticed, arriving by mid afternoon within sight of Providence.

From the cover of a heavily wooded ridge, we faced the Quaker capital across a broad salt marsh. Overlooking the grass choked cove and the narrow thread of river that snaked through it, dozens of houses stood clustered atop a steep hill. The day was raw, the sun concealed behind a wall of gray, and a stiff wind knifing in from the bay. Strangely, however, despite the cold, not one of the town's houses breathed smoke from its chimney.

After carefully descending the high ridge overlooking the wide salt cove, we crept through the tall sea grass to a place where the river narrowed to just several yards across. We kept close together this time, Wantonka with a dark blanket pulled over her head, the boy with his hand in mine, trying to look like any other Quaker family returning from a day of digging shell fish.

For the next long minutes, fording the narrow channel and climbing the steep hill, we were exposed to view from the town. If sentries were posted, we could be shot. And with my free hand, I squeezed the soft flesh of my princess's arm above her elbow, knowing that as long as I felt the warmth of her breast against the back of my hand and the steady pulse of her heartbeat under my fingers, we were alive.

When at last we crested the hill, the scene that met my eyes did little to allay my fears. All was chaos as the citizens of Providence scurried to evacuate their town. Oneka's suspicions about survivors returning with news of the massacre in the Blackstone Valley had apparently been correct. The citizens of the Quaker capital knew an enormous Indian army was near. And despite the esteem in which the natives held their leader Roger Williams, all knew the time for dialogue between our people had passed.

"To Aquidnet Island," one man hollered when I asked his destination. "Better get there quick yourself if you want to keep your hair."

"It's Cononchet himself," another shouted from his heavily laden horse. "Come to take his vengeance for the Great Swamp fight."

"They slaughtered near a hundred at the falls of the Blackstone," a wild eyed Quaker woman shrieked. "A hundred Christian souls lost to those heathen cowards while we were praying at meeting."

Wantonka pulled her blanket close around her face.

"We must find Roger Williams," I told the Quaker woman. "Canonchet will heed him."

"The old man refuses to leave," she answered. "He sits alone in yonder house."

She pointed to a tidy shingled cottage at the edge of the narrow main street. Then she heaved a large cloth bag to her shoulders and struggled off.

Roger Williams was waiting at his door when we arrived. Dressed all in black, his tall staff clasped firmly in his hand and his dark eyes brooding beneath the wide brim of his hat, he looked like any of the humorless Puritan elders who had banished him here.

"Where am I to go?" he asked when I begged him to gather his things. "I'm seventy six years old. I have no family and am unwelcome in the other colonies. I did not start this trouble and now it comes to me."

"Go with the others to Aquidnet," Wantonka tried.

"No," he said. "This is my home. I will remain here and speak with Canonchet. Someone must stop this madness."

Ducking under his low eave, he stepped across his narrow swath of lawn to the edge of the street.

"There." With his long staff, he pointed behind me in the direction I'd just come with my family. "They come."

Across the great salt cove, along the high ridge from which we'd first sighted the Quaker capital, hundreds of natives were spilling down from the forest. In a dark wave, they advanced as the women of Providence shrieked and ran in every direction.

"I must go to him," he said striding forward. "I must save these people and their homes."

"These people will save themselves," I told him.

Already the streets were emptying. By the time the first of Canonchet's braves managed to cross the cove, the people of Providence would have escaped to the Seekonk River to the east. There, intrepid Quaker boatmen from Aquidnet would carry them to safety just as one had done for my cousin and me during the ambush at the Pocasset pea field.

"Canonchet must understand," Williams was telling us, "that by destroying these homes he will engender English hatred toward his people that will never end. Go," he said. "Follow the others to Aquidnet. No harm will come to me that God does not intend."

But stepping across the road, he stumbled over a stone and fell against me. I was struck by how light he was. Even his oak staff hit me with greater force than the old Quaker himself. Beneath his long, dark cloak and enormous black hat, Roger Williams was a straw man.

"We will come with you," Wantonka told him. "Canonchet will not harm us."

"And you, Daniel?" With weary eyes, he looked up at me.

"I have been through much," I told him. "Canonchet has had many chances to take my life. He keeps me alive to tell the story of his people."

At the foot of the Providence hill, elements of Canonchet's vast army had already begun crossing the river above and below the salt cove. As we descended, the first war parties swept past us on either flank. With Williams between us and the boy walking ahead on point, Wantonka and I inched toward the center of the Indian advance. There, at the place where we'd first crossed from the forested ridge, where the river narrowed to a few dozen yards, Canonchet stood waiting.

What hypocrisy, I thought, when I saw them. The Indian leaders were dressed in the finery of the English they wished to sweep from their land. As we closed the distance between us, I saw Weetamoo's heavily jeweled arms sparkle in the sun. Canonchet himself was dressed in a brushed ox hide jacket with silver piping stitched to the collar, cuffs and lapels. Behind him, several of his war captains stood with gleaming English cutlasses fixed to their beaded belts.

"Why?" Williams shouted out when we stood at last across from them. "Why do you turn on those who have been neighbors to you?"

Between us, the narrow band of river threaded sleepily past.

"You are men of God," the old man railed. "Yet you run around the country as wolves, tearing and devouring the innocent and peaceable."

Behind us, flames were already beginning to consume the first of Providence's proud homes.

"This home of mine now burns," he cried. "And yet these past few years it has sheltered and fed many of you."

But Canonchet refused to mind the elderly Quaker.

"You have the blood of the Narragansett on your hands, old man," he answered. "Though you didn't raise your hand against us, you aided those who did."

"No," Williams spat. "You will not accuse me for your own convenience."

Stepping forward, he broke free of my hold, standing tall, shaking his long staff as his town burned behind him.

"Planting time approaches," he warned. "Return home and tend to feeding your people or it will be from your own hand they will perish."

One of the other Indian leaders strode boldly into the river, Sagamore Sam, from the valley of the Connecticut.

"We will live off those English that we kill," he roared. "For these ten years or more, it will be us that will take from you. Go yonder," he pointed behind him, across the wooded ridge he'd just descended. "Go to the valley of the Blackstone. Look upon four score English dead who yet lay unburied."

"You fight like women," I shouted. "Meet the English in the open, if you dare, not with cowardly ambushes."

But Canonchet just laughed at me.

"You are my friend, Daniel," he said. "In time I may come to you and talk of peace. But now, tell your captains to hide their women and children inside their garrisons and castles. This next month, we will go from this place to burn the homes and barns of all Plymouth."

He then signaled to the others to cross the river with him and join him up the hill to the conquered city.

"Stay far from the burning homes," he shouted back to us. "Keep close to the water when you leave this place. And do not return."

The old Quaker sagged against me once more as he watched the native leader disappear toward the smoke blacked crest of the hill.

"I bought this land from that man's father's father," he whispered. "With this act, all the good we accomplished here is lost."

But I was thinking instead of the harm yet to come once Canonchet's formidable army was loosed on Plymouth.

"Food is their weakness," Williams pronounced. "Though these fighters might be able to live off what they pillage from our homes, their women and children will starve without their men to provide for them."

Tightening his grip on his staff, he straightened once again.

"It is by their own hands that the seeds of their destruction will be sewn," he said. "Whether their army is victorious or not, without their women to raise the next generation, the Narragansett and the native people of the Valley will die out."

It was just what the land hungry among the English longed for.

"I'm glad I will not live to see that day," Williams told us. "Though I fear that I and all the English in this land will have a reckoning before the Almighty because of it."

XIV

Heeding Canonchet, Oneka, Wantonka and I led Roger Williams north along the river in the direction the Indian army had just come. Taking the sachem at his word that he intended to point his murderous force toward Plymouth, we followed the safer path to Boston.

Once more Oneka took the lead while my wife and I followed with the old man. We hadn't spoken a word among ourselves since we'd turned our backs on the burning city on the hill. We moved slowly, occupied by our own black thoughts, expecting little trouble.

Our tiny band was just approaching a shallow hill where I intended to have the boy turn us east, away from the river, toward Pawtucket and the path to Boston Leaving Wantonka to stay with Williams, I was hurrying forward to give our watchful scout the signal to change our course when I saw him drop suddenly to his knees.

"Narragansett," he whispered. "There."

Kneeling, I followed the boy's point, my gaze straining through the heavy thickets toward a place where the river turned slightly west. At first I saw nothing through the leafless tangle of trees and vines. But then a sudden wind gust drove a cloud of dark gray smoke across an empty apron of stone at the river's edge. Leaning closer to Oneka, following the smoke trail toward its source, I saw a flash of color.

"Squaws," the boy breathed.

On hands and knees, we moved forward, careful not to disturb the dried leaves that covered the forest floor. Slowly, we approached the Indian cooking fires, stopping when we were close enough to hear the voices of the women. Gathered in a wide clearing, five squaws tended a solitary cooking fire before a familiar brightly colored wigwam.

"Canonchet," Oneka whispered.

With the greatest care, we crept away, returning to Wantonka and our guest. Together we retreated several hundred yards downriver before we dared to speak of what we'd seen.

"Canonchet has made his camp ahead," I told them.

Williams slumped to a fallen log. With his staff in his hands, he rested his head against the burnished wood.

"It's a small camp," I reassured him. "Only for the sachem and his squaws."

"But why?"

"The seed corn," Wantonka answered. "Canonchet has promised the Valley sachems he would send his squaws to them with seed corn hidden near here."

She bent to touch the old man's shoulder.

"We must leave the river," she whispered to him.

He sank even lower under her touch.

"We must go now," she said. "Before Canonchet returns."

Still the old man didn't move.

"What lays behind us and before us is evil," he said. "Only here in this place is good being done."

Then he stood, his staff grasped firmly before him.

"Continue north," he ordered. "Tell the English of this place and bring them here. I will help the women gather their seeds and hurry them back to their children. When you return, I will be gone. Then you will capture Canonchet."

His jaw tightened. With both hands, he lifted the staff and drove it down hard at the ground between us.

"Go quickly," he barked.

Once we left the river and the old man behind, the forest folded itself around us like a heavy blanket. But the close, quiet feel I'd so cherished as a child had been forever changed by this war. Where I'd once found peace, I now sensed danger, behind each tree and rock, and in the once soothing silence.

Deeper and deeper we went, penetrating the wilderness gloom until at last we came to a second river, the Seekonk, crossing at the narrows where it descended from the dense Pawtucket woods. The sun was low, the day nearly spent when we decided to make our camp in the shelter of some rocks at the water's edge.

Careful to conceal ourselves from view of either bank, we lit a cooking fire and fished among the trout and salmon that darted near the water's edge. Despite the ever present dangers that filled the forest around us, our privacy was uninterrupted. And we fished and ate more than we had all winter, slaking our thirst with clear, cold April water.

Just before sunset, Oneka brought a purple crocus to Wantonka. After watching me place the flower in my darling's hair, he then left us to lay his blanket in a hidden corner of the nearby rocks. It was the first time Wantonka and I had been alone in months. And with the chill night air closing in around us, we rolled ourselves together in our blankets, breathing each other's nearness.

"When the war is ended, we will have a child," Wantonka whispered to me that night. "A child of the land, neither red or white."

I felt my heart pound.

"You will teach it the ways of the English," she murmured. "And I will teach it the Indian ways."

"Mother," I called her.

Feeling Wantonka shudder beneath me, I looked up at her silhouette against a startling red moon, catching the glint of tear drops on her cheeks.

"What is it?" I asked.

"You call me mother," she answered.

"Yes?" I reached to wipe away the dampness on her cheek.

"What of my mother?" she asked. "Is she ever to return to me, ever to see our child?"

We both knew the answer to that hard question. Events had doomed Weetamoo as certainly as they had Philip.

"You will see her again," I lied. "Peace is nearer between us than you think."

Wantonka said nothing. And in the moonlight, I saw another tear drop from her eye. Though we both knew Weetamoo must die, perhaps soon, I prayed Wantonka would be spared witnessing her mother's death.

"What will happen to us, Daniel?" she asked me later that night. "When this is ended, where will we go? Where will we live?"

Again, I felt her shudder.

"In Sakonnet," I answered at once. "With my cousin and our neighbors."

"No," she murmured. "There have been too many war fires for our English neighbors to forget this year."

I tried explaining to her the Christian notion of forgiveness.

"The God of the English demands they forget," I promised.

Wantonka shook her head, a lingering tear spilling from her cheek to mine.

"I have seen this Christian forgiveness," she said. "It is for white people only. For my people, the English have the musket and the sword."

I feared she was right.

"We must become English now," she told me. "My baby and me. You must help us, clothe us in your whiteness."

Gazing across the water at the dark wall of hills that rose against the moonlit sky, I wondered at the vastness of the land that lay beyond them. Certainly there was more than any man could need, red or white. Perhaps this conflict would be forgotten and trust restored between us when we all were spread more evenly across it.

"There is great hunger in your people." She spoke as though seeing my thoughts. "None can feed it."

Comfortable in the shelter of the rocks, lulled by the sonorous rush of the water, Wantonka and I enjoyed a restful, if sleepless, night. It was yet one more oasis of blessed quiet amid the din of war. And though our bodies, illuminated by the silver sky, may not have enjoyed much sleep, our spirits found comfort and release.

The next morning, Oneka and I left Wantonka to bathe in a quiet pool among the rocks at the water's edge. Taking ourselves further upriver, he and I washed and then waited shivering in the cold for Wantonka's signal that she'd completed her own bath. It was a gray morning and, after nearly an hour, a dreary rain began to fall. Thinking we'd missed the signal from my wife, that the rushing river current and the chatter of the rain on the dried leaves of the forest floor had masked it, we turned back to our camp.

With Oneka following at a modest distance, I had just rounded the wide bend in the river that led to the rocks where we'd camped the previous night when I saw the apron of river bank and shallow pool where we'd left Wantonka was deserted. Suddenly, the boy was past me, rushing to the spot where we'd last seen my wife. Dropping to his knees, he pointed to a cluster of boot marks on the soft mud.

"Soldiers," he breathed.

Although the ground around him was badly torn by the heavy feet of several men, Oneka still found the imprint of one of Wantonka's tiny moccasins. From the looks of the broken ground around the place where she'd stood, Wantonka had been surrounded, swept off her feet and carried away. Rising again, Oneka followed the river bank to the north indicating to me the direction taken by the departing troop.

"They are near," he whispered.

And he knelt once again to touch the smoldering ash of spent pipe tobacco.

At once, I was running. This time I made no attempt at stealth. I was a white man. I had no near fear of the English, only of what they might do to Wantonka. Soon the boy had fallen behind as I swept through the forest at the river's edge. Hurdling the large rocks strewn along the bank, I ran hard for more than a mile, my lungs heaving, the crisp air biting my cheeks.

The shore was irregular, but the water sufficiently shallow that I could ford at the places where it blocked my path. At one point, I stumbled over a submerged tree limb, falling to my hands and knees. Water splashed my face and in my eyes, momentarily blinding me. Pushing myself to my feet, I wiped my shirt sleeve across my face and was just starting to run again, when I spotted something moving in the trees ahead. A small number of white shirted Englishmen marched single file about fifty yards away.

"Stop!" I shouted.

When they turned, I saw Wantonka standing upright in their midst. With a look, my darling stilled my beating heart. Rather than fear or exhilaration, she showed the same quiet calm I remembered seeing when our eyes met the night she was rowed to the ghostly slave ship in Boston harbor.

"I am Daniel Church," I shouted. "Cousin to Benjamin Church of Sakonnet."

Having just bathed the mud from my face and shirt, I was certain these men would recognize me as English.

"That woman is my wife," I told them. "Where do you take her?"

"To Captain Denison yonder," a small man pointed over his shoulder.

"We are English, Mohegan and Niantic," a second, taller soldier added. "Two hundred and a few. Just marched this month from Connecticut."

"This woman has news of Canonchet," the first man said.

With the same calm look in her eyes, Wantonka nodded reassurance to me.

"There is a Mohegan boy with me." I motioned Oneka to my side. "We will accompany you and tell your captain of the place where he will find the Narragansett sachem this night."

That was all it took. By now, word of Canonchet's return had spread among all the English of the area. Anxious to be the ones who captured such a valuable prize, the soldiers hurried us with them to their camp.

Captain George Dennison was a quiet, cautious man of scholarly appearance who upon greeting us, listened carefully as we explained the opportunity he faced.

"Canonchet has hidden stores of seed corn underground near here," I told him. "He has sent his main army on to Plymouth and remains behind with several squaws who will gather the corn and carry it to Nipmuc territory for planting."

Looking up from the map I'd made for Dennison in the mud between us, I saw Oneka staring hard at one of the Indian men standing with the Connecticut captain. The man, a Mohegan I guessed, was dressed as the English but wore the same distinctive hawk feather as the boy, fixed in his braided hair.

"Canonchet's camp stands between the Blackstone River and a small hill." I carefully drew it on the ground. "If you can reach the crest of this hill by nightfall, you will have the advantage on him."

I looked up in time to catch a spark of recognition flash between the Mohegan warrior and Oneka. Studying the older man's face, I saw a shadow of resemblance to another Mohegan war captain I'd encountered, the son of Uncas who had fought so well at the Nipachuck Swamp the previous summer. Could this man before me be the brother to the other Mohegan, another son of Uncas, father to the boy perhaps?

"You cannot hope to stop the Indian army," I told Dennison as I stood before him. "There are more than a thousand of them. But if you succeed this day in taking Canonchet, you will have done much to end this war."

Blessedly, there would be no discussion. Taking time only to arm themselves and douse their cooking fires, the battle force of red and white sprang forward at a determined trot. Oneka joined the Mohegan troop which ran ahead, taking his place at the side of the man with the hawk feather in his hair.

Watching the two of them disappear into the forest, I was certain I saw the same squaring of their shoulders and lift of their legs, the same forward tilt of their heads and thrust of their arms. Whether they were in fact father and son, they mirrored each other's movements as they led their swift force.

This time, we followed a more direct path than the one we'd taken retreating from our enemy's camp the day before. Keeping the hill which overlooked Canonchet's wigwam as our target, we covered the distance in half the time it had taken Wantonka, the boy and me to do so. With the wide prominence between ourselves and the Blackstone, its great bulk shielding the sounds of our approach, we wasted little effort at stealth, crashing through thickets and over dried leaves without concern.

It was afternoon, the sun settled just above the distant tree tops when we took our positions overlooking the river. Before extending his line, Dennison issued strict orders that not a shot was to be fired. If scouts were sent out from the Indian camp, they were to be killed or captured at knife point, presumably by our Mohegan allies. Nothing was to be done to indicate our presence to the enemy or to show the strength of our force until Canonchet was in sight.

Once his battle line was extended more than a hundred yards across the top of the hill, Dennison signaled the soldiers and Mohegan braves forward. The sun was in our eyes making it difficult to see more than several dozen feet ahead. For that reason, we moved slowly, creeping from tree to tree, inching down the sloping ground until two enemy Indians were spied approaching from the river.

At once, our entire force sank down into hiding in the heavy underbrush. Where an advancing line of armed men had been, there was suddenly nothing visible but the trees and rocks and leafless tangles of thickets that concealed us. And like the game these seasoned woodsmen hunted daily, Canonchet's scouts continued their approach, sensing nothing until several of our Mohegan allies sprang on them.

In that mad and terrible instant, knife blades flashed, determined men grunted, and the two enemy scouts fell immediately lifeless before us. Then Dennison stood and signaled his men to leave the bleeding bodies and continue their advance. He was about to follow them when I caught his arm.

"Wait." I pulled him to a stop. "Without his army, Canonchet won't stand and fight you."

From experience I knew the Narragansett sachem was a stout and resourceful leader. But like Philip and the other native leaders whose battle tactics favored ambush, Canonchet could be expected to seek his own escape from ambush any way he could.

"He cannot cross the river without being shot," I told Dennison. "His only chance will be either north or south around the base of the hill."

It was quickly decided, therefore, that two small groups of Mohegan would be dispatched well to either side of our advance to intercept the enemy war captain should he try to run our flank. Determined to do my part to see this rebellion ended as soon as possible, I followed the Mohegan party led by the man I'd assumed to be Oneka's father.

Having nearly lost my darling for a second time, I kept Wantonka with me as we left Dennison behind and hurried to his north most flank. If for some reason, the Narragansett chief, was able to outrun these sons of Uncas I accompanied, then it would fall on me to capture the man who once had held me captive.

We reached the base of the hill just as the first musket shots sounded from where we'd left Dennison's force behind us. In minutes, a man flashed past our position crashing through the thickets at the edge of the river.

"Canonchet," I managed as I spied the distinctive silver piping on the war chief's jacket.

Immediately, there were three of us in pursuit, myself and two Mohegan. But our quarry was far swifter than I'd figured and my comrades quickly fell behind. By the time I accelerated away from them, Canonchet had opened a lead of fifty yards or more. As he ran, he discarded his jacket and wampum belt. I watched them sweep past my racing feet like bits of debris carried by a river in flood.

The ordeals of the past few months had hardened me as much as him. And though my lungs burned, I knew he would not best me in this race as long as I kept him in sight. Crossing a broad apron of open ground, I saw him turn once to look back at me, a sure sign he was tiring. And I lowered my head and forced my legs to churn even faster. I was Windracer. I could outrun any man alive. Even if I chased the Narragansett sachem past the setting of the sun, I knew I would somehow gain the advantage. All I had to do was keep going, inching closer.

Once we left the open ground, we raced for half a mile through a shadowed stand of pine. The soft pine needles provided welcome cushion underfoot. And as I sped through the trees and into a second expanse of open ground, I saw I'd closed the gap between myself and him. Now my enemy was only twenty yards ahead. But what would I do if he turned and raised his musket or drew his knife on me? We had left my Mohegan allies far behind. Was I any match for the war chief on my own?

When Canonchet turned a second time to look back, I was certain he recognized me. It was my moment of greatest risk. Not near enough to fall on my enemy before he took aim at me, I was still close enough to provide him with an easy shot. We were splashing through the shallow water at the very edge of the river. Canonchet took one more look behind and darted sharply to his left. Whether he'd intended to turn on me or change his course, he took one step toward the middle of the river and his feet flew out from under him.

The water was deep enough to soak the war chief's musket. Rising to his feet, he eyed me carefully, standing no more than five or six feet from the barrel of my own weapon, struggling to catch his breath as water streamed from his face.

"Kill me," he gasped, dropping his useless musket to the water at our feet. "End my story, English, as you were chosen to."

"No," I breathed. "But if you run again I promise I will shoot you down."

Together we gulped the cold air, great clouds of vapor from our breaths catching fire in the dying sun. And in the anxious interval while we waited for the other runners to catch up with us, I wondered if the Narragansett sachem would test me. I steadied my aim and firmed my grip on my musket.

"Then it must be," he said at last.

And he dropped his knife and spread his arms, standing tall before me as the first of the Mohegan warriors burst from the forest behind us. In minutes, Canonchet was stripped of his shirt and bound with stout leather straps. He then was marched the long mile we'd raced together, back to Captain Dennison. The Narragansett camp was sacked, the half dozen braves accompanying the war chief executed and the brightly colored wigwam burned. After a thorough search revealed Roger Williams was no longer in the area, I reported to Dennison that the old Quaker must have gone north with the squaws, as he'd promised. The captain then ordered a withdrawal, persuading Wantonka, Oneka and me to join him to Connecticut with our prize.

Though shaken still, I felt great pride in what I'd done. Until now, I'd been little more than an observer in this fight. Except for helping free Wantonka from the pirates and keeping my cousin from bleeding to death at the Great Swamp, I'd done nothing but chronicle the Narragansett story, as Canonchet had directed. There was one last act to be played out, one final chapter to be written. For that reason, I agreed to accompany the Connecticut soldiers with their prize.

XV

At Stonington, Connecticut, Wantonka and I had our first true glimpse of the ocean. Born at Plymouth Bay, raised on the shores of Mount Hope Bay, I had never before seen such unfettered wildness as the sea displayed in surging against that rugged stone coast.

While our prisoner was interrogated by the military leaders of Connecticut, my family and I fought the stiff April winds to walk the beach before the greatest of God's wonders. Glimpsing the ocean's extraordinary fury, I understood at last why nothing of this land could intimidate the sons and daughters of those intrepid voyagers who'd crossed it, why men such as Canonchet had been doomed the instant they chose to stand against them.

As far as I could see, the wind tortured sea heaved and crashed, the thunder of the surf making it impossible for us to speak. But I could tell from the looks of the others, their eyes shielded to the wind yet unable to turn away, that they felt as insignificant before the spectacle as I. For hours, we remained, numbed by the vision, yet cleansed by it. And later, when I returned to learn the fate of my captive, it was with a clearer vision of my own destiny and the destiny of all men in this land. We'd never conquer it. We'd never own it. We would only share its bounty peacefully among ourselves or perish.

Canonchet had been given one choice to save his life. The Connecticut elders had made him a fair offer, to return to Philip and persuade him to end this war. But the surly Narragansett had refused.

"No Indian will yield," he told his enemies. "Not to me or you."

Canonchet was then sentenced to be executed by the same Mohegan who had captured him.

"I like it well," he said during my final audience with him, "to die now before my heart grows soft and I speak words unworthy of me."

It was a credit to the man who had brought so much misery to the land that he faced his own death with such equanimity. Within hours, a firing squad was prepared of Indians from the three tribes loyal to the Connecticut English. With the sun high in a brilliant blue sky, braves of the Ninigret, Pequod and Mohegan stood before the Narragansett chief, their muskets at the ready.

"Do you wish to speak?" one of the Connecticut officials asked him.

"This was a fight I did not want," Canonchet told them. "Killing me now will not end it."

Once more, he stood tall, his arms spread wide as the balls of half a dozen muskets ripped his chest. His head was cut off, his body quartered by blows from heavy Mohegan war hatchets. And as the fire was stoked to burn Canonchet's remains, I turned my family away, carrying with me, as I'd promised, the last of the Narragansett story.

"We have done our part," I told Wantonka. "Perhaps we should remain here until the war has ended."

"No," she answered.

"But with Canonchet's army in Plymouth, we can't return home."

Wantonka took my hand and led me to a low stone wall that stood at the edge of a wide, muddy field. The sun which had shone so brightly hours earlier was now hidden behind a wall of menacing black clouds. The wind had once more stiffened, blowing in from the ocean as my wife motioned me to sit with her on the smooth, flat rocks that lay atop the wall.

"That English woman, Mary Rowlandson," she said. "Many times I have thought of her and her children."

I shivered at the recollection of the poor white woman, her dead daughter, her starving children and all the other prisoners we'd left behind with Monoco and Philip at Northfield.

"We must do something to help them," Wantonka told me.

When news reached the Nipmuc of Canonchet's death, perhaps they'd consider using their English hostages to broker for peace.

"But we can't return there," I told her. "They will know of our part in this."

I pointed toward the distant smoke cloud rising from the fires that had consumed the body of the Narragansett war chief.

"Today, the Nipmuc and the Pokanoket bark like angry dogs," my princess said. "But by summer when there is no corn to green their fields, they will change their ways."

Perhaps she was right. Perhaps later in the season we would find an opportunity to gain the release of Mary Rowlandson and Monoco's other English prisoners. In the meantime, we faced the greatest of risks by venturing back to the frontier. With most of the wilderness settlements abandoned, Nipmuc and Pokanoket war parties would likely move east toward the same settlements where Wantonka intended us to journey.

"Marlboro, Sudbury and Concord," she said. "There we will find English garrisons strong enough to shelter us until the western frontier quiets."

It was a dangerous gamble, to risk our lives once more to free a woman we'd known for only a few weeks. But in my darling's eyes I saw such determination I dared not argue. As Roger Williams had said, it was our Christian obligation to illuminate the shadows of evil with our own good deeds.

By nightfall, therefore, it was decided. And at dawn the following day, accompanied by Dennison and his intrepid force of English and Mohegan, we left Stonington and returned north to the Blackstone where the Connecticut captain would resume his duties pursuing Canonchet's fractured army.

Reports had been received of several attacks in the Rhode Island and Plymouth Colonies. Each time, however, the enemy had appeared in numbers considerably less than the invincible force I'd seen at Providence. With their leader lost and many of their war captains fallen in battle, more and more of Canonchet's warriors had abandoned their rebellion and returned to their land. In the meantime, the frontier north of the Blackstone remained as treacherous and hostile as ever. Once we left the protection of the Connecticut force, we were exposed to danger from the western Indians under Monoco and his war captains.

"My path is to the east toward Plymouth," Dennison informed us at the end of our second day of travel.

We had reached the Pawtucket, at a place on the river not far from where we'd first encountered his Connecticut troop.

"Will you continue on with us?" he asked.

Next to me, Wantonka kept her eyes fixed on the dense forest into which the river disappeared ahead.

"We will go north," I told the captain. "To Sudbury."

Nearby, Oneka stood with the Mohegan leader. In all the time we'd been together, not one word had been exchanged between them. Until now their startling resemblance to one another was the only clue we had that they might be father and son. But the ease with which the boy faced me, not moving from the side of the Indian war captain as Wantonka and I gathered our things to leave, confirmed what I'd suspected.

"I will stay," Oneka told us at last. "With my Mohegan father."

Next to him, the older Indian folded his arms across his chest, waiting as Wantonka hugged his son to her before departing.

"If you see my cousin," I shouted after him, "inform him of my plans to return here in the summer."

Oneka turned and gave a brief salute.

"He and I will host your father and you at our farm in Sakonnet," I promised.

Like summer sun flashing from behind a disappearing thunderhead, the boy smiled back at me.

"We will eat together and tell our stories there." I raised my musket over my head, watching as Oneka did the same. "And we will laugh."

I had known the boy just a few months, but I felt something tear inside me as I watched him leave to join his father.

"Farewell, my brother," Wantonka whispered as the Connecticut soldiers marched behind the disappearing shapes of their Mohegan allies.

By midday, Wantonka and I found ourselves miles north, crossing the familiar rolling hills east of the Nipachuck Swamp. The land was much changed from when we'd last been here. Two seasons had passed since we'd pursued Philip's army along these paths. Then the valleys had burned with the dying colors of fall. Now the lower elevations swam with rolling clouds of pink and white as the fruit trees of the valley blossomed.

Though caught between two enemy armies, my wife and I did our best to enjoy the peaceful respite. As I picked bouquets of daffodils and other early wild flowers for her, Wantonka knitted blossoms in her hair. The image we created then was of Mother Nature, the goddess Aphrodite stepping indomitably over the blooming ground. No punishing winter winds or warring hand of man could defeat her. She would rise again and again, celebrating each spring in fragrance and color as if it were the first on earth.

At night we lay together in a single roll of blankets, warming ourselves in the mutual heat of our bodies. Though we never shared it in words, I imagined we kept a common thought those nights, the possibility of new life someday growing inside my princess. Even now though, in the relative safety of the empty forest, we did little more than cling to one another, breathing in the fragrance of the blossoms with which we'd perfumed ourselves. But there was an uncommon life force emanating from this land. The colors were brighter, the fragrances sweeter, the ground itself rich smelling and warm. Perhaps it was the war, the nearness of death. But with Nature reaffirmed in everything around us, it was easy to believe we'd been blessed by Her ourselves.

The next day, journeying further north, we encountered even greater silence. By then, we'd joined the Connecticut path, trampled more than a foot deep into the forest floor in some places. As welcome as the quiet was, it was unusual to find the heavily traveled path empty, even in war. With the frontier pushed back to the garrison at Marlboro and more families crowded into the scattered communities between it and Boston, I'd expected to meet at least one or two other parties during our journey.

The closer we drew to Sudbury, the more concerned I became that the silence indicated some danger. Without watchful Oneka ahead on our point, we had to move with great care. Arriving at the last piece of high ground between ourselves and the meandering Sudbury River, Wantonka and I staggered to a halt before a view of unspeakable devastation.

Rising from the west bank of the river, a mile or more distant from where we stood, smoke enveloped a fire scorched hill hundreds of feet in elevation. Not one acre of the steeply sloped ground leading to its summit had been left untouched by flame as the twisted remains of scores of burned trees smoldered over the black ground.

On the east side of the river, opposite the hideous dark mountain, smoke from more than a dozen smaller fires filled the ashen air. Something terrible had preceded us here, I knew. But other than our own panicked breaths, the oppressive silence remained unbroken.

"Monoco," I whispered at last.

"Yesterday," Wantonka responded. "Or maybe the day before."

Pointing with an unsteady hand, I indicated a clearing only a half mile from where we stood.

"A garrison," I said. "Untouched by the fight."

With little certainty that our enemy had departed, we took up our muskets and blanket rolls and began our descent into the smoke choked valley. It may have been courage that pulled my princess forward. For me it was the desperate hope I might find survivors to shelter us from whatever demons had visited this place. And my heart didn't quiet until we'd left the densely forested hillside and stood on the cleared ground before the astonished women of the isolated garrison.

"Where have you come from?" one of them asked.

"From Connecticut where Canonchet was executed," I told them.

But even that glad news did nothing to soften the grim faces before me.

"Had you come a day earlier," another of the women said, "your hair would be hanging from the belt of a Nipmuc murderer."

From the destruction I'd seen across the valley, I'd guess Monoco and

Philip had arrived here with all the Nipmuc and Pokanoket warriors that had remained in Northfield when we'd left there in March.

"I am Mrs. Brown," one of the younger women said.

Separating herself from the others, she approached Wantonka and me with her hand extended.

"You are welcome to rest here with us," she told us. "Or I can take you to my husband and the others who are seeing to our many dead."

Placing our blankets at her doorstep, we chose to follow her toward the smoldering hill nearly a mile to our north.

"The first of them came three days ago," Mrs. Brown told us as she led us along the wide cart path. "They burned several empty homes in the village before crossing the river to attack our neighbors hiding in Deacon Haynes' garrison."

Unable to penetrate the huge Indian army to help his neighbors, the woman's husband, Captain Thomas Brown, sent word to Marlboro for reinforcements.

"Captain Samuel Wadsworth of Milton," she spoke the name of the officer I had hoped would help us in our quest to obtain the release of Mary Rowlandson. "He'd dined with us only the night before, on his way west from Boston. His troop had hardly settled into their blankets in the Marlboro garrison before they were summoned back to help us."

We had traveled nearly half the distance to the scorched hill. Stepping from the forest onto the wide flood plain of the river, I saw teams of men and horses crossing back and forth through the tall, brown grass.

"Nearly sixty dead," Mrs. Brown told us. "Ambushed at the foot of yonder hill."

Finding themselves surrounded and outnumbered, Wadsworth's troop had valiantly fought their way to defensible ground at the top of the hill. Staring up at the rock strewn summit, I recalled my own experience crouched in terror behind the tumbled stone wall at the Pocasset pea field.

"Philip, it was," she coughed against the acrid, smoke filled air. "He lighted fires in the dried brush to drive the English from the hill."

From her window, Mrs. Brown had watched the soldiers of the ambushed relief column, run into the open of the flood plain in a desperate attempt to flee the flames for the safety of her garrison.

"They were shot down like dogs," she gasped. "Right before our eyes."

Stopping at last, Mrs. Brown pointed with shaking hand toward a group of men clustered in the high grass just a hundred yards ahead.

"My husband stands yonder," she said. "If you must go forward to meet him, do so. But he informs me that is no place for a Christian woman to be."

Casting a pained glance toward Wantonka, she turned and began hurrying back the way we'd come.

"I will go with her," my wife informed me. "I will wait for your return with the others at the English house."

I knew it was not fear of what lay ahead that caused Wantonka to turn. Rather it was respect for the lost souls. There was no place among them this day for any red skinned native, friendly or not. Even I felt it irreverent for me to intrude on such sacred ground.

Within a dozen or so yards of leaving the women, I came across the first of the English dead. Stripped of his clothing, his scalp ripped away, his limbs and torso mutilated from the blows of heavy Indian war axes, the body of the fallen soldier looked less than human. Someone's husband or father, perhaps, this simple man had rushed to the aid of his neighbors, fought great odds to claim the high ground overlooking the river. And now, thanks to cunning and deceit, some among his enemy would have his scalp for their trophy.

Plunging the broken end of a willow limb into the muddy ground, I marked the spot of the fallen soldier's body. Lowering my eyes, I murmured a simple prayer, even as I questioned Heaven's purpose for such an atrocity. Then, with my eyes still lowered, I continued forward, careful not to overlook any of the dead still concealed in the tall grass around me. Ahead, the muted voices of men collecting the fallen were punctuated by the sounds of shovels working the soft earth.

"We will inter these fallen heroes together," Captain Brown informed me when I introduced myself to him at last. "In that way, they will ascend to the Almighty in the company of brothers."

Before us, a mass grave was being excavated, six feet square. As bodies were retrieved from the field, they were laid together, stacked in tiers at right angles to one other, each man embracing his fellow with what remained of his tortured, broken limbs.

"Captain Wadsworth of Milton." Brown solemnly read the names from a fistful of blood soaked commission documents taken from the officers among the dead. "Captain Brocklebank of Rowley. Lieutenant Sharp of Brookline."

The grim procession continued as dozens of bodies were collected from the grassy plain and placed together in the mud black hole.

"They were ambushed there." He pointed to a narrow divide where the path from Marlboro passed between the fire scorched hill and its neighbor. "There were hundreds of Indians concealed here."

Starting at the base of the farthest hill, he waved his arm across the entire plain.

"Wadsworth formed a square and fought for hours," he told me, "repelling one attack after another. The Indians lost many dead, we think. But as is their way, they carried them off with them before we arrived here."

Another body was carried in, one more torn and bloodied document handed to the somber Captain.

"Wadsworth had made it to the top of the hill," he said reading from the still neatly folded parchment in his hand. "And they might well have lasted until night if not for the fires lighted by those heathen swine."

I could imagine the chaos as panicked men ran from the hell of smoke and flames into torment far worse.

"The miracle is that most of our Sudbury citizens were saved," he whispered. "Thanks to these brave men, those the Indians had come to kill remained safely in our garrisons."

He shook his bloody documents at the sky.

"Thirty here," he pronounced. "A dozen more along the Concord Road to the north. Sixty English officers and men."

He looked at me at last, his eyes red from smoke and grief.

"Please tell me that you bring better news," he cried.

"Canonchet is dead," I told him in a voice loud enough to be heard across the plain.

And a murmur went up among the others, not of joy, but of relief.

"Know this," Brown said above the twisted bodies of the fallen. "This tragedy that has befallen you in this place is no victory for the red man."

That night, Wantonka and I joined the Browns in their crowded garrison. As was the situation in every garrison left standing on the frontier, dozens of families were confined in a space meant for but a few. On the hard dirt floor, children tangled together in play while their fathers took turns watching over the scorched land from fortified windows on the second story. And as the women of the garrison struggled to hide tears of grief behind their trembling hands, they worked together at the wide hearth that was now the heart of their community.

Captain Brown had been right. The Indians had failed to achieve the victory here their war chiefs needed. Though bent, the spirit of the English was hardly broken. Canonchet was lost. The great army that had boldly descended on Sudbury had killed many, but failed to remove these determined families from their land.

"This war will end." Brown spoke as though he'd known my thoughts. "But these black deeds will never be forgotten."

In the corners of the room, the children continued to play. In time, they would learn the truths their parents worked to keep from them this day. Through them this infamy would live. Through them the red man would be made to pay for his hollow victory here.

XVI

By the middle of the following morning, I found myself again crossing the battlefield. Wantonka accompanied me this time and we pointed north toward Concord, carrying what belongings had been recovered from the men of that town who had died here. All was quiet, as I paused by the newly turned black earth of the mass grave, whispering a prayer to the Almighty that the brave deeds of the men interred there might earn them a place at His side.

Following the river, we passed the garrison of Deacon Haynes, its sides peppered with the holes of scores of Indian musket balls. The smell of smoke and charred wood was everywhere. Even after we moved clear of the last of the burned homes of Sudbury and into the empty swamp where the eleven bold, but reckless men of Concord had been ambushed, the stench remained with us, on our clothes, in the pores of our skin.

Despite the lingering reminders of the horrors we'd seen, however, all remained quiet. And we traveled in relative peace for most of the day, following the meandering river north and east. Shortly before nightfall, we crossed a broad meadow toward a cluster of wigwams and ramshackle pole barns thrown up at the edge of a sleepy mill pond.

"Concord," I whispered.

Once more Wantonka and I were subjected to angry glares as we made our way among the temporary shelters, past scores of panicked refugees gathered from across the frontier. Major Simon Willard, I learned, had just returned with a caravan of survivors from an attack on Groton weeks earlier. The sight of an Indian in their midst, even a woman, must have brought chilling reminders of what they'd endured.

"Monoco, it was." One kind hearted woman spoke up at last. "They all fear he will come here next."

But when they learned we carried news of Canonchet's death, even the most hostile of them relented.

"We have misjudged your intentions," a swarthy faced man offered. "Let me take you at once to Major Willard."

The old warrior's home stood on a pine covered prominence overlooking a broad turn in the river. A formidable two story structure, the garrison had a view that extended for miles along the river, from the encampment by the mill pond at the center of town, past homesteads and fields that flanked the shallow hills to the north and south.

"These oak beams," the gray haired officer said as he welcomed us into his parlor, "have sheltered my family for forty years."

With his cane, he pointed to the smoke blacked rafters overhead.

"My children fished with the Indian children of the Musketaquid at Egg Rock." Again with his cane, he indicated the corner of the room that faced the river. "Now the children of those children fight one another to drive us from this place."

He sank heavily into a rocker placed near the hearth.

"Groton has been abandoned," he said. "Brookfield. Lancaster. The garrison at Springfield is under siege."

Extending his hands, he leaned closer to the fire.

"I've been in the saddle all winter," he sighed. "By now the cold has settled so deep in my bones that even with the approach of May, I can't move far from this hearth."

After sharing our news of the burning of Providence and the execution of Canonchet, Wantonka and I listened as the old man spoke of the suffering at Groton.

"Those people you saw by the Mill Pond have lost everything," he said. "Forty families saw their homes burned with all their worldly possessions. Monoco himself slept one night inside Nutting's garrison, while Captain Parker crowded dozens of families into his."

The two structures were so close, Willard told us, that throughout the long night the Nipmuc war chief conversed with his English enemy.

"Monoco boasted he'd burn Concord, Chelmsford, Watertown, Cambridge, Charlestown, Roxbury and Boston."

As he leaned farther forward, the old man lost grip of his cane and it fell to the floor with a clatter. Immediately, Wantonka slipped from her chair to retrieve it. Kneeling before Willard, she was just placing the burnished ironwood shaft back in his hands when their eyes met.

"'What me will, me do.'" Willard spoke directly to my wife. "That's what Monoco said."

Cocking his head to one side and then the other, our host studied Wantonka's face as if he were looking there for an answer to the riddle of her people.

"Young woman?" he quietly asked her. "Do you think Monoco can do as he says?"

"I do not," my princess answered at once. "But he believes so."

"Then he will keep trying." Willard lowered his chin to his chest. "And more will die because of it."

"Perhaps not," I said, helping my wife again to my side. "With so many to feed at Menemesset and Northfield, the Nipmuc are starving."

I told Willard how the Indian army had been divided.

"Canonchet took one thousand warriors east to Rhode Island," I said. "Now that he is dead, those will disperse. As for the ones remaining in the west, with so many lost at Sudbury, the end may be nearer than they know."

I then told our host of the English prisoners we'd seen at Menemesset and of Monoco's plan to use them to barter for peace.

"The Nipmuc know you can never gather an army large enough to march west against them," I said. "When their losses are confirmed and their people are dying from hunger, they will treat."

"Reverend Rowlandson's wife?" he breathed.

"She is alive," Wantonka told him. "Her daughter has died. But she and her two other children live."

"Thank the Almighty," the old man whispered clasping his hands together. "Thank the merciful angels of Heaven."

Before we left his home, Simon Willard promised to arrange a meeting for us with a man who would accompany us west to Wachusetts. John Hoar was his name, an Englishman from Concord who had contracted with Reverend Rowlandson to return his wife and children to him.

That night, we camped a mile north of the Mill Pond on a small elevation overlooking the river at a place called Punkataset. We had traveled far and seen much. But our respite there was most pleasant.

Despite the depredations of March and April, Major Willard's scouts had convinced him that our enemy had retreated dozens of miles from where we lay. Oneka had returned to his people. Unlike our earlier moments together on the frontier, we were entirely safe, alone, and free, night and day, to share the most intimate closeness without fear of interruption.

For nearly a week we waited for our summons to Willard's home. I had no idea what caused the delay but I welcomed it. Perhaps John Hoar was in Boston where Reverend Rowlandson had removed himself. Perhaps our guide was seeking to employ one of the neighboring Praying Indians to assist us. Because they were free to travel the frontier far easier than we could, because they knew the ways of their red brothers and because their loyalty had been proven with the Plymouth, Rhode Island and Connecticut militias, the value of these friendly Indians was growing, even among the most skeptical of the English.

Together my wife and I fished the river and hunted the forests. We built our fires, cooked our bounty and slept in the open under the stars without fear of notice. It was early spring. And though diminished, the west wind still carried an occasional chilling rain. But on the days when the clouds parted, the sun warmed and invigorated us. Soon the snow white blossoms that filled the fruit trees were replaced by leafy clusters of green and the constant singing and chatter of birds dwarfed the sweet rush of the river.

There was a small homestead on the plain between the river and the hill on which we camped. During the day, Wantonka and I would hear the English children laughing and shouting as they ran in play across the acre of cleared ground that fronted their cabin. And at dusk we would sit together watching the smoke from the settler's hearth fire smudge the silver sky.

It was a fragile hold we had on this land I realized as I gazed down on that rugged square of ground. In an instant, the life that so illuminated the homestead and its occupants could be extinguished. But as I listened to the words of a fervent Protestant hymn ring out from inside the distant cabin, as I touched my fingers to my darling's shirt front, thinking of the new life that might sometime grow there, I realized the dangers that cursed this place, blessed it as well. The greater our losses, the more value we would place on what Fate continued to provide.

It was nearing the end of the first week of May when a rider summoned us to the Willard home. Knowing we weren't likely to return to Punkataset, we carefully packed our things along with several bunches of blossoms taken from the trees around our campsite, rolling them together in our blankets in order to keep the fragrance of the magical place with us.

Once more, Major Willard welcomed us to his hearth, pulling his rocker close to the fire. The sun burned through the unshuttered windows casting a warm glow across the room. But our host remained dressed in his heavy coat, sitting as close to the flames as possible. With him, three men awaited our arrival. The first was introduced at once.

"John Hoar," Willard told us. "As stout a frontiersman as you'll find in all New England."

Like my cousin, Hoar was lean and tall. His eyes burned with the same brightness as Church. And his enormous hands clenched and unclenched as if they were anxious to be somewhere else, at work at some other industry. Standing with him were two shorter, swarthy skinned men. Praying Indians, I guessed, dressed in English clothes and boots, with their black hair cropped close like Hoar's.

"Tom Doublet and Peter Conway." As Hoar spoke their names, the two men bowed deeply to Wantonka.

"Princess," Doublet whispered.

"I have seen your mother," Conway added, "and she is well."

Hoar then explained that Doublet and Conway had moved several times that winter between Menemesset and the English garrison at Lancaster.

"Though they are trusted by Monoco," he told us, "they provided valuable information to our army of the Nipmuc evacuation north to the Connecticut in February and Canonchet's march south in March to the Blackstone."

I then reminded these men that Wantonka and I had also been present on those marches.

"My wife and I spent considerable time with Mary Rowlandson," I told them. "We are anxious to assist in returning her and her sons to her husband."

I waited for Doublet and Conway to respond. Though thousands of Indian refugees had accompanied us that winter, I still thought it odd I'd never seen either of these two men before. Not trusting them entirely, I watched their eyes for some hint they may have recognized me. But other than their words to Wantonka, they seemed equally distrustful of me, remaining at a distance, refusing to look up at me.

Since Hoar was anxious to start early the next day, it was decided we would remain together that night at the Willard home. The air was hot. And though it was dangerous to do so, Wantonka and I left the window to our room unshuttered, listening to the river rush among the rocks beneath the garrison.

The peaceful whispers of the water, mingled with Wantonka's gentle breaths, were reassuring. Still, I could not sleep. My mind was full of worry at the risk I faced returning to Philip's camp. Though none but Canonchet and Captain Dennison of Connecticut knew of my involvement in the capture of the Narragansett sachem, Canonchet had been my protector among the Indians. Without him, I was at the mercy of the others, Philip, Anawan and Monoco.

Like my cousin, John Hoar was a bold man. I knew he would proceed with his mission whether we accompanied him or not. But if my suspicions regarding his companions were correct, he could be making a costly gamble with his life. I had no choice, therefore, but to heed Wantonka and join with Hoar, as risky as it seemed. Though certain Weetamoo would let no harm come to her daughter, I had only fortune to watch over me and the distant hope that Anawan might stand for me.

XVII

By dawn, we were on our way, traveling the well trod path used by English soldiers coming and going from the critical Lancaster garrison. Hoar, Wantonka and I stayed together, while Doublet and Conway remained ahead and behind. Watching our red companions share food with us that morning, seeing each pack a worn bible in his bed roll, helped me relax my concerns somewhat. Both seemed gentle, dutiful men. But this war had opened deep chasms of mistrust in me. Hereafter, on this frontier it would take much for any unknown man, red or white, to put himself beyond my suspicions.

At Lancaster, we met Thomas Sawyer, Major Willard's son-in-law. Despite the ravage inflicted on the town at the time of Mrs. Rowlandson's capture, Sawyer's garrison had been spared. In providing shelter during the interceding winter months to the many soldiers coming and going from their posts in the west, Sawyer had learned of Philip's return to Wachusetts.

"There you will find Mistress Rowlandson," he told us. "Along with the entire Indian army."

According to Sawyer, word of our mission had preceded us.

"All military activity on the frontier has ceased," he informed us. "No troops will march from Hadley or Springfield until you return."

I glanced briefly at Doublet and Conway.

"But this could be a ruse," I said. "Philip could be using her and us to buy time to plant his crops. Once he's fed his army there will be nothing to keep him from launching a summer campaign."

"Then we must act quickly," Hoar spoke up. "Keep to the plan and keep moving."

That evening as Hoar and our two Indian guides gathered provisions for the second, more difficult leg of our journey, Sawyer agreed to lead Wantonka and me to the Rowlandson garrison. Unlike the scorched landscape of Sudbury, much of Lancaster's devastation was already covered over by new spring growth. It wasn't until we arrived at the site of the Rowlandson garrison, therefore, that we saw evidence of the real destruction unleashed by Monoco's braves.

Nestled against a shallow hill, only the fire blacked remains of a wide stone hearth and four stout corner posts stood out from the nest of leafy vines that enshrouded the Rowlandson homestead. Nearby, the tumbled foundation of a second structure, a barn perhaps, was identifiable only by the brilliant sea of yellow flowers that surrounded it.

"Daffodils," Sawyer told us. "Reverend Rowlandson had them sent from England. Tulips too. Though, by the look of it, rabbits must have gotten those."

Wantonka was on her knees at once among the flowers' smiling faces. Carefully grasping the pale green stem of the largest, she plucked the flower from its resting place. Opening the leather pouch at her belt, she pulled out a folded piece of white cloth which she spread on the ground next to her. And as Sawyer and I watched, she carefully pressed the chosen daffodil on the cloth, enclosing it in the white linen folds and then placing back in her pouch.

"I will carry this yellow flower to Mistress Rowlandson," she said rising to her feet. "It will warm her memories of home."

I was certain my wife and I shared the same thought at that moment. With horrible visions of the Lancaster slaughter still in her mind, Mary Rowlandson might never find the courage to return to this place. Above where we stood, on the flank of the hill beyond the fallen barn, several fresh wooden crosses marked the burial places of her brothers and other relatives who were killed that terrible day. Death had touched this place, but as Wantonka proved, it was the life that continued to overflow from the land that blessed it.

That night, however, when darkness hid the bright faces of the flowers, it was the ghosts of the dead that returned to haunt Lancaster. As a stiff wind raked the trees outside the Sawyer garrison, their shadows danced and their cries echoed through the ravaged settlement. It was a terrible sound, like the wailing of children, continuing until dawn when the wind at last ceased and the tortured spirits of the dead returned to their resting places beneath their crude wooden crosses.

By then, we were up and started on the final leg of our journey. Soon, the squat, black outline of the Wachusetts mountains was visible on the horizon. We had just ten miles to cover to reach them. Yet it seemed a journey to another continent. This was Indian land, uncontested since the abandonment of the frontier settlements. Uncivilized, I wanted to believe. But with Wantonka's hand in mine, I found it hard to believe our enemy was any less intelligent and calculating than our English brothers. In war, each side abandoned lofty purpose, each became primitive.

By mid-afternoon, despite my earlier concerns, Doublet and Conway led us in safety to the far western flank of the mountains and into the heart of the Nipmuc camp. There our arrival was greeted as little more than a curiosity by the hollow eyed survivors of the winter famine.

This was my first visit to Wachusetts, though Menameset where I'd spent my winter of captivity lay only a dozen miles further west. At first I thought we'd stumbled upon a lesser village of the Nipmuc empire. Even after considering the hundreds of warriors Canonchet had removed east with him in March, those who circulated among the littered encampment before us were far fewer than I'd expected.

Perhaps battle losses had been worse than I'd speculated. Though signs of victory were everywhere - scalps hung from hideous drying poles, braves carrying English cutlasses and wearing ornate bands of polished gold and silver - there was no glow of triumph on any of the shadowed faces we encountered. In three brutal months of campaign, the condition of our adversary had grown more desperate than before.

Despite the uncaring looks we encountered on the hollow cheeked faces of the people of Wachusetts, however, their leaders had expected us and sent their braves to summon us at once. Inside Monoco's elaborately painted wigwam, we found the Nipmuc sachem together with Quinipian, the surviving leader of the Narragansett, his wife Weetamoo, Philip and Anawan.

As usual, Philip looked away from me as Quinipian and Monoco gave Hoar perfunctory greetings. The war captains behind them stood with their arms folded, their eyes inscrutable as always. Foremost among them, Anawan gave me a respectful nod. But when Weetamoo met my gaze with the same fierce contempt as before, I knew some among our adversaries were still far from conceding their rebellion.

"Daniel." Monoco was first to speak. "Come close."

With a wave of his hand he signaled Hoar to step aside for me. By now I was certain they knew of my presence at Canonchet's last stand. Whether they knew also of my direct involvement in his capture, I could only guess.

And I approached the council on unsteady legs wondering if it were my death sentence I was about to hear.

"You were with our brother Canonchet." It was Quinipian who now spoke. "Tell us of his end."

There was not a hint of treachery or anger in his flat, dark eyes. As Canonchet had pronounced, I was simply the teller of his story, lacking sufficient currency in the eyes of the Narragansett to even be considered a threat to them. First, I told them of the ambush of the English soldiers at the falls of the Blackstone.

"Canonchet then marched on Providence." I was careful to leave out the part about my desertion from the Narragansett force. "There he met Roger Williams who pleaded that his homes be spared."

The others continued to stare back at me with the flat, uncaring eyes of men who had seen much of this already.

"Canonchet spoke harsh words," I told them. "He said he hadn't wanted this fight, but the English brought this war to him so Providence would be destroyed."

I spoke of Williams watching from the great salt cove as his own grand house was burned.

"Then Canonchet sent his army east to Plymouth," I said. "He himself returned to his camp on the Blackstone to retrieve the seed corn for your people."

Monoco turned to Philip, grunting something I couldn't hear.

"He was ambushed there," I said. "He was chased north along the river and nearly escaped."

I spoke of how the great warrior was captured only because his foot slipped on the wet rocks and he fell into the water.

"With his powder wet, it was impossible for him to fight," I told them. "So, he was captured and taken to Connecticut.

A murmur went up among the others.

"The English chiefs gave Canonchet one chance to live," I said. "If he renounced Philip and the war, he would be allowed to go free."

I waited until I again had their full attention.

"He refused and was sentenced to death."

I told them of the firing squad of Pequod, Mohegan and Ninigret Indians assembled on the Stonington common.

"He was given one last chance to speak," I recounted. "But Canonchet simply said that it was a good time for him to die, before his mind grew weak and he spoke words that would dishonor him."

Even Weetamoo had relaxed her hostile glare to fix me with a rapt look.

"Then he threw his arms wide as the shots pierced his chest." I said nothing of the quartering and burning of the body. I left it in their minds only that their leader and comrade had died a brave death.

For several minutes, no one spoke. Then from outside the wigwam, a low wail began. At first just one or two squaws could be heard, a sound like the distant crying of children. But soon it swelled to fill the entire encampment, hundreds of native women taking up the doleful lament.

Without my knowing it, some of the camp's women had overheard my words through the skin walls of our shelter, as may have been intended by Philip and Monoco. One by one, the sachems stood and left the wigwam with their war captains following them. Nothing was said to Hoar of his mission. He, like us, was left to determine what next action we should undertake. It seemed ill-advised to pursue the native chiefs, to intrude on whatever special moment we had brought to them. But it was equally impossible for us to remain here much longer without seeking out Mistress Rowlandson and informing her of our intentions.

Once again, Wantonka seemed to know my thoughts. Taking my hand, nodding to Hoar, she led us from the wigwam into the campground where the people of the Nipmuc, Pokanoket and Narragansett tribes were gathered in a vast circle around a single brightly colored coat I'd once seen Canonchet wear. As the women continued their wailing, the men began to chant, some low, some shrieking their terrible war cries. Collectively, they created a symphony of sound which rang from the sides of the mountain.

As the circle of mourners slowly closed around the lone, discarded garment, a woman separated herself from the others. Approaching the center of the circle, she removed a colorful blanket from her shoulders and, bending, carefully laid the blanket over Canonchet's jacket. Once she'd stood and returned to her place in the circle, another person, a warrior this time, came forward with a war hatchet to rest on the ground beside the blanket.

One by one, others stepped into the circle adding to the items in the center. There were weapons, beaded belts, more articles of clothing, even a grotesque dried scalp. I couldn't be certain what these offerings were, gifts perhaps, or other belongings of their lost leader. As the circle closed and the last of the offerings was placed on what was now a pile three or four feet high, wood was placed around it and a fire lighted.

Suddenly, the chanting ceased. The flames gained in intensity. And the circle of Indians widened until the fire consuming the offerings to their lost war chief raged before them.

"They release the spirit of Canonchet," Wantonka whispered in my ear. "They free him from the things he carried with him in this world."

I watched the smoke from the fire climb among the tree tops that covered the mountain. I recalled the evil black smoke cloud that had filled the air when Canonchet's remains had been burned at Stonington. The smoke this time was far less dark, more pure against the sky. The difference made me consider the man, the good and evil I had seen in him. In death, both spirits had been released. As the English had gotten their demon, now the natives celebrated their hero.

"Come," Wantonka said, taking my hand. "Let us leave them to their prayers."

Unnoticed by the others, we left the circle and pointed toward a shimmering light visible through the trees at the edge of the camp, the first of the sunset's orange reflecting off a still pond.

"We will find her there," my wife said.

XVIII

Before us, dozens of prisoners, red, white, men, women and children, prisoner slaves of the native alliance, were arranged along the rocky shore of a tree lined pond, washing the clothing of their owners. It was a statement of their abject misery that, even with their owners occupied mourning for Canonchet, not one of them dared escape. Weary, starved and broken, they knew they wouldn't last more than a few hours before they would be hunted down and killed.

From a distance, the bent, straw like shapes seemed indistinguishable from one another. If Mary Rowlandson were among them, it would take searching to find her. Drawing close, we peered into the faces of the first of the filthy ghosts. Their eyes were small and hard, focused so deep inside they didn't seem to notice us.

Slowly we went, from one poor wretch to the next, careful not to disturb the delicate silence in which they'd immersed themselves. Who had these people been, I wondered? Farmers, mothers, soldiers? Their identities had long ago been lost to the harshness of their existence. What a pity it was that, seen even in the most hopeful light, we could only consider rescuing a few. The rest would have to endure until the end of the war.

At last, Wantonka stopped before a stooped form. Wrapped in a torn blanket, head covered, the unrecognizable figure bent before a pile of dripping rags.

"Mistress Rowlandson?" Wantonka leaned close to study the down turned face. "We have returned for you."

It was only because Mary Rowlandson's body stiffened at the sound of my wife's voice that I felt certain we had found her. In the weeks since we'd left her, the last of the starving woman's life fire seemed to have been extinguished.

Struggling to raise her head, she stared at us with flat, unseeing eyes. When Wantonka took her hand and placed a strip of dried venison in it, the poor woman didn't seem to know what to do. Even the others around her paid no attention to us or the food we carried. Instead, they remained bent over their wash, working slowly, accomplishing little.

"Mary," Wantonka breathed. "It's time for you to leave your work and come with us."

"I cannot," the beaten woman begged. "I cannot leave my work."

Her eyes were wide with fright.

"Weetamoo will beat me and my children."

"Where are they?" I asked her. "Your children? Where do they keep them?"

Now Mrs. Rowlandson turned to me.

"I don't know," she wailed. "I don't know if either is alive. They won't tell me. They beat me when I ask."

Wantonka took Mary's hand and raised it with the slender strip of meat toward her mouth. Even then, Mrs. Rowlandson didn't seem to know what to do with the food we offered.

"Come." Wantonka gently drew her from the water. "Eat."

And as she led Mary away from the others, she placed the venison against the starving woman's lips.

"Eat," she whispered once more.

At last, Mrs. Rowlandson opened her mouth and tasted the dried meat. She chewed slowly, tentatively, as if she were using her jaw for the first time. At a nod from Wantonka, she swallowed and took a second bite, her eyes beginning to show some warmth. Soon, she had what was left of the meat strip in her mouth, chewing faster, her eyes darting toward the pouch at my wife's belt.

"More?" she asked, her voice the sound of dried leaves.

Wantonka produced a second strip and, handing it to her charge, coaxed the other woman to follow us back to the camp. At first, Mrs. Rowlandson cast about her for her laundry. With frightened eyes, she considered the path before us.

"I cannot," she rasped, attempting to break free of Wantonka's grasp. "I have my work."

But the more she struggled, the more fiercely she stared at Wantonka's food pouch. Incredibly, none of the other prisoners seemed to have noticed us. They remained bent over the water's edge, struggling with their damp rags, seeing and hearing nothing.

"Mary, you remember me," Wantonka whispered, urging the other woman forward. "I'm Wantonka, daughter of Weetamoo."

Mrs. Rowlandson' feet, barely covered with torn pieces of blanket, were filthy and bloodied. With eyes now wild with fright, she attempted a step and stumbled against me, as weightless in my arms as a breath of summer wind.

"Let me," I said, lifting her in my arms and turning with Wantonka toward the camp.

As my wife continued feeding the wretched prisoner, we entered the wooded fringe of the encampment, seeking an empty wigwam where we could shelter her. The people of the tribe were still assembled in their circle of mourning. Only Hoar spotted us as we approached. Rushing to our sides, he took Mrs. Rowlandson from me.

"They have offered us shelter there," he said, indicating a rugged pole barn. "Our guides will gather blankets and wood for a fire." He hurried forward with the woman he'd come to ransom in his arms.

With the help of Conway and Doublet, we clad the walls of our new shelter with blankets. After struggling to build a suitable fire from the damp wood the two men had gathered, we laid blankets before the flames on which we placed Mrs. Rowlandson. By then, she'd eaten several strips of meat and a handful of cornmeal. Soon, the simple effort of digesting real food had rendered her nearly unconscious from exhaustion. The two guides then left us. And as Hoar and I averted our eyes, Wantonka carefully stripped away the white woman's filthy clothes.

"Daniel," my wife said after several minutes of grunting exertion. "You must help me."

Respectful of Wantonka's request, I reluctantly turned to face the half dressed invalid. Not wanting to cause Mrs. Rowlandson embarrassment and shame, I kept my eyes turned to the side as I attempted to help my wife remove her matted bodice. I held her by the shoulders while Wantonka undid the few remaining buttons that held the soiled garment in place. Other than my wife, I had seen no other woman unclothed. I did not want to do anything that would arouse the slightest suspicion that my intentions were improper.

Mary Rowlandson was so thin, however, and felt so brittle in my hands, that I was soon forced to watch more carefully that I didn't bruise her. It was when I looked on her at last that I realized how thoroughly captivity had bled the poor soul of her womanliness. She was little more than shapeless skin and bones, with nothing to excite the smallest reaction but pity in a man.

"Remain with her," I told Wantonka when I was at last able to pull away from them. "I'm going to search for her children."

I had little idea where to go or how to proceed. But the helpless woman's condition made it impossible for me to not try at least to find her surviving offspring.

"Anawan," Wantonka whispered. "He will help you."

After learning from Doublet that he'd seen the Pokanoket war captain return to the chief's council with Philip, I waited outside Monoco's lodge for him. The great crowd of braves who had gathered to mourn Canonchet had dispersed to their wigwams. And but for a few children and scavenging dogs, the village was empty.

A warming wind brought the fragrance of budding fruit trees from the hill. And in the distance, the weary band of slaves was returning from the lake, their backs bent beneath their loads of washed clothes. It was then that angry shouts flew from the council lodge.

I understood little of what was said. From the tone and the few angry words I recognized, it appeared an argument had broken out among the Indian leaders concerning my mission to free the captured white woman. After a year of fighting, one great chief and hundreds of braves lay dead. The combined peoples of four nations had been pushed to the edge of the frontier. To the south and east, their European neighbors longed for retribution. To the west and north, the powerful Mohawk formed an impenetrable wall preventing any further retreat. And in desperation, the council members continued to lash one another with shouts, until the entrance flap opened and wild-eyed Weetamoo appeared. Seeing me, she stormed before me, her fists in the air, her jewelry laden arms jangling.

"You will not take her," she shouted. "My husband will never allow her to be ransomed."

Like most of the others, the Pocasset sachem had shrunk. Under her stolen finery, my wife's mother appeared as despairing as her prisoner.

"Where are her children?" I asked.

"At Ashquoach," she spat. "Planting seed corn with the women and old. By now, the boy is infested with lice and the girl is ill. Does this woman really want her children back, such as they are?"

No matter how much I'd come to loathe Weetamoo, this uncaring outraged me more.

"As you say, she is their mother," I shouted. "And Wantonka is your daughter."

I no longer cared that some of my enemy might hear my harsh words to their sachem. I no longer cared what any of these savage people thought of me or my mission.

"What has become of you that you forget the most basic of life's purposes and needs?" I challenged.

"What, you ask?" She growled like an animal of the forest when she turned on me. "I've become as the English have made me. If I appear worse to you than I was, you have only to look inside yourself for the reason."

Starvation and want had made her this way. Still, she was the mother of my wife.

"You have power here," I said to the sachem. "Use it to help this poor family, and a woman who, except for the color of her skin and the English God she worships, is a mother same as you are."

Behind Weetamoo, the flap again opened on the council lodge. This time, several native war captains came out. Among them, I recognized Quinipian, the surviving Narragansett sachem. Leaving the others, he came quickly to his wife's side.

"Daniel," he interrupted. "What value does the English woman place on her life?"

I had no idea how to answer him.

"Take me to her," the Indian chief instructed me. "I will ask her my question."

"She's ill," I told him. "She can't talk now."

"Take me to her," he insisted.

Ignoring Weetamoo, he pulled me with him toward the pole barn where I'd left Wantonka and Hoar to care for Mrs. Rowlandson. Leading the way, Quinipian ducked behind the flap and entered before me. Inside Mary was resting beneath her blankets. Her eyes were wide with terror the instant she saw her master. Throwing off her covers, the frightened woman attempted to rise when Wantonka held her back.

"What value do you place on your life, woman?" the sachem repeated his question.

"This is outrageous," Hoar stepped forward, but the Indian shouldered him aside.

"Come," Quinipian ordered.

Ignoring everyone else, he took Mary's hand, pulled her from the floor and, with Wantonka still clinging to the white woman's shoulders, swept the two of them with him into the bright sun outside the barn. Though not a large or powerfully built man, the sachem had so taken us by surprise that neither Hoar nor I was able to stop him. By the time we followed him outside, Quinipian was leading the two women across the village toward the place where we'd left Weetamoo standing.

"What is the meaning of this?" Hoar tried.

But Quinipian could not be deterred. Head down, he hurried forward, pulling the two women past his wife and into the council lodge.

By the time Hoar and I caught up with them, Mary Rowlandson stood with the Narragansett sachem in the center of the enormous, smoke filled room. Before her sat the council of the chiefs.

"Tell them," Quinipian ordered her. "Tell them what you are worth to the English for exchange to me."

As before, the other chiefs stared forward with flat, unseeing eyes.

"He has no right to negotiate value for this woman," Hoar said, stepping forward.

But Sagamore Sam, newly arrived, raised his hand to silence the stubborn Englishman. Rising, the bandaged Nipmuc war leader crossed the room to stand at Mary's trembling shoulder.

"I am sorry to have done much wrong to you," he said to the terrified white woman. "When Metacom began this fight with the English in Plymouth, I did not expect it to reach this far."

Only Philip showed any emotion. Shifting restlessly on his blanket, he cast angry glances at Hoar and me.

"Some of my brothers think it is wrong for you to be returned to your husband in Boston," Sam said. "But this is the home of the Nipmuc. We have chosen."

Raising his hand once more, he placed it on the shoulder of Quinipian.

"You belong to this man," Sagamore Sam said to Mary. "It is he who must decide."

Slowly, Mary turned to face the Narragansett chief. Briefly, their eyes met. Quinipian's chin was set, his jaw clamped shut. But something about his impassive pose seemed to ease the English prisoner. Drawing a long breath, she straightened. And with her eyes still fixed on her captor, she whispered to him.

"Twenty pounds sterling," she said.

There was a sudden stirring among the council members as each considered the number.

"Mistress Rowlandson?" Hoar started.

He looked helplessly from her to me.

"Why ...?" He swallowed hard. "However did you determine such an amount?"

But the question came far too late for it to have any significance. If there had been any purpose to her choosing such an amount for her ransom, it was instantly lost in the flurry of activity it inspired.

Some nodding, some grunting, others shaking their heads, the members of the war council stood as one.

"Her children?" I shouted. "Her son and daughter? What of them?"

But the interview was ended. No one heeded my words. Even Mrs. Rowlandson herself seemed too fixed on the moment to have heard me.

Following Quinipian outside the entrance flap of the lodge, I was accelerating my pace to catch the Narragansett when I felt a hand on my arm.

"Daniel," Anawan spoke at my ear. "Come."

Unable to pull away from his fierce grip, I felt myself yanked to the side and hurried from the council lodge, through the center of the village to a nearby fringe of woods.

"Philip is against this ransom," the Pokanoket war captain told me. "You must remain here and stand against him in order to free the woman."

Turning, I saw that Hoar and Wantonka had remained inside the lodge with Mary. There was no one to witness our conversation.

"Forget these English children for now," Anawan whispered. "Fight for this woman. Her life is important for the peace."

We had just entered the forest and stopped behind a wide oak. By now, the other chiefs were leaving the lodge, Monoco, Sagamore Sam, Philip. But shielded behind the trunk of the towering oak, we remained hidden from view.

"Once the woman is free, I will help you find the children," Anawan promised.

He looked over my shoulder, staring deep into the forest. At first, I thought he'd heard someone approach. But following his gaze I saw only the tangled pattern of shadow and light that marked the wilderness.

"Too many young have already been lost to this fight," he said. "I have lost one of my own sons, and because of that I may one day be forced to return my father's belt to you for keeping."

He turned to me.

"Do you understand?" he asked. "Metacom is already dead. I am dead. Weetamoo and all the others who began this fight are dead. There is no use making these children suffer longer."

123

XIX

Joining Wantonka and Hoar, I settled in to watch over Mary Rowlandson's hoped-for recovery. No one dared ask the white woman how she had determined the value of her ransom in sterling. But the amount, though large, was hard to argue against the enormity of her suffering. And, in daring to state it before the Indian war council, she seemed to have so convinced herself of her own worth that she returned to her bed of blankets with renewed spirit.

That afternoon, as we sat in our crude pole lodge watching Mrs. Rowlandson sleep, we heard the sachems collect their people for another ceremony. Dressed in their finery, the sachems, Monoco, Sagamore Sam, Quinipian, led their people once more into the trampled circle of black earth outside the council lodge. Quinipian wore a white shirt adorned with silver buttons and lace trimmings stitched into the sleeves and hem. His legs were covered in short woolen pants above white stockings with garters hung with polished silver coins.

Weetamoo, as before, wore every piece of jewelry she possessed. Beneath a dark woolen coat adorned with wampum belts, her arms and neck were covered with bracelets and chains of gold and silver. Her cheeks were painted, her ears covered in jewels. Yet, even with powdered hair, red stockings and white, heeled shoes, the wild haired sachem of the Pocasset still looked more like a creature of the forests than any civilized lady of the east.

For hours they danced and chanted, seeking the help of their gods in arriving at a proper decision regarding their captive and the potential peace. Only Philip refused to participate. Whether by choice or at the insistence of the others, the man who had started this conflict now found himself further removed from it. If the Nipmuc and the remaining Narragansett chose to move toward peace, Philip would be forced to stand alone against the English. In seeking the release of the Rowlandson's, therefore, Hoar and I now found ourselves closer than any other white, Pilgrim, Puritan or Quaker, to ending the war.

Throughout the remainder of the day and into the evening, the Indians continued their ritual, seeking whatever guidance they could derive from dance, prayer and alcohol. Not once did Philip join in the proceedings, confirming our suspicions that he was still opposed to the ransom. It wasn't until hours after nightfall that he again made his presence known by sending orders for us to bring Mary Rowlandson to him.

Though significantly recovered in body and spirit from the first moment we encountered her, Mistress Rowlandson seemed shaken by the request for an audience with her tormentor. Trembling once more, she stood with us before the rebel leader in his lodge. Philip was seated, as always, at the feet of Anawan. It was a fitting pose, I thought, the weaker man, the king, ruling from the shadow of the stronger man, his champion.

"This ransom you offer Quinipian is not enough," Philip groused. "What more will you give me to speak well of you before the council?"

I felt Hoar stiffen at the outrageous request. With my eyes fixed on Anawan, I held back my friend's hand.

"What do you want?" Mary asked bravely.

"Two coats, twenty shillings, a half bushel of seed corn and some tobacco," the sachem replied.

It seemed the most shameful of all the acts committed by the man who'd started this mischief.

"What say you to this?" Philip barked.

Again I felt Hoar ready to object. And again I held back his arm.

"Is this what Metacom wishes?" I asked, stepping between Mary and the sachem. "Does he wish that the people of the Nipmuc, the Narragansett, and the other tribes know of this outrage?"

Outside, the chanting grew louder.

"Have they not fought and suffered together with you?" I shouted. "How does the chief who began this ridiculous war dare tell his people he now demands separate payment for their captured English prize?"

Philip refused to look at me. For several seconds, he sat with his eyes averted.

"You hate me," he finally said to the terrified white woman. "But what do you know of me?"

Still trembling, Mary gathered herself sufficiently to raise her eyes to him.

"I do not hate you," she managed. "I pray for you."

Philip's eyes darted in confusion. His mouth opened and he began to speak, but the white woman interrupted him.

"You are the son of Massassoit, savior of the English." Her voice steadied. "Your brother Alexander died at the hands of the Plymouth Governor Winslow."

"He was poisoned," Philip barked, pushing himself to his feet.

"And so were you," Mistress Rowlandson answered. "By hate. And that is why I pray for you."

Philip stalked to the far corner of the wigwam.

"What of your English?" he spat. "It is they who hate. They take my father's land. They murder his children."

"Yet you were raised a Christian, same as them," the emboldened woman replied. "Do wish to be judged by our God to be no better than the English you fight?"

Again Philip appeared ready to speak. This time, he couldn't find the words.

"I have been treated badly here," Mary continued. "My children were taken from me. I am starved and beaten like a dog. But in the land of the English across the sea, my enemy would have done far worse. You are the son of Massassoit, not of the English. And I pray you will see your father's face in what you do, not the face of your enemy."

Stunned to silence, Philip turned and stormed past us to the door of the lodge, leaving as I'd seen him do so often in the past when confronted by someone bolder than himself.

"He can't be serious about this new demand," Hoar finally spoke.

"He was," Wantonka told him. "But now that Mistress Rowlandson has spoken, Philip will say no more of this."

"Well done." Hoar took Mary by the shoulders. "Now let us return this poor woman to her bed."

Outside Philip's wigwam, the ceremony had grown in intensity. The chanting of the Indian braves had been replaced by drunken howls and shrieks as dozens of shadowed shapes lurched this way and that past the enormous fires raging at the center of the encampment.

"This night will see the end of me," Mrs. Rowlandson wailed.

Before us, her slender shadow twisted grotesquely in the dancing firelight.

"There is none here who will harm you," I promised. "Listen to them. They celebrate your freedom."

But in my heart, I wondered. This was a wild and unpredictable people, driven to extremes of passion. Once unleashed, there was no reckoning with their emotions.

"Remain strong," I offered Mary, knowing full well that no strength of man or God could contain their anguish.

"Sleep," I begged her. "Sustain yourself in the belief that you have friends near."

But there would be little sleep for any of us. Throughout the night, Quinipian came and went from our shelter, his mood changing with each visit. Once, he proposed a toast to Hoar. Raising a brimming clay pot, he drunkenly splashed corn mash drink over all of us.

"You are a good man," he told my comrade on his first visit to our shelter.

"Hang him for a rogue," he shouted on his next visit to us.

Back and forth Mrs. Rowlandson's emotions went. With her physical self shrunk, it was little wonder her emotional self had any means to support her.

It was well past midnight when Quinipian paid his final visit to us. This time, the sachem was so drunk, he could hardly stand without the help of a young woman who clung to him mischievously. After waking us with more of his threats and curses, he proceeded to chase the spry young woman around our cramped lodging. With his polished shillings jangling at his knees, he lurched and stumbled, nearly falling on the still reclining form of his white captive.

"Why do you shame yourself?" Hoar shouted.

Quinipian fixed him with a stunned look.

"The woman," he slurred. "You have paid for her and she is yours. Now I must have my woman."

With a giggle, the young Indian girl sprang past us and out the tent flap.

"Ahh, you see," the drunken Indian said. "I have lost her. Now I must go to my old squaw to warm me."

Long after Quinipian left us, the revelry continued outside. Though the fires dimmed, the shadows of our enemy continued to dance across our walls, the endless stream of grotesque imagery making it impossible for us to sleep. By dawn, the ground was covered with sleeping revelers. Not one native stood to block my way as I prepared Hoar and Wantonka to lead Mary Rowlandson to freedom. Even Philip was absent, fearful no doubt that we might speak to Monoco and the others of his selfishness the night before.

By mid-morning, however, as the last of our preparations was completed, a brave approached us with a message from the chiefs. A final council was to be assembled by the great rock at the edge of the village. There, with the towering stone as their altar and the greening mountain bearing witness to their gods, the sachems would make their pronouncement.

Once more, Mary Rowlandson's spirits fell. After assurances from us that no one would deny her freedom, the frail white woman reluctantly allowed us to carry her before her tormentors. Her head bowed, her spirit nearly broken from her ordeal, she made yet one more brave attempt on trembling legs to listen to Sagamore Sam.

"Tell this to your English husband," he said. "Tell him we have chosen to return you to him."

At my side, I heard Mary breathe a whisper of thanks.

"But tell him," the war chief continued, "the fight he and his brothers have brought to our people is not ended."

Weakened by his own ugly wounds, Sam directed his brave sounding words to the hollow-eyed few of his people arrayed around us.

"Tell them," Sam shouted, "that many more will die before this evil is ended."

It was absurd, I thought, a threat made empty by speaking it.

"Tell your white neighbors that the people of the Nipmuc and our brothers will feast on the harvests of another English summer."

Watching Mrs. Rowlandson lean heavily against my wife, I realized this boast would cow none but her.

"Tell them their women and children will never be safe from our scalping knives," the Indian chief railed. "Tell them they are few and we are as many as the leaves in the forest."

Perhaps he meant to so convince the poor woman that she would beseech our people to sue for peace.

"Say they will be thrown from our land and swallowed by the sea."

Mary Rowlandson might tremble, I knew, but no son of an English father would heed any of these empty words.

"I have spoken," he said.

We had won. In minutes, Wantonka and Thomas Hoar would be free to carry the white woman to safety. But my anger at Sagamore Sam's words made it difficult for me to stand silent before him. I'd seen such horrors on both sides of this war, I had to hold my mouth clamped shut to keep from cursing his false bravado.

They were all lost souls, I realized as I looked from one member of the war council to the other. The words they spoke, the breaths they took, would be among their last. Urgent for respect, they would be swept from the land, with no one to remember them or their brave words but me. I longed to speak, to tell them this. I drew a breath and formed the words. But then I felt Wantonka take my hand.

"Come," she whispered. "It is done."

It was hard for me to believe that the people I'd once considered my brothers and sisters I now so loathed. I had taken one of them as my wife, after all, and continued to love her more than any person, red or white. It was not, therefore, a simple question of skin color, although this war was about little else. And it was not an issue of right or wrong since both sides were equally to blame for what had happened between us.

What then?

As I squeezed Wantonka to me one last time, as I took Mary Rowlandson's bony hand in mine and nodded to Hoar to be off, I considered the bonds of trust that existed between us. I trusted Hoar and his guides to deliver my wife and Mrs. Rowlandson to safety. In turn, they trusted me to retrieve the lost Rowlandson children. It was this same bond of trust that had existed once among all our people. It was what had enabled both to survive. Now that it was broken, things were changed forever.

With Conway and Doublet arriving at last, Hoar prepared to leave. Handing me a small, tightly packed leather pouch, he shook my hand.

"There are silver coins and tobacco there for you to use in exchange for the children," he told me. "God speed."

But before she would allow herself to be led off, Mary turned once more to Wantonka.

"I have been separated from my husband for many months," she breathed. "So many I can no longer count them."

With trembling fingers, she took my wife's hands in hers.

"I cannot allow you to separate from your own husband to help me," she said. "I will leave you. Both of you together. I will travel with these men and will be most grateful to them and you for my freedom."

Straightening at last, she glanced from one of us to the other.

"But you and your husband," she told Wantonka, "must remain together."

"You are strong enough for this?" Wantonka asked.

Incredibly, Mary Rowlandson laughed, her face at once transformed. Her eyes flashed briefly as they filled with tears.

"After everything I've endured," she answered, "I should think I am."

Embracing each of us for the last time, pressing her bony frame against ours, she joined Hoar and the two scouts on the path toward Lancaster. Not once did she turn to look back. Mary Rowlandson was finished with the frontier. Without her having said a word to me about it, I was certain she and her husband would keep their family in Boston. This place, this wilderness most certainly had consumed too much of life's fire for them to ever return here.

Once the party of travelers was out of sight, once they'd paid for their freedom and vanished into the dark forests that pressed the eastern flank of the mountain, Anawan at last made his appearance. At his side, the Pokanoket war captain carried his musket and his blanket roll.

"You have kept your promise," I said to him.

With a nod to Wantonka, he spoke.

"Will the princess come with us?" he asked.

Again he gave a courtly nod to Weetamoo's daughter.

"I will," she answered him.

Together, my wife and I collected our things for the journey west to the Old Fort at Ashquoach. Joining Anawan beside the great altar stone, we quickly followed him away from the camp.

"Metacom is angered by your visit here," our guide informed us as we sped west. "But for Monoco and the others on the council, he would have had you killed."

He delivered this as flatly as if it were the weather he discussed.

"Once you have the white children, you must return to the land of the Sakonnet," he said. "Only there will you be safe from him."

Philip was a powerless leader, I reasoned. With his surviving warriors absorbed among the Nipmuc and the Narragansett, he was forced to abide by the decisions of their sachems. With Anawan defying him now, Philip's threats were even more empty than before.

Still, I was many miles from the nearest English outpost. But for my wife and Anawan, my situation was hopeless. Though peace seemed near, I knew now more than ever that my war would never end as long as Philip drew a breath.

"Philip is a dying dog," Wantonka said. "More dangerous now than ever before." It was ironic, however, that the farther west we traveled, the safer I felt. It wasn't just the company of Wantonka and Anawan. Nor was it the distance I was placing between myself and Philip. But with both English and native attention focused on the narrow frontier that separated them, the heart of Indian territory was at peace. Like the distant English coast, the dark interior offered too few accessible targets for any attacking army to risk itself.

With a soothing sense of relief, therefore, I traveled with my wife in the protection of the Pokanoket prince. None would bother us here. Though some might challenge my princess and me, none would dare stand against Philip's war captain. And for the first time in more than a year, I was able to rekindle some of my boyhood wonderment at the spectacular beauty of the land.

The further west we moved, the more sharply defined the terrain. The rolling hills of Wachusetts were soon replaced by steep climbs to craggy summits and sharp descents into gloomy caverns cut deep into the granite flesh of the land by torrents of tumbling water. If God had a favorite prayer, I believed, it was the commingled sounds of this holy place, the birds, the rushing wind and water, together with our own panting breaths as we hurried forward on our mission.

XX

By mid-afternoon, the sun was full in our faces when I spied the Indian encampment of Ashquoach. Perched on a distant hill, silhouetted against the cloudless sky, the far prominence had been cleared of all trees. Shining in the low sun like the head of a bald man, the naked hilltop stood above the same winding river as the southern camp of Menemeset. A small, pole stockade and a cluster of wigwams was all that covered the shallow summit. Surrounding them was the largest corn field in the Nipmuc nation, nearly a hundred acres of black earth being planted by the tribe's women and slaves.

Steadily, Anawan led us forward. Confident that none would challenge us, I kept my eyes fixed on the elevation ahead looking for some sign of the children we'd come to rescue. From the compact size of the stockade and the small number of shelters, I guessed there to be no more than one hundred people living and working there. With the lateness of the season and the dryness of the weather, I knew that all would be consumed with the cultivating and sewing of seed.

Advancing up the shallow slope, I saw several groups of planters scattered across the wide expanse of newly turned ground. Bent to their task, their eyes on the ground before them, the workers, red and white, had not noticed our arrival. Even as we left the cover of the surrounding forest and crossed the open field, none stood to challenge our arrival. It was as I'd reckoned. We were so far removed from the embattled frontier that none here considered themselves at risk of surprise or attack.

Anawan did not slow his pace. Pointing us toward the largest cluster of workers, he strode briskly forward. And, blinded still by the sinking sun, my feet twisting and turning in the furrowed ground, I struggled to keep up with Wantonka and him. As we came closer, several of the women looked up from their buckets of seed corn. Soon, one of the older of them stood.

"I am Anawan of the Pokanoket," our guide shouted out to her. "I have come for the children of the white woman."

Scowling, the old woman raised her hand, pointing where a slender figure knelt at her side.

"There," she gummed, indicating a child whose filthy skin was barely lighter than the earth beneath him.

"And there." Again she pointed, this time at another cluster of planters on the far side of the field.

Quickly, Wantonka knelt beside the white boy. Lifting his chin with her fingers, she offered him another of her venison strips.

"Eat," she breathed.

The boy trembled before her. Except for the milky blue of his eyes, he was barely recognizable beneath the dirt caked on his face.

"What is your name?" my wife asked him when he took the first strip of meat from her.

Whispering something unintelligible, the boy began chewing tentatively.

"We have come to take you to your mother," Wantonka told him.

But the boy saw only the second strip of meat she'd pulled from her pouch. Looking away, I noticed the old woman approach Anawan.

"Who will do this work?" she asked.

Standing one by one, the other women eyed us closely.

"We will pay you," Anawan told them.

And, at once a cry went up from the old woman. Soon, planters came running toward us from each end of the field. Behind them, a flock of children stumbled over the torn ground, struggling to keep up.

As the others gathered around us, they began jabbering in their native dialect. It was difficult to determine from their heated talk whether they were pleased or not at Anawan's offer. Only the warrior's stern face kept me from worry. I watched Wantonka help the frail boy to his feet and felt Anawan take hold of the leather pouch containing what was left of the sterling silver coins Hoar had brought with him to ransom the Rowlandsons. With a nod toward me, the tall brave then assumed control of the negotiation.

As the Pokanoket warrior spoke to the gathered women, I scanned the many faces, young and old, looking for the second child. It was nearly impossible to tell one of the captured children from the other. All were covered with filth. Their hair was tangled and knotted with bits of twigs and straw. Shapeless in their dirty, loose fitting shirts, the boys and the girls were even indistinguishable from one another.

Some of the desperate urchins looked back at me with wild, starving eyes. Most, however, were too worn and wretched to even raise their heads. Suddenly, I realized the enormity of the task I'd taken on. It would be impossible for me to rescue just two of these poor children and turn my back on the rest.

"We cannot leave them," I said taking Wantonka's hand.

Anawan had opened the pouch. Squatting before the oldest of the squaws, he began to lay the contents, one item at a time, on the soft ground at her feet. Already, several coins gleamed in the sun. As the crowd murmured, the woman reached to pick up one of the tobacco tins Hoar had packed for us.

"Mother," I said at once. "We want all the white children."

I counted nearly a dozen.

"All," I repeated.

To the astonishment of both Anawan and me, Wantonka then produced a second coin purse from under her shirt. Fixed by a leather string around her neck, the unexpected prize caused a great stir among the squaws. Opening the small cloth pouch, my wife further astounded us by displaying several gold and silver chains inside. They were the same chains I had seen hung around her mother's neck at the great council fire the night Mary Rowlandson was freed.

With his eyes fixed on Wantonka, Anawan carefully stood. Never before in the brief period I'd known him had I ever seen a look on his face that made me so fearful. Showing neither annoyance nor anger at my wife's intrusion, the Pokanoket warrior, our champion and guide, regarded her with utter bewilderment. With his head tilted to one side, backing slowly from her the way a small animal might distance himself from a larger, more dangerous one, Anawan allowed the squaws to close around Wantonka and her treasure.

Now was the time for me to take action, I realized. With our Pokanoket ally suddenly removed from our circle and the native women distracted clamoring for Weetamoo's stolen jewels, I quickly moved to gather the slave children to me. By offering scraps of meat and corn meal scooped from my own food pouch, I quickly collected a ragged herd.

Nearby, the Indian women squawked like geese. Their hands flew in the air above Wantonka. But none seemed to any longer consider their white prisoners. It was Wantonka and her prize of gold and silver they wanted.

Seeing this, stepping cautiously among the squirming cluster of starving kids, Anawan drew close to whisper to me.

"But those fine things belong to the wife of Quinipian," he said.

"No," I told him, careful to share my small food stock equally among my anxious charges. "Those jewels were stolen from the parents of these children. And I know they would gladly trade them for their freedom."

The bickering among the squaws grew louder as, one by one, each piece of jewelry and coin was distributed among their clutching hands. At last, the empty pouches we'd brought with us were flung high in the air from the center of their group. That's when Wantonka appeared, pushing herself free of the greedy crowd. Her hair and shirt were ruffled. But a smile illuminated her face.

"Come," she said taking the hands of two young girls. "Let's leave this place."

With an eye on the distracted group of women, Anawan and I helped her move the urchins toward the forest fringe at the near end of the field. Once we were clear of Ashquoach, we could set up camp and see to the needs of our new family.

Together, we traveled for two or three miles north and east of the native fort, arriving at last by the edge of a quiet pond secure in a dense stand of pine. Here we rested the children and prepared two crude pole structures to shelter them. As Anawan and I cut and lashed together the trunks of several dozen saplings, Wantonka began the enormous task of tending to the children.

The early summer air was sufficiently warm that my wife was able to strip her charges of their filthy clothing and bathe them in the clear, spring fed pond. With the help of the older and stronger of her brood, Wantonka first washed the weak and the young, laying them afterward on beds of soft pine needles before a warming fire. Next, she had the older children strip and bathe themselves as she washed all their dirty rags.

By nightfall, our shelters were complete, our fires bright and, as their clothes dried, our charges lay together beneath the blankets Anawan, Wantonka and I had carried for ourselves. Fish and game were plentiful. With Anawan's guidance, we'd tracked and caught three rabbits, a pheasant and a string of plump trout which we gutted, cleaned and cooked at once to feed our new family.

If the tall Indian resented his role in helping us free the children of his enemy, he never showed it. Instead, he helped us manage their wellbeing with diligence and care. At night, he watched as we slept. And in the morning, he disappeared into the forest to scout the surrounding ground for signs of trouble.

As for the children, they were at first passive toward ourselves and one another. For them, the shock of rescue seemed just as difficult as capture. And they clung to one another like new born puppies as we fed them and clothed them once again in their newly cleaned clothes. It wasn't until the evening of our first full day together that color returned to their gaunt faces and their tiny voices at last were heard. Being among the oldest, the Rowlandson boy was the first to speak.

"Have you seen our mother?" he asked Wantonka. "Is she alive?"

Watching the young boy sob and shiver waiting for an answer to his question, I realized how much he'd risked in asking it. Perhaps all that had kept him going was the belief that Mary Rowlandson had survived and that she waited somewhere for his return. Daring to learn otherwise had taken every ounce of his courage.

"Yes, I've seen her," Wantonka cried. "She is well and awaits your return."

It was at that moment that I fully appreciated the tragedy of their ordeal. More than the starvation and the filth, greater even than the terror they'd experienced at the hands of their captors, was the excruciating hopelessness of their situation. Watching the Rowlandson child throw himself into Wantonka's arms and hug himself to her, I felt the enormity of his relief at finally letting go of the suffocating grip captivity had forced on his innocent spirit.

XXI

For two days more we lingered beside that quiet pond. As our charges rested and fed, their energy returned sufficiently for them to begin at last to frolic as children. Delighting us with their laughter and play, they chased and splashed one another at the water's edge, collapsing at the close of each day into a deep slumber that carried most of them through the night. Some of the younger children, however, continued to be tortured by nightmare images of their ordeal. Waking with shrieks of terror, summoning their lost parents with the most pitiful cries, they kept Wantonka and me from sleeping ourselves.

One night, the darkness close around our dying fires, I had a sudden vision of my own mother holding me as I held one of the frightened children. It was a memory from so long ago, I'd forgotten it entirely, a prize left behind by my dead mother, hidden deep inside my mind for me to find. Discovering it, I realized, was my reward for helping these poor boys and girls, a gift from Heaven for their recovered souls.

"Does this remind you of your childhood?" I later asked Wantonka.

We lay together in our blankets, so close I was certain I didn't need to speak, that in the quiet my darling could hear my thoughts.

"No." Her voice was sharp, her whisper hissing in my ear. "I had no childhood such as these."

Wantonka stiffened in my arms, and for several seconds she didn't speak,

137

her quickened breaths the only indication she gave of the troubled thoughts I'd stirred in her.

"My mother is no different now than she's ever been," she said at last. "The evil she has done this last year is what she's always done. She fought with my father, Alexander, and with my father's father, Massasoit. She wanted the power they had and wasted no time being mother to me."

I squeezed her closer, holding her trembling shoulders as I considered her words.

"All this time that I've been orphaned," I finally breathed, "I never dreamed that things might well have been worse for me, that having a parent could be a curse as easily as a blessing."

"It can be so," Wantonka answered. "For children. And for their mothers also."

At first, I didn't understand.

"Children a burden to their mothers?" I asked her.

"Yes."

She nuzzled closer, until I felt her breath hot in the folds of my unbuttoned shirt.

"Do you think Mistress Rowlandson would have suffered so if not for her worries for her children?" Wantonka questioned. "Do you think life is truly blessed for those who bring children to this troubled world? I wonder."

She stopped and breathed her warmth against me.

"You birth them," she continued. "You watch them struggle and die. For some it is too hard."

It was a terrible logic I'd never considered.

"Do you think you were a burden to Weetamoo?" I asked her.

"She told me so," Wantonka answered. "Many times."

It was the worst tragedy of all, worse than being orphaned, worse perhaps than being kidnapped and taken from one's family.

"Abandoned by the woman who gave me life..." But Wantonka shuddered, unable to finish.

"And you?" I asked. "Do you want children of your own?"

I suffered waiting for her answer.

"I want your children, Daniel," she murmured. "With you by my fire, we will be happy. Always."

Breathing a last long breath against me, she fell into a deep sleep. And we were, for the time, at peace. But at the first light of morning, as our tiny family woke at last, a few of our children were so shaken by the visions that had assaulted their night that it took considerable coaxing by their mates for them to forget themselves again in play. We were still a long way from safety, dozens of miles from Marlboro, dozens more to Boston. But even farther removed from any conclusion to their ordeal were those poor children who carried such terrible memories with them.

The weakest of our group was the Rowlandson girl. No more than eight or nine, Betsey Rowlandson had survived the burning of her home and the massacre of several of her brothers and uncles. She'd shivered at her mother's side as her infant sister had perished from her wounds. And she'd endured months of cruel captivity separated from her mother and surviving brother. What little of her strength remained after her long emotional ordeal, starvation and a lingering, untreated winter fever had melted from her bones.

Little Betsey Rowlandson was the reason we remained so long camped by the pond. While the other children frolicked, Betsey lay with her head in Wantonka's lap barely strong enough to raise herself to follow her brother with her eyes. To travel with her in her weakened state would have been murder. To return without her would doom our mission.

On the evening of our second day camped by the pleasantly shaded pond, Anawan approached the fire where Wantonkla and I sat together.

"Princess," he addressed my wife. "Your mother will be angered by what you've done. Because of this it will not be safe for you to come to her again. Do you understand me? She will have you punished for this. You and Daniel."

Wantonka refused to bow her head.

"You are a great war captain," she told our guide. "It is because of you that Philip and Weetamoo still live. You fight for them. And you protect them when they run. But they have done much wrong with the life you've given them."

Gazing past our fire, she watched the insects dance across the pond's unruffled water as if reading some message in the swirling patterns they created on the mirrored surface with their wings.

"I have nothing to fear from my mother," Wantonka stated flatly. "The next time I see her, she will be dead."

She turned and faced the tall warrior.

"You and I will not meet again in this life," she promised him. "If I live to see these children returned to their parents, then it will be you I will next see killed."

For several minutes, Anawan said nothing. Then he lowered his eyes to the fire, taking its light full on his leathery face.

"See me now, woman," he finally said. "Look long at me this night. And then, no more."

By dawn the next day, I awoke to find Anawan gone. He'd done what he could to help us, but his place, as Wantonka had said, was at his sachem's side. With the Nipmuc inclining toward peace, Philip would be forced to return east with whatever warriors remained loyal to him. As the war captain of the

Pokanoket, Anawan would be depended on to carry out the fight as long as his leader wished. Our respite from the war had been brief. If we were to meet again, I knew it would not be in peace.

In Anawan's absence, Wantonka and I grew more anxious to leave our camp and speed our family toward the English settlements of the east. Even in this quiet place, our safety was not assured. Only in the company of my brother Englishmen and the surviving members of their families would these children find true peace.

By twining and knotting together slender pine branches, my wife and I fashioned a sturdy backpack in which we could sling the invalid Rowlandson child for carriage. I'd carry Betsey while Wantonka and several of the older children divided the rest of our supplies. By mid-morning on the day following Anawan's departure, we began our journey. With the sun in our faces, we followed a path south and east, wide of the Nipmuc camp at Wachusetts, toward the English garrison at Marlboro.

The children were most cooperative. Clinging to our sides, they walked without complaining for more than an hour at a time, stopping to rest only when Wantonka signaled them to and then resuming their march with enthusiasm. Betsey Rowlandson was feather light. The only way I knew she was on my back was from the whispered song with which she entertained me. Despite her weakened condition, her tiny voice, once released, continued unrelenting through much of our journey.

By the end of the first day, we'd covered nearly fifteen miles, stopping to camp on the quiet shores of the lake of the Quinsigamond. Blessedly, we'd seen no one. And if we'd been spotted by our enemy, the presence of a white man in the company of an Indian woman and a group of half starved white children had apparently proved to be of too little interest for them to bother intercepting us.

We were at least a dozen miles from Marlboro, still deep in frontier wilderness. But for the children, the miles we'd come from their place of captivity did much to comfort them. Even little Betsey managed to raise herself from the bed Wantonka had made for her on the pine needle floor of the lake shore. With the help of her brother and one of the older girls, she took herself to the water's edge where she waded tentatively into the cooling lake.

Not yet fished or hunted by whites, the waters and forests of Quinsigamond abounded with game. And with the help of the older children, I was able to keep our family well fed. As Wantonka oversaw the play of the younger kids, two of the bigger children, a boy and a girl, astonished me with their skills at fashioning traps and weirs. So effective were they at their newly learned trade that we had only to sit and wait for all the rabbits, squirrels, trout and pickerel we could want to find their way into our lair.

Something about our restful sanctuary seemed to even calm the children's restless sleep. That night was the first where neither Wantonka or I were we awoken by the cries of tormenting night terrors. By morning, as a result, with our entire group able to rest and eat in comfort, the strength of our charges seemed doubled. And we banked our fires, circled the north end of the lake and attacked the path to Marlboro at a far quicker pace than the day before.

Even Betsey chose to walk much of the distance that morning. With her brother and a friend leading the way, scouting our flanks as Oneka used to do, she followed the others, alternatively taking my hand and then Wantonka's. Clutching and pulling at every new marvel she encountered along the path, her fierce grip assured us she would survive.

For a while that day, it was possible to look at the land and see it with the same wonderment as the children. Each crying bird or startled quail made my heart beat fast as the kids cried out with glee. Their voices had returned. And the music that they made was strong enough to silence almost every other worry. Not until we crested the last hill and stood looking across the unplanted fields of Marlboro did I even think of war. Before me that evening, rather than the welcoming face of our longed for haven, however, I saw only bristling palisades.

There was no celebration to welcome us in fortress Marlboro. To the anxious soldiers of the garrison we were just another tiresome band of frontier refugees to be fed and clothed and passed on east to Boston.

Taken together with my report, there was now every indication that the Nipmuc would be compelled to sue for peace. But with the peace, Philip would be forced east again with Anawan and the other surviving Pokanoket. The mood in the garrison was dark. As war returned, they would be the first to feel its brunt. Exhausted already from numerous campaigns, these poor men now faced the awful prospect of the war coming home to them.

After finding shelter for our brood in a deserted wigwam just outside the stockade, I sought out the commander of the garrison. Leaving my wife to quiet the children and to watch over their sleep, I stepped inside the stockade to present myself to Major Thomas Hammond, a Plymouth man whom I'd known before the war.

"These children?" he asked. "How is it they are in your company?"

I told him the story of the Rowlandsons' capture and struggles and of Thomas Hoar's efforts to ransom them.

"Mary Rowlandson?" he beamed. "She has recently returned to Concord. We've had news of it just yesterday."

Bowing my head, I whispered a word of thanks to the Almighty.

"These are her children?" Hammond asked.

"Two of them. The rest were taken in other raids across the frontier. I haven't had time to even learn their names," I confessed.

In Plymouth, Hammond had been a public figure, a teacher and a leader of the church. He'd struck me as a good man, not one I would have expected to see here in the midst of the fighting but, like Roger Williams, a fair and respected Christian.

"And what news of my cousin?" I asked him.

"He is home, I'm told. When he wasn't given command of the Plymouth forces, your cousin retired to his wife and new child."

"A child?" I'd been away so long, I'd known nothing of Alice's pregnancy.

"A son," Hammond told me. "Constant. Named after Alice's father."

"Then Church is finished with this war, I trust."

"Perhaps not," Hammond offered. "There is talk in Boston that the Puritan governor will release the Praying Indians being held at Deer Island."

Church had often spoken of forming an English and Indian army to track Philip. With the help of the Praying Indians, he might have his chance.

"Join them," Hammond said, taking my arm. "Take these children to their families in Boston. If you leave tomorrow, you'll arrive as the internees from Deer Island land in Boston. Meet with them. Beg them to help us."

Hammond eyed me closely.

"That Indian woman you travel with?" he questioned. "You risk much being with her now."

"She is my wife." I straightened.

"Weetamoo's daughter?" he asked.

I nodded, my mouth suddenly too dry to speak.

"Then she will persuade the Praying Indians to help," he said. "Her skin is red, but her soul is Christian, same as you and me."

His hand still on my arm, he pulled me to him, turning me so that I could see what he had seen. Behind me, outside the stockade gate, Wantonka was visible through the blanket covering the opening to our wigwam. She was seated before our fire, bent over a reclining shape. It was Betsey Rowlandson, I knew, Wantonka's constant companion since we'd left Ashquoach.

"The way she behaves with those white children," Hammond breathed into my ear. "It's more than kindness. It's as if they were her own."

Watching my darling, seeing her lips move in a quiet lullaby, her hands stroke the honey colored tangle of hair in her lap, I knew he was right.

"Some distrust her," he warned me. "But many, like me, respect and admire her."

That night was the most pleasant of our journey. Though I could see fear in the eyes of our hosts, the children were unaware of it. Instead, the company of the anxious white soldiers of Marlboro so eased the terrors of the youngsters that they enjoyed the most peaceful sleep. So still were they, so lost in slumber, that Wantonka and I were able to lay together ourselves, touching, kissing, unafraid of rousing their curious eyes.

XXII

Boston
May, 1676

Much was changed since my last visit to the busy Puritan capital. Rather than being forced to sneak past the reinforced gate at Roxbury Neck, this time the children and I were welcomed through it. Accompanied by four mounted soldiers, Wantonka and I passed through the towering portals to the salutes of the guards. The horsemen, dispatched by Governor Leverett, had met us at Dedham Plain and escorted our little band, some of the children riding in the saddles themselves the last half dozen miles across the Roxbury Hills.

Word of our arrival had preceded us. Even on the newly planted ground of the town's south end, crowds gathered to stare in wonderment at the spectacle of so many freed children. Once again, I saw Betsey Rowlandson clutch at Wantonka's hand as a broad view of the harbor opened before us. Most of these boys and girls, I realized, had never seen the ocean, the town, or the tall ships anchored before its docks. Some of the kids' parents or other family members awaited them, I was certain. But this was no homecoming for any. Their homes had long ago been destroyed, their frontier towns burned to the ground with all their worldly possessions.

With the four horsemen leading the way and a crowd of curious spectators following us, we crossed the base of the Common where the bodies of a dozen Indian captives twisted beneath the crude wooden stocks from which they'd been hanged, left no doubt as a sign to those who doubted the might of Puritan resolve. Reaching the North End, halting on King Street in the shadow of the Governor's formidable new quarters, we were next greeted by a group of somber Puritan elders. Before them stood Mary Rowlandson, her eyes searching frantically among the confused but smiling faces of the children.

"Betsey!" she cried at last.

Breaking free of the black cloaked older men, she ran to Wantonka's side. There, she knelt to sweep the frail, wriggling Betsey into a fierce hug.

"Mother," her son then spoke from the midst of the other children.

Seeing such relief on the poor woman's face, bathing in the radiance of her smile, was more reward than I'd dreamed. As several of the other children were welcomed by their parents, as kids and family swept together in a numbing rush of emotion, even the dour elders warmed.

"You have brought me Heaven on Earth," Mrs. Rowlandson gasped taking Wantonka's hand. "Were I the wealthiest soul in the Colonies, I could never repay you for the return of my darlings."

Mary's sudden show of gratitude toward my wife seemed to stun the rest of the crowd. As their eyes moved from Wantonka to me, I knew many of the adults in the growing throng found it hard to believe they had a red woman to thank for the deliverance of their children. In the silence that followed, I saw the elders hesitate. Some even started to turn away when a noise sounded behind them.

"We meet again, sir," a bold voice shouted out.

Turning, I saw the great oak door of the Governor's quarters thrown back and Leverett himself staring across the stone apron that separated us.

"I might have known you and your Indian woman would be at the center of this commotion," he growled.

Without his great coat, dressed only in a white canvas shirt, Leverett seemed to have shrunk. His face nearly as gaunt as some of the enemy I'd seen in the west, he stared back at me with the dark, brooding eyes of a beleaguered commander.

"Or is she by now your wife?" His cheeks reddened. "Well done, sir."

And, grinning broadly, he marched through the others to shake my hand.

"You will find us crowded here," he told me. "With the gathering of refugees from the settlements in the west, most houses host two or more families. But you are welcome to squeeze yourself in wherever you wish."

Without the slightest hesitation, he then dropped my hand and took Wantonka's.

"Princess." He bowed. "Since you were last here, attitudes in the capital have changed toward you and the other Praying Indians. With my apologies to you, I offer you thanks for the deliverance of these innocents."

With a slight bow of her own, Wantonka acknowledged his compliment. Then, at a nod from the Governor, Mary Rowlandson stood. Taking her two children by the hand, she signaled Wantonka and me to join her as she crossed the cobble stoned square toward the lone figure of a man. He was slight, bespectacled, with a gray beard and thinning black hair that hung to his stiff white collar. Standing well away from the others, his eyes welling with tears, he watched us approach.

"Father," the Rowlandson boy spoke taking the man's hand.

For a moment I was stunned the man hadn't run to his children as his wife had. Watching his face melt in tears as he knelt to cradle young Betsey to him, I wondered how he'd managed to contain himself.

"Oh, my poor children," he sobbed. "I'm so very sorry."

With pitiable moans, he repeated the apology again and again.

"I should have done more to keep you from such a fate as you have endured," he murmured into the little girl's shirt front.

Glancing around at the stern faces of the others, I realized the poor man was shamed by what he'd allowed to happen to his family. I'd seen such horrors inflicted by both sides in this war. Until then, I'd not realized the despair suffered by those who'd survived them.

I knew Rowlandson's enemy. They were strong and they were savage and they arrived unannounced in such overwhelming numbers that no man could protect even his wife and children from them. I had no idea what kind of man the Reverend Rowlandson was, evil or good. I had no idea why he moved with a limp or held his right arm limp at his side as he embraced his son with the other. But I knew for certain the father had no cause to blame himself for the torments endured by his children.

"John?" Mary whispered, gently squeezing her husband's damaged arm with her fingers. "This is Wantonka," she told him, "and Daniel, her man."

Rowlandson looked up from his children with such a pained look on his face that I wanted to vanish from the spot. Where Mary had warmed me with the widest of smiles, her husband's embarrassment hurt me deeply.

"Thank you," he managed, fighting himself to his feet.

Around us, other families were reunited with laughter and shouts. Though ours was the most somber of the reunions, the welcoming look on Mary's face convinced me it was perhaps the most heartfelt. My suspicion was immediately confirmed when, despite the cold looks from his elders, John

Rowlandson then circled his arm around Wantonak and squeezed her tightly to him.

"You will join us for dinner this evening," he told her. "After that, you are welcome to stay with us as long as you wish."

As we soon discovered, the Rowlandsons had taken up residence with relatives in a large, single story home on the edge of the mill pond. Snug on the flank of the Beacon Hill, the home stood by the swampy path Wantonka and I had followed the night of our escape from the black slave ship.

With most of Boston's other structures clustered further away in the town's north end or across the river in Charles Town, the home and its tiny half acre of garden were most serene. Miles distant from the wilderness, centuries removed from the savagery of the frontier, the formidable, oak beamed house was an oasis of culture.

In one corner of the home's large main room stood a harpsichord constructed of dark mahogany. Unlike any of the rude church organs of home, the top and sides of this fine instrument were fashioned with gay patterns of polished gold inlay. Wherever I stood, the harpsichord was visible, filling my mind with wonder at the heavenly sounds it must make. If the music it played were half as pleasant as its appearance, I thought, it must echo the voices of angels.

Once more, I was taken how quickly the young Rowlandson children settled into their new surroundings. Although Betsey clung fiercely to her mother as she'd once done to Wantonka, both children seemed as comfortable with their siblings and parents as if they'd never been separated. As I watched them talk and play together, I saw their father separate himself from them and come over to me.

"You have an eye for our treasure I see," he said.

With his right arm hanging limp at his side, he inclined his head toward the harpsichord.

"We brought it from England and settled it here with my cousin and his family. Lancaster, as it turned out, was no place for it."

At my side Wantonka shifted restlessly. Certain she felt as awkward here as I did, I took her hand and pulled her closer.

"I used to play," Rowlandson was saying. "But now I'm afraid what little talent I had is lost for good."

He touched his good hand to his limp arm.

"An Indian musket ball shattered my shoulder," he said. "I fell where I'd been working in the fields and didn't recover my wits until my home was burned, my brother killed, my wife and children taken from me."

The setting sun, beaming through the open door, cast a warming glow on his family. But the doleful tone with which Reverend Rowlandson told us of his ordeal cast a shadow over the blessed reunion.

"Until you have children of your own," the reed thin gentleman said, "you will never know how great a service you've done."

I glanced down at Wantonka. Perhaps there was something about my princess, the color of her cheeks, the light in her eyes, that had told the Reverend we didn't have long to wait for an infant of our own.

Suddenly, my wife dropped my hand and crossed the room to the harpsichord. Carefully, she pulled back the simple pine bench. Watching her seat herself before the keys, I caught my breath. It was simple curiosity, I guessed. The ornate instrument had drawn her, I was sure, by the uniqueness of its appearance. Even I had only seen such things in books. But then Wantonka astonished us all by placing her hands on the ivory keys and playing.

"My Lord," our host gasped.

At once the great room filled with the most exquisite sounds. Wantonka seemed transformed. With her eyes half closed, her head inclined forward, she was joined to the instrument. Only the music that she played was more harmonious than the vision she presented.

"Why, it's a Trinity hymnal," Rowlandson whispered. "How on Earth?"

But the unanswered question was quickly lost in the delight that overwhelmed us at her skillful playing. Soon, the children were gathered around my princess singing words in Latin to the music she was playing. Perhaps she'd learned to play at one of the Christian meeting houses of home. Still, she was a splendid mystery, like the country that had birthed her, a wellspring of wonder and surprise.

The evening was warm, so we built our cooking fire outside the house. As the children splashed and frolicked at the pond's edge, the women, Wantonka, Mary and the prim mistress of the house, knelt by the growing fire. Rowlandson's cousin, a burly, robust Scot, filled and lighted pipes for us, a ritual I remembered from my captivity in the Great Swamp and again at Menemesset.

Smoking in silence in the corner of the yard, watching our women tend to our supper, we could have been our enemy. Our clothes were different, the color of our skin, even our gods. But we were men, just the same, standing shoulder to shoulder, casting our shadows across the cherished ground that nurtured us.

From time to time, one or two men from town wandered from the gathering darkness to join our group. Hardly any conversation was spoken between us. Occasionally, Reverend Rowlandson or his cousin would make a perfunctory introduction. Our uninvited guests would then stare with curiosity at Wantonka and me before politely excusing themselves and returning to their homes.

"They are intrigued by you," my host confided in me. "As am I."

It seemed unlikely.

"It is I who should be intrigued," I told him. "I've known nothing but the simple life of the wilderness. Now my own wife astonishes me with her gift for music."

"Yes," he agreed. "Wantonka intrigues us all as well. Many of these people have never spoken to an Indian, man or woman. To them, they are a mystery, made savage by the stories told of them."

I knew it was true. I could see fearful wonder in the eyes of these Puritans of Boston.

"But you are a white man," Rowlandson continued. "An Englishman, no different than them. Yet you've gone into the wilderness, faced our red enemy and brought our children back to us."

As he spoke, I stared at his stiff shirt collar, wondering at its incredible whiteness. Never in my life had I possessed such a garment. How had he managed to keep himself so clean, I was wondering? To me, it reflected a godly state I could only aspire to.

"There is no person more elevated this day than you," he was saying to me.

I looked down at my leather breeches, torn and stained from scores of scrapes and tumbles.

"There is not one among you who would not do as I have done," I answered.

Beneath his graying beard, a smile shone. Reaching his good hand toward me, he squeezed my arm.

"You are very wrong, sir," he whispered. "There are none here who could accomplish one tenth what you have done. Whether you choose to believe this or not, you are a hero to us all. God sent."

Clapping me lightly on the back, he signaled me to join him with the women at their dining table. Never had I felt my legs so weak as I crossed the apron of gravel toward the table that had been set by the pond. All my life, I'd relied on heroes like my cousin, Anawan, even Wantonka. I had succeeded only because they had. To be included among them now, to be called to the forefront of men, was more than humbling. It was terrifying to realize that people such as Rowlandson depended on me now, as I had once depended on my cousin.

Sitting before the enormous feast the women had prepared, I reflected on the extraordinary circumstance that saw Wantonka and me welcomed at a table set on the same rocky ledge where we had scrambled for our lives less than a year before. Though our world had descended into chaos in that time, this moment saw us elevated.

"Trial by ordeal," Reverend Rowlandson was saying to the people seated before him. "These times will see many fall in the eyes of God. For these two we honor here this night, however, their deeds will surely earn a place with Him."

Mary Rowlandson bathed us with her eyes. Like the other Puritan women of the time, I knew she would not speak in the presence of her men. She would join her husband in silent thanks instead, the look on her face and on the faces of her children gathered nearby, speaking volumes more than their reverend father.

The night continued warm. After dinner, we spread our blankets on the shore of the pond with the Rowlandsons. Watching the last of the dying lights of Charles Town across the river, I heard a tiny voice cry out.

"Sing to us, Princess." It was little Betsey calling out to Wantonka for the lullaby my wife had sung to her when we first carried the child from Ashquoach.

"She insists no one else sing to her," Mary Rowlandson spoke from the shadows. "She whispered to me that your voice is like an angel's."

And so, Wantonka sang us all to sleep that night. And I dreamt we floated on a cloud, all of us together, far above the earth and its churning tangles of conflict.

XXIII

Plymouth
June, 1676

The first truly sultry day of late spring found Wantonka and me aboard a sloop descending the coast from Boston. Our destination was Plymouth where we hoped to meet with my cousin. Word had been received in Boston that Philip had returned from the west with one thousand Pokanoket and Narragansett braves. Taunton had been attacked, Swansea burned to the ground. In response to this new threat, a war council had been convened in Plymouth which Church was expected to attend.

Tacking on a feeble south wind, our ship approached the slender strand of green that sheltered Plymouth harbor from the main body of Massachusetts Bay. My wife and I sat together atop a tangle of anchor lines, watching the rocky shore slip slowly past when we caught a glimpse of Scituate. Weeks earlier, the town had been attacked. Twenty homes had been burned, their charred beams standing stark against the bright sky.

"Where we go," Wantonka whispered against my shirt sleeve, "war follows."

Somewhere beneath the unbroken canopy of trees, beyond the scorched town and the shallow hills that ran west from its ruins, Weetamoo and Philip were hiding with the last of their rebel army.

"It is the end," I heard myself tell her.

The Nipmuc had already sued for peace. Knowing he would likely be a valuable prize to Monoco when it came time for him to bargain with the English, Philip had returned to Plymouth.

"The end, yes," Wantonka answered. "But Metacom will be even more dangerous than before."

"So will the English."

Already, the colonies were swarming with volunteers. Every one had a brother or cousin who'd been killed. Vengeance drove them as murderously as desperation drove Philip.

After what seemed an eternity, the weak breeze carried us at last to the docks of the town. Much of the day had been consumed. The sun lay low and hard in our eyes as we scanned the beachfront dwellings for our destination. Across the matted sea grass, a large group of soldiers was already gathered at the Plymouth meeting house, waiting for the orders of their commanders. Eying Wantonka suspiciously, they quickly closed around us, blocking our approach.

"What business have you here?" one of them asked my wife.

"I am Daniel Church," I spoke up. "I have come from Boston to find my cousin, Benjamin."

The soldiers scowled.

"He's inside yonder," another of them barked. "Meeting with the Governor, General Bradford and Captain Moseley."

He grinned when he saw Wantonka stiffen at the name of the hated pirate officer.

"You may leave her here with us," he grinned. "And go inside to find your kinsman."

I counted nearly a dozen of them. From their dark bandanas, their pants ballooning from their buckled boot tops and the jewel bedecked handles of their cutlasses, I figured them to be more of Moseley's villains.

"Stand aside," I told them. "I carry orders from Governor Leverett."

It was a lie. After his greeting my arrival in Boston, Leverett hadn't summoned me again.

"This woman and the other Praying Indians have been pardoned," I told them. "Let us pass."

I was a hero now, Reverend Rowlandson had told me. I'd been twice to the frontier and returned. What fear had I of scoundrels such as these?

"Let them be," another of the pirates spoke up. "Can't you see the squaw is pregnant?"

Glancing to my side, I saw Wantonka had pressed the leather of her shirt front tight across her belly. By arching her back, thrusting her hips, and clutching her stomach with the palm of her hand, she was able to make her natural rounding more prominent than before.

"She may be heathen," the soldier said. "But by the looks of this poor fool with her, I'd wager the baby is white. Let them pass. They sicken me."

A hero knows when to stand and fight, I reasoned to myself, and when to retreat in dignity. Taking my wife's arm, I elbowed my way through the foul smelling group and into the shadows of the meeting house.

Once inside, it took a while for my eyes to adjust from the harsh sunlight. Although the shutters had been thrown open against the heat, the meeting house was dark as a cave. I heard voices at the front of the enormous room, one of which sounded like my cousin. But, blinded, I was unable to be certain.

"I have made my decision," one of the voices spoke harshly. "I will not be questioned about it any further."

I heard a shuffling of boots. When my eyes finally cleared, I was able to see several men standing in a group before the rough hewn wooden lectern from which the minister gave his Sunday sermon. Foremost among them was red haired Governor Winslow.

"The Praying Indians will be invited to join General Bradford's army at once," the Governor said. "As for you, Benjamin, I urge you to consider enlisting your support as well."

At last, I was able to recognize my cousin's familiar stance. His face was full and tanned. And although his hand was bandaged, he stood tall, recovered from the wounds he'd received at the Great Swamp.

"But I deserve a command of my own," he stated. "A fast moving force of friendly Indians can take the fight to Metacom instead of waiting for him to destroy more of our towns."

"And General Bradford will lead such a force," Winslow pronounced.

I knew what Church was thinking. We'd served under Bradford on the Pokanoket Peninsula. It was the General's annoying cautiousness that had allowed Philip to escape capture a year before. There was nothing in the old war horse's nature that would adapt him now to the fighting tactics of his enemy. Not even the service of the Praying Indians was likely to speed the deliberate pace of his army. But before my cousin could further caution him, Winslow dismissed the meeting.

"Benjamin," I shouted stepping forward.

"Daniel!" He leapt at me, catching me in a fierce embrace. "Princess."

With his bandaged hand, he then gathered my wife to us.

"I am renewed seeing you." He squeezed us so tight I almost couldn't draw a breath. "You must tell me of your travels."

And without another look toward the Governor and his war council, he swept us with him out the door of the meeting house.

"Let these old dogs have their say," he beamed, elbowing his way through the surly pirates still gathered there. "We will gather a force of our own and get ourselves back in this fight."

One of the pirates stood as though trying to block our way. Without slowing his stride, my cousin flashed his knife from his belt.

"Step aside," he shouted, knocking the larger man to the ground with a blow from his shoulder. "I am an officer of the Governor's war council. I'll have you shot if you attempt to interfere with me."

Without bothering to look at the others standing to either side of us, he led us boldly past them. Snickering, he thrust his knife back into his belt. Then closing my arm in his, he leaned close.

"Make no mistake," he whispered to me. "They're stout fighters, those pirate swine. Let's pray none of them comes after us."

Still chuckling, he increased his pace, leading us from the center of the village, not stopping until we were standing by the harbor's edge, well out of sight of the meeting house. Blessedly, none of Moseley's men had followed us.

"So, tell us at once," he beamed, "what news of the past year?"

We found a shady place beneath a gnarled sea pine. Sitting on the rocks, our feet thrust in the soft sand and the harbor a shimmering carpet at our feet, Wantonka and I told our story. Stopping only to gather wood for a fire as the sun disappeared at last behind us, we related all to my earnest cousin.

"After I left you at the Great Swamp," I told him, "Wantonka and I were forced to travel with Canonchet to Menemesst."

I told of the ordeal of our winter of capture, our discovery of Mary Rowlandson and her children and our return east in the spring.

"After burning Providence," I said, "Canonchet was captured by Captain Dennison of Connecticutt."

Wantonka interrupted to describe my role in locating and pursuing the Narragansett war chief.

"I'll wager it was a hard race," Church grinned. "Not many can outrun my cousin in the forest."

We spoke of the tragedy at Sudbury and our return to the territory of the Nipmuc with Thomas Hoar.

"Twice to the capital of the Indian confederation?" Church marveled. "And twice returned?"

And through it all, I threaded the marvelous story of Anawan, from the return of his father's belt to the Pokanoket war captain's aid in freeing the captured white children.

"Still, he's a man to be reckoned with," my cousin cautioned me. "A dangerous fighter. In time you may be called upon to kill him."

I recalled Anawan's words before we parted.

"He says he's dead already."

In the flickering light of our fire, I saw Church cast his somber eyes on Wantonka.

"And your mother?" he asked.

Wantonka scowled and kicked the sand with her bare feet.

"She is dead also," my wife spat.

"You will be a mother soon yourself." Church assured her.

My princess nodded.

"Then you will have the chance to right Weetamoo's wrongs," he whispered. "A child sprung from both sides of this conflict will right many wrongs."

We sat together for several minutes more, not speaking, enjoying each other's presence. It was something I'd come to appreciate in its absence, the company of family. I'd seen it in the eyes of the Rowlandsons when we'd reunited them in Boston, a fire that burned more brightly than any inspired by God.

"What will you do now?" I asked Church at last.

Before he answered me, my cousin studied his bandaged hand in the firelight.

"This wound," he said, raising it for me to see. "I cut myself with the blade of a hewing axe. I nearly bled to death before I was able to bind it."

He frowned and cradled the wounded limb against his chest.

"It made me think," he continued. "If I was going to kill myself, I might as well do it in battle as in my yard with my own tools."

"But you will not serve for Bradford?"

He shook his head.

"What then?" I asked.

"Why not a force of my own?" His eyes narrowed. "Tell me the names of all the sachems you saw gathered with Philip."

The suddenness of his question made me pause.

"Monoco," I stammered. "Anawan. Mattoonas."

With Wantonka's help I added several more.

"Quinipian. Weetamoo. Sagamore Sam."

"And Awashonks?" he spoke the name of the female sachem of our closest neighbors, the Sakonnet."

Both Wantonka and I shook our heads. Until then, I hadn't thought of the gray haired chieftess.

"I thought as much," my cousin breathed.

Taking a stick from the ground between us, he began poking at the center of the fire sending a shower of fiery ashes in the air that illuminated the water at our feet.

"I think she has returned her people here," he said. "I've seen signs of it in the forests near Mount Hope."

He continued with the stick until the air around us seemed to have ignited.

"If we can find her," he whispered. "Perhaps she will provide us fighters for a force of our own."

"Sakonnet fighters?" Wantonka cried. "But have they been pardoned by the Plymouth elders?"

"Not yet," Church answered with a dark smile. "Not yet."

XXIV

With one horse between us, a splendid animal Church had borrowed days earlier for his trip north, we retraced his steps to Cape Cod. Wantonka rode most of the way as Church guided us, first to Sandwich, and then across the belly of the Cape to Saconessett where a sloop waited to return him to Newport.

At Saconessett, we spent the night in the lodging of some Cape Indians recently released from Deer Island. Good Christians who had stood beside my cousin and me during the early days of the war, these loyal friends had been swept from their homes and returned to Boston at the same time Moseley had taken Wantonka to the pirate slave ship. Against all logic, however, they bore no bitterness toward us or the English who'd detained them through the winter. After relating grim tales of deprivation that rivaled even my experiences with the Nipmuc, several of the younger men among them offered to travel with Church and me, to join our force in pursuing Philip.

"You would do this for us?" I asked them, "after everything the English have done to you?"

With a quick look to Wantonka, the other Indians lowered their heads without responding.

"They know no other way," Wantonka spoke for them. "The English are their brothers. Some are good. Some are bad. The same is true of any tribe."

The other Indians murmured in ascent. And it was decided they would follow us in two days to our home in Sakonnet. The next morning, during our crossing to Rhode Island, my cousin and I hatched a plan for locating Awashonks and securing the help of her fighters.

"Aquidneck Island is where you'll find her," Wantonka interrupted us. "If she has left Philip, as you say, then her home is where she will return."

Church considered her suggestion and agreed.

"We'll stop in Newport first," he said, "and secure a grant of pardon for any who will help us fight."

By late morning on our second day traveling from Plymouth, our sloop was rowed into the wide cove of Newport and pulled up before the sturdy fishing shacks that lined the sandy shore. Though the beach and the village beyond were empty, the forests rang with the sounds of woodsmen's axes.

"They prepare their palisades for attack," Church told me.

For the next long hour, he and I struggled to gather the military leaders from their scattered work parties. By the time Captain Taylor and his officers were assembled, however, it was clear we would get little support from them. Grousing bitterly at our interruption, Taylor barely listened to our proposal.

"This garrison is vulnerable from both land and sea," he barked. "I cannot spare any men from preparing my defenses."

Exasperated, my cousin repeated his request.

"I believe the Sakonnet will provide me all the men I need," he said more carefully. "I require only that you grant them pardon in exchange for their service."

"Sakonnet?" Taylor's face reddened. "It is they we build our defenses against."

"Benjamin and I will go to them," I offered. "Once we put our plan to their sachems, I'm certain they will join us."

I'd reluctantly advised Wantonka to remain behind when Church and I approached the officers. I hadn't wanted to risk yet one more tense encounter between my wife and the mistrusting whites of the colony.

"My cousin and I both know Awashonks," I went on. "She will listen to us."

But my words sounded hollow. And I wondered if I'd made a mistake not bringing my princess to confirm my standing with her people.

"The Sakonnet chose to follow Philip," one of Taylor's officers countered. "They made their choice a year ago."

"Choice?" I cried. "What choice? To be collected like swine and herded onto slave ships bound for the Indies?"

It didn't matter what I said. The officers remained intractable.

"What now?" I asked when Church and I were again alone.

"Rum and tobacco."

Undeterred, he strode briskly toward the home of a bay trader we'd done business with in the past.

"These fools won't stop me from doing what is right," he laughed. "We'll gather gifts for Awashonks. Once we have persuaded her to join us, Taylor will be glad he no longer has her as an enemy."

Dusk saw us at last in Church's canoe paddling our cargo of trade goods across the bay to Aquidneck Island. The evening was fair, the water calm, the sky the hue of glowing embers. With Wantonka seated between us on the damp bark floor of our vessel, my cousin and I paddled toward the garrison of Captain John Almy where Church's wife Alice was waiting.

Never had I been so anxious to see my cousin's wife, and to introduce her to my princess. When I'd last seen Alice, it had been to bid her goodbye as I bounded alongside Benjamin toward Taunton and the first meeting of militia. Since then, I'd taken a wife, journeyed to the frontier, and been called hero by some. Though I was anxious for her to see the new man I'd become, more than anything, I wanted to meet her new baby. I'd witnessed enough of death. With a child of my own due soon, I was anxious to look new life in the eyes, to hear its bold cries, to celebrate its arrival among us.

With our backs bent, our paddles biting the frothy surface of the bay, Church and I were one, our canoe gliding under us as if it were driven by a single powerful force. But the joy I felt at being with my cousin was slight compared to the excitement I felt when the first wailing sounds of Church's baby could be heard across the water. Fearful of Philip's murderous war parties, Alice had kept herself watchful for her husband's return. Spying our canoe at last, she'd carried her baby in her arms, wading knee deep in the gentle surf to meet us with an exuberant kiss for Church.

"Alice!" he cried, breaking from her strong arms. "Look what I've found."

In that first instant of welcome, Alice's gaze settled on Wantonka. Showing no hint of recognition, she nonetheless bathed my wife in the warmth of the most welcoming smile.

"Thank you," she breathed, "for bringing my husband home."

Turning the same grateful smile to me, squinting against the dying light, she suddenly clutched her baby to her breast.

"Daniel?" she breathed. "Can it be you?"

Catching her breath, she leaned for an instant on the shoulder of her man.

"Can this day be any more happy?" she gasped.

There were five of us now, more family than I'd ever known. And the fullness I felt when we were joined together at last on the apron of beach that fronted the Almy house was beyond anything I'd experienced. A lasting portrait was fixed in my mind that night, possibly in the minds of all who sat together on the beach by the Almy's cooking fire. The baby had just finished nursing when Alice surprised us all by passing him into the arms of my wife.

"Hold him," she whispered. "It would please us."

Perhaps it was the firelight. Perhaps it was the pale European coloring of the infant contrasted to Wantonka's tan face and arms. But, bent toward the slumbering child, my darling's face glowed as if from light within.

"Once we capture Philip, our kids will grow together," Church vowed. "Their birth will mark the end of conflict between our people. There will be no more red and white, Indian and English. There will only be American."

It was bold talk stirred by the joyous moment. I prayed it was true. But in my heart I feared that if my child were birthed with my wife's skin coloring, he'd never be welcomed in any America created by Europeans. If Wantonka harbored the same fears, she refused to show it. Instead, she cradled the new born life in her arms as though it were the most prized treasure.

"If Sakonnet remains unsafe at the end of the summer," Captain Almy announced. "Then you will stay here and have all the children you wish right here with us."

A tall man, he smiled down on us. But as the giant beamed, my cousin's face grew shadowed.

"Thank you for your kindness," he told our host. "Your offer is most welcome as Daniel and I have much work to do before things will be safe again in Sakonnet."

The sudden mention of our mission quickly darkened the spirits of all.

"It's true then," Alice sighed. "This visit home is to be brief."

There was no need to answer her. My cousin's down turned face told all.

"We leave tomorrow," he said, "to find Awashonks and enlist her aid in tracking Philip."

Alice gasped.

"You can't," she breathed. "You won't."

But her somber tone confirmed she'd already resigned herself to the inevitability of another of her husband's brave schemes.

"You're a father now," she tried once more. "Both of you."

I watched Wantonka for a sign of support. But my wife simply cradled the white child closer.

"Leave the fighting to others," Alice pleaded one last time.

Church said nothing. There was no need. Alice was a formidable woman. Like Wantonka, she'd endured the dangers of the frontier with enthusiasm. When my cousin and I departed the next day, she'd speak the brave words she'd always spoken to us. She and my wife would stand together, shoulder to shoulder, and watch until long after we had vanished in the distance. Tonight was to be enjoyed for what it was, not a prelude to our separation, but a blessed respite from it.

Although the heat of the day didn't diminish with the lengthening of the hour, the threat of Indian attack made it impossible for us to remain much longer outdoors. Laying our blankets together on the wide pine floor of the Almy's great room, therefore, we shuttered and secured the windows and doors against the cooling bay breeze.

It was a marvelous feeling, being united at last under the same roof. It wasn't until the moment I settled on my bedding and listened to Church and the others breathing quietly nearby that I relaxed at last the hold I'd held on myself. For the past months, I'd been constantly on my guard. Only then, secure in the Almy's house, surrounded by the others, did I realize how tight that hold had been.

But with the baby's constant stirring and the dense, sultry air inside the house, sleep was impossible. Soon, we were conversing, couple to couple, concealed in the dark, secure in the comforting embraces of our spouses.

"Tell us of the west," Alice whispered.

And the others quieted, waiting for me to tell of the frontier where, among them all, only Wantonka and I had ventured.

"There has been terrible suffering there," I told them. "Thankfully, Wantonka and I were spared much of it."

I told them of the struggles of the Narragansett after Great Swamp.

"The trail of blood from their wounded and dying," I said, "made a highway of red dozens of yards wide in the forest."

I spoke of Philip's disastrous journey across the mountains to the valley of the Mohawk.

"He lost hundreds of his braves," I continued, "and returned to Menemesset a broken chief with only half an army."

I related my encounter with the masterful war generals, Monoco and Sagamore Sam. I told of the massacres at Sudbury, Lancaster and Northfield.

"Wantonka and I were spared the violence of these fights," I confessed. "But we bore witness to the destruction that had occurred when we passed through nearly a dozen burned towns from Providence to the river of the Connecticut."

I spoke of the wretched survivors we'd seen, the starving English captors enslaved and treated like dogs by their native masters.

"One English woman saw her home burned, her brothers slain, her husband wounded, and was made to watch helplessly as her infant daughter bled slowly to death in her arms."

There was not one other sound in the room but that of my voice. I spoke to the shadowed rafters, reliving in the theater of my mind each terrible image as I related it.

"Mary Rowlandson," I whispered the name so dear to Wantonka and me. "She was captured at Lancaster and kept prisoner throughout the winter and spring."

I spoke of Thomas Hoar and our return with him to Wachusetts to ransom the English woman and her children.

"Thank the Almighty," Mrs. Almy whispered from a far corner of the room.

But I couldn't help wondering if the reverent woman's God had eyes for such a wild place as we'd been.

When the first slivers of gray light were seen through the chinks in the shutters, we opened the door on our friends, the two Cape Indians who had agreed to join Church and me to Sakonnet. At first, their presence squatted beside the rekindled fire, shocked Mrs. Almy into a startling shriek. Even the two natives seemed as alarmed by her unexpected outburst as we. Lunging for their muskets, they turned with their backs to the house ready to defend themselves as well as us from whatever menace our hostess had spotted.

"Why, Emily," Captain Almy told his wife. "It's just Thomas and One-Eyed Jim. Our friends from the Cape."

Mrs. Almy smiled in embarrassment.

"I'm so sorry," she said. "I didn't know what to think."

"They've come for us," my cousin told us. "After breakfast, we'll paddle together to Sakonnet to look for Awashonks."

The arrival of the two friendly Indians put a sudden end to the peaceful interlude we'd enjoyed that evening. There would be no more talk of past adventures. Our minds were now focused on the immediate future and our mission. And we moved in deliberate silence, not wanting to break the delicate hold each of us held on ourselves. The women were particularly careful, not even allowing their eyes to meet mine. Theirs was a far more difficult task than ours, I knew. Awaiting our return all day, every fear would be magnified, every danger more intense in imagining it than in confronting it.

"What say Taylor and the others at Newport of this venture you plan?" Captain Almy was the first to break the silence, asking the question I'd been fearing since we'd arrived the night before. "Did they grant you the authority to negotiate for them?"

Squatting next to his wife, he scooped warmed cornmeal from an iron pot.

"I'm sure they'll welcome a treaty with Awashonks," Church lied.

"Indeed?" Almy gave me a wink as he handed me a bowl of the fragrant porridge. "And do they even know of your intentions?"

Church coughed loudly

"We spoke to them of it, of course," my cousin answered, careful to skirt the Captain's question.

"Well, I guess we do things differently here than in Newport." Almy continued serving our breakfast from the pot the women had prepared. "Why ask for something before you're certain you can have it?"

Church coughed again, catching my eye this time.

"We should leave at once," he told me. "Hurry with your porridge. Thomas and I will prepare the canoes."

And he was off before our host could question him further.

"You watch over him, Daniel," Alice told me when her husband had retreated out of ear shot. "I believe your successes prove you a more level head than him. Don't let him lose his hair this day."

"He has a rather high regard for the Sakonnet," Almy said. "And they for him. But beware. The events of the past year have certainly cast all Wampanoag as our enemy."

I expected Wantonka to interrupt, to assure us of Awashonks' intentions. When she didn't, when she looked at me instead with the same grave look in her eyes as the others, I realized for the first time how risky my cousin's plan might be.

Our departure was as difficult as anything I'd endured throughout the war. Despite their attempts to keep themselves steady, both Alice and Wantonka clung to my cousin and me with tears soaking the fronts of our shirts. It wasn't until Captain Almy stepped forward and eased the two women back that Church and I were able to gather up our muskets.

"We'll cross the river to Sakonnet," Church told them. "We'll remain safely off shore, searching the usual fishing places until we find someone to carry a message to Awashonks. By nightfall, I will send Thomas back here with news of our progress. I swear it."

His plan sounded simple and safe. If an enemy war party attempted to pursue us by water, we all knew they'd never catch Benjamin and me. Even with his injured hand, my cousin was a sturdy paddler. Never had the two of us been headed. Still, it seemed a dangerous gamble leaving the safety of our homes.

"This has to be it," I told the others, trying to keep my voice calm. "What we do now must end this for good."

The two women stood clinging to one another. I waited for each of them to nod that they understood me.

"Today, we will send a message to the Sakonnet," I said. "We'll meet with Awashonks and get the help of her braves to hunt Philip and capture him."

Even I took strength from these words. Only this action remained between us and peace. I felt it in my bones. Moving swiftly, we crossed the narrow beach to launch our canoe, joining Thomas and One-eyed Jim who had already stood out several yards from shore. We didn't look back, nor did we speak. Determined movement forward was the tonic we needed.

XXV

After paddling most of the morning, we were approaching a rocky promontory extending several dozen yards from shore when Thomas spied what we'd been searching for. Rising in the stern of his canoe, the tall Indian signaled with a wave of his hat toward three Sakonnet braves who were fishing from among the distant rocks.

"We guessed right," my cousin whispered. "Awashonks has returned."

Bending once more to our paddles, we pulled ourselves forward as fast as we could manage. We worked hard, but the strong tides and rolling ocean swells coming from the wide bay made it difficult to keep our point. And after losing valuable time to several steering corrections, we were finally spotted by the fishermen who dropped their poles and vanished into the forest.

"We've lost them." I shouted forward.

"Perhaps not."

Church nodded for me to help him paddle closer.

"I am Benjamin," he shouted. "Friend to the Sakonnet."

Gesturing with his hands toward the dense curtain of green beyond the rocks, he signaled anyone who might be hiding there to come forward to meet him.

"Bring me to the left." He pointed toward the tip of the promontory.

Steadying himself, he resumed his awkward hand signals.

"This could be a trap," I cautioned as I eased the canoe closer to the rocky shore.

"Indeed." He didn't stop.

"We're well within musket range of the trees," I reminded him.

"Then they'll have little trouble seeing me." Waving one last time, my cousin leapt across the bow to pull our bark the final distance to shore. "Stand and show them you're unarmed."

I did as he asked but still saw no movement beyond the wall of trees. Behind us, the two Cape Indians had remained well off shore and out of range. If we were attacked, there would be no support from them.

For several minutes, my cousin continued signaling, exposing himself in the open to anyone who might be concealed ahead of us. I'd seen this kind of bravado before, at the pea filed in the Pocasset Swamp when he'd defied Philip's shooters to boldly retrieve his cutlass. I'd been astonished then, and perhaps impressed. But now he was a father, and so was I. After the horrors I'd witnessed in the past months, this risk taking seemed terribly reckless.

I held my ground only to avoid the shame I knew would haunt me if I deserted my cousin here. I was thinking of the shots that would come, just crouching low to avoid them, when an Indian showed himself at last at the fringe of the trees. It was a man I recognized at once, an old Sakonnet friend named Honest George. Ignoring my cousin, he strode directly toward me.

"Daniel?" he asked. "Did you bring our princess here with you?"

He kept walking forward until he stood directly in front of me, stooped, craggy faced, with warm eyes and a crooked, sphinx like smile that concealed his intentions.

"She is here," I answered. "On Aquidneck Island at Captain Almy's house."

"We saw her with you at Menemesset." Honest George spat between his broken teeth. "It is good you have made her your woman. It is good you have kept her from her mother and Metacom."

Church approached from the side.

"You've left Philip?" he asked.

George nodded, still smiling in his inscrutable way.

"We've come to plant our corn," he said. "Not to fight."

If only it were that easy, I was thinking. Unless Church and I prevented it, Taylor and the others at Newport would soon sweep in on these unsuspecting natives.

"Is Awashonks with you?" Church asked.

Again George nodded.

"Then we must see her," my cousin said.

Still George's smile didn't waver.

"Go to her," I begged. "Ask her if she will meet with Benjamin and me."

For several seconds, Honest George stood before us, his thoughts concealed behind his amiable mask. Then as suddenly as he'd appeared, the old Indian turned and vanished in the trees from where he'd come.

"Will he do it, do you think?" Church asked me.

"Of course he will," I answered at once. "But will she?"

For the remainder of the morning and into the afternoon, we waited. Church and I stayed by our canoe, keeping watch. Thomas and One-eyed Jim refused to come closer than they were, preferring to oversee the river front from the safety of the channel.

"I can't help thinking," Church said to me at some point during our wait, "if we had gotten to her in time last year, Awashonks might never have joined Philip."

"Perhaps not," I answered. "But then her people would have been sold to slavery as Wantonka and the friendly Pokanoket."

I thought once more of the poor souls Wantonka and I had left behind the night of her escape.

"We'd have no one to ask to join us now." I glanced over my shoulder at the two Cape Indians. "And I'm afraid those two won't be much help by themselves."

"There." My cousin stiffened. Gripping the barrel of his musket, he pointed to the forest. "He comes."

As reckless as Church might have been, there was no man, red or white, more cunning and watchful. Seconds later, Honest George burst into view, hurrying toward us from the trees where my cousin had pointed.

"You will follow," the excited Indian gasped.

And then he turned and started back in the direction he'd just come.

"Where?" I shouted after him.

But the Sakonnet was gone from view again . Taking my arm, my cousin pulled me with him toward the same curtain of forest where our messenger just fled.

"It could be a trap," I tried.

But there was no slowing him. After more than a hundred yards of running, dodging trees, struggling to keep Honest George in sight, we broke into sunlight. Before us, at the edge of a broad field, Awashonks was seated on a wide flat rock. To either side of her, two braves stood in waist deep sea grass that covered the sloping ground behind them. One I recognized as Peter, Awashonks son. The other was the Sakonnet war captain Nompash.

"Mother!" Church shouted gaily.

But as soon as our running carried us to her, Awashonks stood, signaling to a Sakonnet war party crouched in hiding in the tall grass. Ambush, I thought, as nearly a hundred armed men suddenly appeared, their faces fierce with war paint, their muskets at the ready.

"We come in peace," my cousin was saying.

But my mind was working to form Wantonka's image one last time before I died.

"It is the custom," Church's voice broke. "It's the custom at times like this to put down your weapons when you meet."

Instinctively, I tightened my grip on my own gun, choosing a target from among the dozens arrayed before me. Somehow, even in panic, my eyes settled on a tall boy perhaps half my age whom I could easily shoot before I was killed. I wondered if we'd met before, either here in the shadow of Mount Hope, or perhaps during our winter in the west. I was considering the rightness of taking one last soul with me to God, thinking how little consequence his death would be to the conclusion of the war, when the sachem raised her arm.

I was prepared to die. But choosing not to resist, I'd just released my grip on my musket, just felt it thump the hard ground beside me, when the first of Awashonks' braves stepped forward. Coming directly to me, his eyes on mine, the same young Indian I'd picked as my target moments before stunned me now by lowering his own firearm and stacking it next to mine.

In seconds, the rest of the war party followed, placing their weapons before me and then retreating to stand again behind their sachem. Daring to glance to my side, I saw my cousin watching wide-eyed as the last of the Sakonnet disarmed himself.

"Thank you, mother," he managed.

And as if I wasn't sufficiently stunned already, I watched in even greater astonishment as Awashonks stepped away from her body guards and came unexpectedly to me.

"My son," she whispered, hugging me to her. "You have returned our princess to us?"

"I have," I breathed against her tunic.

This was war, I reminded myself. She was my enemy, and I was hers. Yet here she was embracing me, calling me son, as if the only difference between us was our age, as if we were neighbors still and all the interceding months of death and suffering had never been.

"You have returned in peace?" Church asked.

"We have," the old woman spoke to him at last. "My people weary of Philip and his war."

"Is Metacom here in Rhode Island?" I asked her.

She nodded, signaling to the men around her to sit down in the tall grass.

"Why was it that you never came to me, Benjamin?" she then asked. "Last year, when this mischief began. You could have gone to the Plymouth fathers for their blessing on us."

"I wanted to." My cousin shifted restlessly on his feet as I recalled the day the pirate captain Moseley took Wantonka and the other friendly Indians to be sold as slaves.

"When you did not come," she frowned, "I could not keep my young braves from following Metacom."

"I tried to come." Church continued to kick his boots at the dry ground. "But Daniel and I were ambushed in the Pea Field."

Suddenly, a young brave leapt to his feet and began shouting and waving his war club at us. Though it was impossible to understand his words, it was clear from the painted warrior's actions that my cousin's mention of the fight had angered him.

"His brother died at the Pea Field," Nompash told us.

The war captain was forced to speak loudly to be heard above the growing shouts of the others. Soon they were all on their feet, raising their clubs, shaking their fists.

"Speak no more of old things," Nompash barked at them.

At his feet was a carved wooden gourd. Reaching for his blanket, Church produced a jug of rum we'd carried with us from Newport.

"Peace," my cousin said.

Taking the gourd from the ground, he poured the rum into it and offered Awashonks a drink. The old woman hesitated. At first, it appeared she thought the rum was poisoned. Behind her, the Indians in her war party watched in restless silence. Pulling back the gourd, Church cupped his hand and spilled a little of the rum into it. With his eyes fixed on the sachem, he sipped the liquid from his hand, poured some more and sipped it also. Then he offered the wooden vessel to Awashonks once again.

"Mother, drink a toast to peace," he said to her. "You have my promise that the Plymouth fathers will welcome you to their fires once they learn of this."

Behind the sachem, several of the younger braves continued to scowl as she took the gourd from Church and drank from it.

"It's decided," Nompash pronounced. "We will join you if you lead us."

Although the old woman and her war captain wanted peace, I remained uncertain of the others. Church seemed to have the same concern. Stepping sharply forward, he spread his arms before the young braves.

"You all know me," he shouted. "When we hunted these forests and fished these waters together, we were brothers. But when you followed Philip and raised your muskets against Daniel and me, we fought you as warriors. Here I

169

am," he shouted even louder this time. "Today I come again as your brother. But if there are those who wish to fight me still, let them stand now."

Nompash glowered at his men. Some had their heads lowered. Some stared fiercely back at Church. But one by one, each man began to slowly nod his head.

"None would stand to fight you," Awashonks told Benjamin. "Instead, we will fill this gourd and each will drink from it."

Several of the warriors grinned at this, nudging those who didn't, encouraging all to enjoy the moment rather than resist it. Immediately Awashonks dispatched her son Peter to Plymouth to seek confirmation of a pardon from Governor Winslow. But because the journey required a difficult circular route to avoid both English and Pokanoket patrols, we resigned ourselves to a long wait for his return.

Deciding to withdraw to Almy's, Benjamin and I were with our wives when word arrived that Major Bradford was advancing with an English force of hundreds. Within days or our meeting with Awashonks, they arrived on the peninsula with such a clatter that our friends the Sakonnet were driven deep into hiding.

From the Almy house across the bay, we learned of daily raids by elements of Bradford's force in the forests around Swansea and Taunton. While Philip remained elusive, scores of his braves were killed or captured. So desperate was Church to reenter the fight now that he very nearly gave up his wait and enlisted with Bradford himself.

"If this new army is credited with ending the war," he cried, "I will be forever shamed."

"Metacom will never stand and fight them," I reminded my cousin.

The presence of Bradford was a blessing, I knew, not the curse Church would have me believe.

"Once we have our own fighting force," I reasoned, "we can use Bradford's army as a hammer to drive Philip to us."

This was to be my new role. I saw it at once. While Church had stalked away from the war after the battle in the Great Swamp, my own experience during the long winter at Menemesset had taught me the value of patience.

"Wait a bit longer," I advised him. "Then you will have the glory you've earned."

"And you," he answered.

But glory seemed an empty prize that day.

"Just promise me," I whispered, "that we are nearing the end of this horror."

XXVI

After just two more days waiting at the Almy house, however, Church could contain himself no longer. Against my protests and amid reports that Bradford had ordered Awashonks and the friendly Sakonnet removed to Sandwich, my cousin set out for Plymouth.

Awashonks' son Peter had been gone more than two weeks. And although Peter's mission and the difficulty incurred by a lone red man traveling so far on foot would have explained an even longer delay, Benjamin could not be dissuaded from following him. After informing Bradford of his plan, my cousin left me to oversee the transfer of the Sakonnet to Sandwich.

"Caution our mother to move her people as slowly as she can," he confided. "That way it will be quicker for us to return here to Aquidneck when I've received pardon for them."

Once more, I would command a refugee army, traveling with yet another displaced tribe.

"In one week," Church informed me, "I will look for you east of Dartmouth. Make your fires by the harbor in the shadow of the great hills of the Acushnet and I will find you."

From Bradford I received a white flag of truce and letters of safe passage with which I was to lead my new flock.

"Beware you don't stray from your path," the major cautioned me. "Or your friends the Sakonnet will find their heads fixed to the end of my army's pikes."

Unwilling to waste a single minute more, Benjamin departed that day, leaving sad faced Alice alone to roam the shadows of the Almy house with her infant. When Wantonka learned of my intentions to lead the Sakonnet east, however, she insisted on joining me instead of remaining behind with her new friend.

"Awashonks has heard too many empty promises to heed even you," she argued. "Because of your cousin, she now fears her own son might have been betrayed by the Plymouth elders."

It was the same concern that had driven Church to Plymouth, the unspoken fear we all shared regarding Governor Winslow's intentions.

"I will go with you to her," Wantonka insisted. "I will speak the words for you that will keep our mother's mind from worry."

By then, though, word was received from Bradford's camp that the Sakonnet had already departed for Sandwich. It was critical, therefore, that we hurry, that we overtake the native band as quickly as possible to convince their sachem to await my cousin's return at the place he'd chosen by the Acushnet. If Awashonks managed to lead her people all the way to Sandwich before Church returned, much valuable time would be lost.

With horses borrowed from Captain Almy, my wife and I set out the day after Church's departure. Riding north to Portsmouth and then turning east toward Cape Cod, we followed the path Awashonks was likely to have taken with her people. With Bradford's formidable army between us and the frontier, chances were slight that we'd encounter trouble from hostile Indians. We rode hard, therefore, covering ground far more quickly than the women and children who would slow the progress of the other Sakonnet. Even in country they knew so well, it would be difficult for them to cover more than half a dozen miles a day.

Despite her advanced pregnancy, my wife had little problem maintaining a swift pace. The ground beneath our horses' hooves was dry and firm. And we flew across the treeless coastal plain like clouds before a stiff wind, arriving at the wide bay of the Acushnet as the sun rested atop the distant hills.

"There," Wantonka pointed toward a smudge of black settled above the embankment on the far side of the water. "Sakonnet cook fires."

I was about to spur my horse, when she grabbed at my reins.

"It will be dark by the time we travel that distance," she reminded me. "If we camp here, we can arrive there in daylight."

And avoid the risk of being mistaken for enemy, I suddenly understood.

"Build no fire," she further cautioned me. "We can lay our blankets there in the cover of those rocks."

Helping her from her mount, I wondered at her lightness. Enfolding my arms around her gently swollen waist, I held her to me for a moment, marveling at how well we fit together, three now, rather than two, but still perfectly matched.

Resting my head in Wantonka's lap that night, listening to the gentle whispers of the water against the shore, I pretended the lovely, rhythmic sound of the waves was the beat of our child's heart coming from inside my wife.

"Mother," I so loved the sound of it.

Feeling Wantonka shudder beneath me, I looked up at her eyes, catching the glint of tears.

"What is it?" I asked.

"You called me mother once before," she answered. "It made me sad, remember?"

"Yes?" I reached to wipe away the dampness on her cheek.

"What of my mother?" she asked, reaffirming the same concerns she'd shared with me months earlier. "Is she ever to return to me, ever to see our child?"

We'd already considered the answer to that hard question. Events had doomed Weetamoo.

"You will see her again," I found myself telling the same sad lies as before. "Peace is near between us."

Wantonka said nothing. She pulled my hand close. And in the moonlight, I saw a tear fall. Though we both knew Weetamoo must be punished for following Philip, I prayed Wantonka would be spared recrimination because of it.

"Speak to me again of our new life, Daniel," she asked me later that night. "When this is ended, where will we live?"

Again, the same troubled questions.

"In Sakonnet," I reminded her. "With my cousin and our neighbors."

"No," she murmured. "Too much has happened here for our white brothers to forgive."

I breathed her perfumed bodice.

"They will," I promised.

Wantonka sighed.

"I have heard this before from you," she said. "It is for white people only. To forgive only with the sword."

I feared she was right.

"Keep us safe," she made me promise yet again. "My baby and me. You must you and you cousin."

Gazing across the water at the forests standing tall against the moonlit sky, I marveled once more at the vastness of the land that lay beyond them.

Certainly there was more than any man could tame. Perhaps this land would prove more welcoming, however, when we all were brothers once again.

"There is hope for us." She spoke as though seeing my thoughts. "As long as we are together as one."

Warm in each other's arms, lulled by the rhythmic lapping of the water, Wantonka and I shared a quiet, night. It was yet one more blessed interruption from our ceaseless war. And though our bodies, may not have enjoyed much sleep, our spirits found comfort and release. And in the morning, we awoke refreshed for the final leg of our journey.

Racing our horses at the water's edge, splashing each other with cooling salt spray, we sped the last two miles to the Sakonnet camp. There our fears were quickly put to rest as Awashonks and Nompash welcomed us with enthusiasm.

"You have returned as you promised," the war captain exclaimed as he hugged me to him. "It seems our people trust only Wantonka and you."

I explained to Awashonks and him how my cousin had gone to Plymouth to speed Peter's return.

"Benjamin wishes you to linger here," I told them, "until he arrives with a pardon from Governor Winslow."

My request was accepted at once. And without further discussion, we settled into the Sakonnet camp. Despite the gracious welcome we'd received from their leaders, however, several of the younger braves remained cautious, even hostile, toward our presence among them. Though we were treated with the familiarity of neighbors by the majority of the Indians, groups of two or three appeared wherever we went, watching us, bristling as though expecting trouble.

"Do you feel you have betrayed your people by helping Benjamin and me?" I asked Nompash when we were out of earshot of the others.

"Yes," he answered at once.

"Then why do you do it?"

"Because I felt the same sadness as this when I first betrayed my English brothers."

Leaning forward, he made a mark in the sand between the rock he was sitting on and mine.

"This is the English," he said, placing his hand beside me on my rock. "This is the Sakonnet." He then touched the rock on which he was seated. "And this is Nompash," he sighed, striking the mark he'd made in the sand between the two.

"Metacom speaks of a time before there were English," he went on. "But I know nothing of this."

He pondered the wide bay.

"Metacom says the English steal our land. But he rides a tall stallion the Plymouth fathers gave him in payment for ground he does not wish to hunt."

Squinting against the bright sun, he drew a long breath.

"Because of his words, we have lost brothers and sons," he continued. "That is why we fight now, because Metacom's words have emptied our lodges of so many of our warriors."

His eyes were bright when they again settled on mine.

"Metacom believes his brother was poisoned by the English," he said. "But it was him that was poisoned, by hate.

Reaching toward me, he again placed his hand on the rock where I sat.

"Now Philip has poisoned others of my people with this hate. That is why I will help you and your cousin."

He took my hand firmly in his.

"I will lead you to places where no English have been," he promised. "Deep into swamps that have hidden our people in earlier wars. There we will find him."

He squeezed my hand until it hurt.

"There the hate will die with Philip," he swore. "And then it will be ended."

XXVII

The night my cousin returned with the sachem's son, a great celebration was held. As the sun dipped low over the bay, an enormous feast was prepared. From dozens of cooking fires, fresh bass, shellfish, rabbit and venison were brought to Awashonks' lodge where they were set before us at the open end facing the shore.

Soon fiery light from the setting sun bled onto the mirror flat bay, silhouetting scores of braves squatting in the sand to take their meals. The air was perfumed with the fragrance of their feast. The sun sank lower, its reflected light growing darker, richer. Then, when the last of the food was consumed, the sun gone and the sky painted blood red, wood was gathered for a council fire.

So busy were the Sakonnet with their ceremony that hardly a word was spoken to Church and me. We could only watch and wonder at the elaborateness of their welcome. First, Awashonks stood and spoke. Then her son and Nompash followed. Next, a fire was lighted, the flames leaping to the tree tops. And as jugs of turgid root wine were passed around, the assembled braves began chanting and beating the ground with their war clubs.

"They ready themselves for battle," Wantonka whispered to us.

One at a time, each of the braves stood and danced around the fire.

With his war club raised above his head, his feet stomping the soft sand, each warrior chanted loudly in the dialect of the Wampanoag.

"Now that they no longer fight you," my wife told us, "they prepare to fight with you."

When one brave finished and returned to his place by the fire, another stood. Over the course of the next hour, dozens of Sakonnet fighters performed the same ritual, the sound of their shouts rising above the chants of the others. Among the braves who stood, I recognized several of the younger Indians who had at first scorned my presence. The safe return of Peter had calmed their worries. Now they were readying themselves to stand with my cousin and me, rather than against us.

"We make fighters for you," Nompash hollered to us. "Soldiers."

The celebration lasted well into the night, driving my wife, my cousin and me at last to the farthest edge of the camp where we laid our blankets in the shelter of a scented pine grove.

"I have enlisted the help of volunteers from Plymouth," Church told me when we'd settled together among the soft needles of the forest floor. "Several whites, good men, who will fit in nicely with these Sakonnet. They will join us here in the next few days."

He then went on to tell Wantonka and me of the panic that still infected the English communities to the east.

"Among ourselves, we know this conflict is just one step from being ended," he said. "But in Plymouth, they believe Philip has returned with every Indian from the west. The talk there is not of Philip's capture but of the annihilation of the whites."

Perhaps the desperation of our English brothers would compel them to finish things at last. One question lingered in my mind, however.

"Bradford's soldiers are conscripts who will be paid by the colony," I reminded Benjamin. "But how are we to pay our fighters?"

"Bounty for the Sakonnet," he responded, "will be their pardons and the plunder they collect from the enemy."

"And the volunteers from Plymouth?" My heart raced. "Certainly you don't intend to allow them to sell our captives into slavery?"

I recalled again the hideous ghost ship riding low at anchor in Boston harbor, its holds crammed full of captured Pokanoket.

"What choice do I have?" Church whispered. "In Connecticut, the paid conscripts massacre every Indian they find. No prisoners are taken. In Boston, there is talk that Sagamore Sam and other Nipmuc who willingly surrendered will be shot or hanged. Forcing the enemy we overtake to lay down their arms, even if it means enduring passage to the Indies, is better than death."

Still, I wondered. Taking Wantonka's hand, I waited for her to respond to my cousin's plan. But my wife remained silent. The night was far too dark for me to reassure myself her eyes weren't troubled. And when I tightened my grip on her hand, I felt no responsive squeeze. Whatever dark thoughts my cousin had provoked in her, my darling chose to keep them to herself. Perhaps she agreed with him that her people were better off as slaves than killed. Perhaps she agreed with the majority of Europeans that Philip and his outlaws deserved punishment. Or perhaps she was far too saddened by the future to even form the words to speak of it.

As the sounds of the Sakonnet celebration quieted, I drifted off to sleep. So deeply did I sleep, in fact, it seemed I'd hardly closed my eyelids when the growing light of dawn illuminated them again. Shielding my face with my arm, I was about to roll onto my side for a precious few more minutes rest when I felt something move beside me.

"Wantonka?" I whispered.

"No," a sobbing voice replied. "It is Oneka."

Opening my eyes, I pushed myself to my elbows, straining in the half light to see his shadowed face.

"Don't send me away," Oneka's voice broke. "Please let me stay with you."

So happy was I to hear his voice, so moved by his tears, that I spread my arms at once and pulled him to me in a gentle hug. As the boy lay in my arms and continued sobbing, I felt Wantonka and my cousin stir awake. Soon my wife's fingers stroked Oneka's matted hair and touched his damp cheek.

"You have been away too long," she breathed. "And you have seen too much."

But the boy was inconsolable. For several minutes, he sobbed and shuddered against my chest, clinging to me as if he'd never let go.

"Who is this boy?" my cousin asked.

"Our son," were the only words I could think to answer with. "And he's come home to us."

By the time Oneka managed to compose himself, the sun had broken free of the horizon and was burning gold upon the surface of the bay, illuminating the boy's scratched and bleeding face.

"I ran all night," he explained as Wantonka wiped away the tear stained blood from his cheeks.

Then I noticed the blood spattered on the front of his pants and shirt. Looking more closely, I found no noticeable wounds. Even his face, once wiped clean, was unscratched.

"It's not my blood," the trembling boy explained. "It came from a captured warrior."

Amid his sobbing, Oneka then related the horrors he'd witnessed since joining his Mohegan brothers who were now part of a force of Connecticut militia led by Major John Talcott.

"We caught many Narragansett," he told us. "Some were braves I knew from the Great Swamp and Menemesset."

According to the shaken boy, Talcott ordered the killing of everyone he caught, men and women.

"Two days ago," he related. "The English father gave one of the captured Narragansett to my brothers to torture."

The unfortunate captive, a man known to us as Smiling John, had helped Oneka locate the missing Rowlandson children during our stay among the Nipmuc.

"I begged my brothers to leave him," the boy stammered. "I went to the English and Mohegan fighters and told them how he'd given me a blanket and fed me from his own food."

With the fingers of his right hand, Oneka began rubbing a small blood stain on the front of his pants.

"My brothers made me stand with John and watch," the boy whispered. "They cut off his fingers and his toes."

Oneka rubbed and rubbed, but the blood was too dried and hardened to be removed.

"Smiling John sang the song of his people," the stammering boy managed. "He stood tall, even when his voice grew weak and his blood flew everywhere. But my brother's knives did not stop cutting him."

He looked so small and wounded, a bird with a broken wing.

"At Sakonnet I learned that you were here," he managed. "I did not stop running until I saw your blankets."

I had spoken little to my cousin of Oneka. I wasn't certain I'd ever encounter the boy again and had seen no need to tell of his days with me. Now I was relieved to hear Church ask no questions of him. A friend of mine was always welcome, his quiet eyes told me. Oneka would be a valuable scout, I knew. Once the boy was settled with us, he would more than repay my cousin's trust.

Within hours, the volunteers from Plymouth arrived. After dispatching Awashonks and her son with the rest of their pardoned tribe to Aquidneck, Nompash delivered us a force of fifty fighters. Some of the men I knew, most I didn't. Many had welcomed Wantonka and me when we first arrived among them. A few hadn't. Now we were all part of Church's army. But before we could begin our new campaign, we had much to learn from our Indian allies.

"Do not go into the forests as the English do," Nompash instructed us.

"To fight my people, you must move like us. Spread your fighters. Each man able to see the face of the man on either side. But no closer."

He taught us to move silently, no talk, careful to disturb little with our feet.

"Coming and going," he insisted, "take a different path with each march."

At first, however, several of the Plymouth men disagreed. Like Moseley and Bradford, they believed in the European style of massing troops for the greatest effect.

"Ambush is the penalty for that strategy," I reminded them.

I recalled my own experience in the Pocasset pea field, and later, watching helplessly as scores of Connecticut men were massacred by Cananochet at the great falls of the Blackstone.

"We are hunters now," Church added. "There is no game that can be caught except by stealth."

How many souls were lost, at Northfield, Sudbury and a dozen other places, how many more could have been saved by advice such as this?

On July 11, our preparations were nearing completion when word of the enemy arrived with the last of the volunteers from Plymouth. A large band of Pokanoket and Narragansett had been spotted north of our position in the vicinity of Assawompsett Pond. Church decided to set out after them at once.

Camping just once during our march, we aligned our force on the morning of the second day as Nompash had instructed. Advancing in stealth, shoulder to shoulder, our English and Sakonnet fighters entered the cool pine forests on the west shore of the pond. We had covered nearly a mile of ground when Oneka suddenly signaled us from his forward position. Following the example of their Indian brothers, our white volunteers dropped quickly to their knees as Nompash, Church and I crept ahead.

With hand signals, the boy led us to a granite crested ridge. There, with sunlight glinting off the distant pond, he pointed out the enemy encampment. From the fires, the clusters of wigwams, stacks of muskets and groups of braves huddled together throughout the camp, it appeared our force was outnumbered by two or three to one. Surprise would be our only advantage and we needed to use the terrain well to insure it.

"We'll break into three groups," my cousin whispered. "Nompash will take half the Sakonnet and circle to the rear of the camp from the left."

With his foot, he cleared the ground before him and began drawing in the sand.

"Daniel will take the other Sakonnet with him," he instructed, "and circle to the right. The men of Plymouth will remain with me holding the front along this line."

Again, he drew in the sand, this time indicating the fringe of woods standing between us and the Indian camp. His logic seemed good. Nompash and I could easily maneuver our experienced Indian force into position while Church's abilities and reputation would be valuable in holding the less experienced English volunteers in line along our front.

"Once the encirclement is complete," Church said, "once Nompash and Daniel join, they will fire a musket to signal the attack."

Without further discussion, Nompash and I departed with our braves, leaving Church to align his volunteers along the ridge where they would await our signal. Once more, I was impressed by the silence with which the Indians moved. So quiet were the fighters I led that I had to turn frequently to assure myself they were still behind me.

For several breathless minutes we advanced, crouched low, the glare of the sun hard in our eyes, listening for any sign that our quarry had discovered us. Outnumbered as we were, divided in groups that could easily be overrun by the enemy, we were dependent on the competence and courage of mates who, days earlier, had been strangers to us.

Passing within a hundred yards of the Pokanoket camp, I motioned to the first of our braves to drop from our column and take a position waiting the signal to attack. On I went, stationing warriors at intervals of twenty or more yards along the right flank of the cluster of enemy wigwams. Arriving at last at the edge of the pond, I then turned to the left, signaling the last of my braves to complete the line behind me as I closed toward Nompash.

So stealthy were the two of us, so careful to keep ourselves concealed from one another that I'd crept to within a few yards of the Sakonnet war captain before we spotted one another. Then the encirclement was complete, the two forces joined in a formidable ring of fire that, together with Church's English, enveloped the enemy.

"Give the signal," Nompash whispered.

I raised my musket. Through the dense stand of pine, I could see the shapes of the enemy fighters squatting by their fires. I thought of choosing a target, but could not. It would be murder, I thought, to kill an unarmed man taking his meal. Instead, I aimed in the air over their heads and fired.

Immediately, several more muskets sounded. Fighters sprang from cover on both sides of me and the air was filled with the shrieks of attacking Sakonnet. Incredibly, however, not one of the enemy was struck. Either the braves to my left and right shared my reluctance at targeting unarmed men, or perhaps they still considered these Pokanoket and Narragansett braves their brothers. Whatever the reason, our first volley went high, leaving a delicate instant in which we were exposed to the returning fire of our enemy.

Racing forward as fast as I could run, ducking tree limbs, bounding over rocks and brush, I kept my eyes fixed on the ground before me. Expecting the air to explode in my face at any time, I counted the seconds it would take for the surrounded warriors ahead to take up their weapons and fire. But not one enemy musket sounded. And when I finally dared to look, I saw the Indians before me standing with their arms raised in surrender.

Our victory was complete. Not one of the enemy even attempted escape. Seeming as relieved as we, in fact, they were easily collected in a circle, their muskets and other weapons gathered. Then Church leapt into their midst and clapped one of the prisoners in an exuberant hug.

"Jeffrey," he exclaimed.

Holding the older Pokanoket at arm's length, he then launched into a heated discussion I was unable to hear. From the enthusiastic tone of his voice, however, it was clear my cousin had found an ally.

"This man is a good friend," Church announced. "He's promised to lead us to a second encampment."

Soon other Pokanoket began conversing with their captors. It was as if Philip and his war had never happened, as if we'd stepped back to a time when we'd all been friends.

XXVIII

True to his promise, our new friend Jeffrey led us to the second Pokanoket encampment. Again, our success was shockingly easy. Springing our trap as before, we overran a group of sixty-five enemy without having to fire a shot. This time our quarry greeted us trembling so violently in fright at our sudden appearance, that several were unable to remain standing as we collected them.

For the next few days, we occupied ourselves delivering our captives to the authorities in Plymouth. Unarmed, closely guarded by their former brothers, the Sakonnet, our Pokanoket and Narragansett captives, offered no resistance. So glad were they of the food and drink we provided them on the scorching trail east that they followed Church's lead as children.

Word quickly spread of our victories. In less than a week, our allied force of whites and Sakonnet had succeeded in removing more of our enemy from the forests of the colony than the combined English forces of Bradford, Moseley and Talcott. Everywhere we went we were greeted as heroes. Even Governor Winslow himself insisted on traveling to Plymouth from his home in Marshfield to deliver his congratulations in person.

"You were right and I was wrong," he told my cousin and me. "If you hadn't persuaded me to grant pardon to these men you fight with, I fear there would have been many more scalps taken here."

At a word from Winslow, Church was given the authority to pardon whomever else he chose.

"Kill whom you will," the Governor directed. "Return what prisoners you can to me. And free any native you feel will help you track more of Philip's swine."

In an instant, my cousin was given the power of life and death over Philip's disintegrating army. But it was only the beginning of our adventures. No sooner had we rested and resupplied ourselves than news arrived of a large enemy gathering at Bridgewater. Just a dozen miles to the east, Indians had been spotted felling trees and attempting to construct a log bridge over the Taunton River. If we moved quickly, we might well arrive in time to intercept whatever force they intended to bring across.

Being the swiftest, I was sent ahead to scout the land and, if possible, locate the main body of the enemy force preparing to assault Bridgewater and Taunton. It was a difficult assignment, choosing between speed and caution. As easy as our initial successes had been, I feared our next encounter might be with a force so driven to desperation they would resist us fiercely.

I knew these brave men we pursued. I'd lived with many, stout warriors like Anawan and Nompash. For every several captives who came willingly to us, there would be more than a few who would fight us to the end. Not knowing who they were and when we were likely to cross paths with them, required that we increase our vigilance as we went forward.

For that reason, though I moved as quickly as I could, I kept my eyes and ears sharply tuned for any sign of trouble. This land had been my home for most of my life, yet I was a blind man among these forests when compared to the native Pokanoket and Narragansett I pursued. Many English had gone to their deaths in just the way I was doing now, rushing headlong toward concealed forces.

I took no comfort from the quiet I encountered. The farther I went, the deeper I penetrated the forests, the greater my risk became. It was for that reason that my heart leapt when at last I spotted the river and the first Indians aligned on its far embankment. I'd arrived in time, before the enemy crossing. Concealing myself, I could watch their movements in relative safety.

At first, I observed several braves coming and going from the trees on the far side, carrying powder barrels. From the number of barrels they carried, at least a dozen, it appeared a large operation was planned. Holding my breath, waiting for the main body of the enemy to show themselves, I watched as the last of the powder barrels was delivered to the river bank. Then all but one of the Indians disappeared again into the leafy wall of trees.

The man who remained, was stooped and slight of build. He wore his hair close cropped above his fleshy, shirtless torso. From his stature and build,

I thought for a moment it might be Philip himself. But the rebel king had had such fine braided locks when I'd last encountered him at Wachusetts that I refrained from firing now.

In a colony overflowing with combatants, perhaps ten thousand men at arms, the lone Indian entranced me with his composure. As my heart raced, I watched him draw a pipe from his pocket. Carefully spilling tobacco from a leather pouch into the stained ceramic bowl, he lighted the pipe, tilted back his head and drew long breaths of smoke from it. He could have been any man, I thought, red or white, alone at peace on a quiet afternoon, a fisherman perhaps waiting with patience for the first pull of his line.

I don't know how long I lingered in hiding watching my fellow traveler. It could have been an hour or only a few minutes. Time hardly seemed to matter, only the unbroken tranquility between us. Soon, I conceived a persona for my new friend. He'd broken off from the others because he'd wanted none of their fight with his English neighbors. Maybe he'd been among the many reluctant followers of Philip I'd seen at Menemesset, men who wanted only to return to the Peninsula in peace.

In my heart I believed that if I showed myself to the reclining Indian now, he'd gladly cross the river to me. Perhaps he'd even agree to lead my cousin and me to the war party that was forming. I could do Church a great service if I succeeded. And I was steeling myself to rise from my concealment when a musket thundered behind me.

At once, the Indian threw aside his pipe, slid from the log on which he was sitting and, splashing up the muddy river bank, disappeared into the forest. Turning, I saw two of my Sakonnet brothers race toward me from behind a dense cloud of gunpowder. Foremost of the two was Nomapsh.

"You are a strange man, Daniel," he gasped.

Standing over me, he kept his eyes fixed on the trees across the river.

"Why didn't you fire on him?" He refused to look down at me. "Do you call that English honor?"

"He was unarmed," I tried.

"Metacom is always armed," Nompash growled.

My cousin was the next to arrive, leading the others on the run. There was no reproach in his look as Nompash described Philip's escape to him. Instead his eyes settled on mine with relief.

"His hair was shorn," I tried, getting to my feet at last.

Quickly, Church dispatched skirmishers along the river bank to cover the crossing of the main body of his force.

"You did the right thing," he then told me. "If you'd fired before we arrived, you might have brought the entire war party across on you."

The others, red and white, who stood around us showed me no regard, either good or bad. Even Oneka kept a stone face. As long as their two leaders were present all would keep to themselves whatever feelings they had regarding my inaction. I wanted desperately to explain myself to them, to tell them even if I'd known it was Philip, I still wouldn't have been capable of murdering the man. Instead, I volunteered to be the first across the river to lead in his pursuit.

Straddling the log, keeping a low profile to avoid being shot by enemy Indians hiding on the far side, I pulled myself across the sleepy current. One by one, the others climbed the log behind me, grunting in the sweltering heat as they crossed. Closer and closer I drew to the impenetrable wall of green behind which an army of Pokanoket could be hiding. Though I knew Philip was likely to be running still, Anawan, Quinipian and the other war captains were stout enough to have formed an ambush for us.

Once I reached the far bank, I squatted with my musket at the ready, covering the others who followed. As each of the Sakonnet braves squeezed himself off the log and took up his position next to me, our eyes met briefly. Incredibly, I saw no recrimination. Rather, each warrior gave a simple nod of his head, a sign, I wanted to believe, that they approved my sparing the rebel king an unheroic death.

Once Church himself had crossed, he signaled me and six of our Indian fighters to follow him immediately into the woods. Bursting through the initial wall of leaves, I spotted the well trod path made earlier by the men who'd carried the powder barrels to the river.

"There," I pointed.

Keeping the path in sight but remaining well off it to avoid ambush, I led the way into the forest. Behind us, I heard Nompash spread the main body of our force for a more careful advance. Should we stumble on the enemy and draw its fire, Nompash could easily swing his left and right flanks into position to complete an envelopment of the ambushers.

This was hardly new territory for me. Many times, my cousin and I had crossed through these same sloping forests during our trips to Taunton. Today, the land seemed foreign to me as the farthest planets. Philip's behavior, his daring to exposure himself to me and then his quick retreat, cried out that we were being led into a trap. With every breath, I tasted fear.

But as I'd learned so many times before, the hidden enemy caused me more concern than the enemy revealed. And when my eyes at last beheld the first wigwams in a clearing just ahead, my mind cleared and my heart slowed. Dropping to my knees beside the others, I scanned the trees to either side of the dozen or so Indians gathered before us.

"Women," my cousin whispered.

Creeping forward on our hands and knees, we closed the distance between ourselves and Philip's camp.

"Return to Nompash," Church instructed Oneka. "Tell him Metacom has already abandoned this place."

Then signaling the Sakonnet fighters with us to circle left and right to be sure the surrounding woods were clear of Pokanoket warriors, my cousin motioned me to stand with him and approach the remaining Indians clustered in the center of the camp. They were expecting us it seemed and remained squatted together as we approached.

"Narragansett," one of the women spoke up indicating a fresh trail pointed east. "They return to their land on the far side of the bay."

Her eyes were filled with tears, as were many of the others.

"And Philip?" Church asked.

They shook their heads.

"But he was killed," the woman said. "We heard the shots by the river where he'd just gone."

After several more questions, it was clear they hadn't seen their sachem since our arrival at the river.

"Philip lives," my cousin informed them at last. "He ran before us."

But it wasn't relief that I saw on the faces of our newest prisoners. Rather the look of resignation darkened their eyes.

"We will continue after him," Church promised.

"He knows," the woman answered. "And he has prepared himself to die."

Hearing the unexpected crack of branches and the shuffle of leaves, I turned in time to see an army of small children burst at me from the trees. Flushed from their hiding places by the Sakonnet we'd dispatched to our left, the children ran shrieking in terror among the women, searching in desperation for familiar faces.

"Their fathers and mothers have abandoned them," the Pokanoket woman explained to us. "Only we would stay to keep with them."

Standing, she gathered several of the smallest children to her side.

"It is the end," she whispered to them. "For all of us."

Their eyes streamed tears as they stared in fright at us. Some, hardly old enough to walk, huddled against their older sisters and brothers.

"And now even the youngest of them will be taken from us," she growled at Church, "to die on your slave islands."

Long after I'd turned away, the image of those fearful children lingered in my mind. Like the Rowlandson children, these innocents had done nothing to bring this torment on themselves. While Philip ran, it was these few who stood alone to suffer for his sins.

But we had little time to mourn their fate. The retreating Narragansett had left us a fresh trail which we needed to follow at once. Leaving the Pokanoket women and children with several of our English volunteers, Church and I hurried our war party from the camp.

Moving swiftly west, we came upon a narrow river where the heavily tramped ground indicated our quarry had just crossed. Forced to wade the sleepy current nearly to our shoulders, using overhanging willow branches to pull ourselves onto the far bank, we quickly found the enemy trail and resumed our pursuit.

After struggling another few miles in sodden leggings and moccasins, I took my cousin's arm and pulled him to a stop.

"This is not the course we need to follow," I told him after he'd halted the rest of our fighters. "The longer we pursue the Narragansett, the farther we move from Philip."

Considering my words, Church called Nompash and several of his lieutenants to his side.

"Our task is not revenge or plunder," I told them. "It is to find Metacom and end this war."

"Daniel makes a strong argument," Church responded. "We may have wasted our advantage chasing the wrong quarry."

"No!" one of the younger Sakonnet barked. "These Narragansett killed my brother."

The bold man's name was Lightfoot. I'd known his brother and him as boys.

"Leave him," Nompash spoke. "Let Lightfoot take his braves and follow Quinipian. I will lead the others with you back to Bridgewater."

And it was decided. Lightfoot gathered a fast moving group of six warriors and vanished without another word into the forest toward Mount Hope Bay. Then Church led us, retracing our steps along the same forest path we'd just taken, through the same deep river crossing, to the sorry group of women and children we'd left behind hours before.

Once we arrived among the Indian women and their band of squalling children, it was agreed we'd spend the night. And in the morning, as we gathered our prisoners for our return to Bridgewater, Lightfoot miraculously reappeared. With him, he brought more than a dozen Narragansett prisoners and news of many more killed. Chattering in his native tongue, he told Nompash of his daring night attack.

"Lightfoot says he arrived like the wind," the older war captain beamed at his young protege. "So fast and hard, the Narragansett thought there were a hundred."

Lightfoot's was our most successful operation yet. Outnumbered by the

Narragansett he pursued, scorned by Church and even Nompash, the young Sakonnet warrior had impressed us all with his skill and pluck. Perhaps Philip had eluded us. Perhaps the rebel king had survived to fight again. But there was now no question in any of our minds that our relentless band of brothers would bring him down, and soon.

By mid-afternoon, after my cousin had dispatched our prisoners under guard to Bridgewater, we resumed our search for Philip. We moved south this time, toward the dangerous swamps of the Pokanoket territory where Philip was certain to have returned. With our fighters once again fanned wide to the left and right, our progress was slow. But as Bradford's force filled the surrounding countryside, our enemy had nowhere left to run. We could take our time, remaining careful of ambush.

After hours of stealthy marching, we passed an abandoned camp, arriving at last by the entrance of the first broad swamp. In the distance, we could hear the sounds of our enemy cutting wood for his fires. We had found Philip, I was sure. But with darkness approaching and the way ahead uncertain, Church and Nompash were forced to halt our force until the light of dawn could guide us.

Throughout the night, our rest was disturbed by the sounds of our enemy. So close were they, so loud were their voices, it seemed we'd camped together, neighbors for one last night. I thought of Philip, less than a mile from where I lay, taking what might well be his final rest. What was he like, I found myself wondering?

In all the time I'd been fighting him, I'd seen and spoken to the Pokanoket king just once. In Wachusetts, on the night of Mary Rowlandson's release, the sachem had struck me as such a crude and common man that I found myself now wishing I could talk with him once more before the end. To have inspired such rebellion, I knew, he must certainly have possessed qualities unknown to the English. But with his end near and his reputation already vilified, the real Philip might never be known to history.

It was fear and restlessness, however, that drove my mind to wonder about my enemy that night. I was a soldier, not an historian. My job was to capture Philip or kill him before more lives were lost. After all, I'd already carried the story of Canonchet's final days to the Nipmuc. And I'd returned the belt of Anawan to its owner. I owed nothing more to any of my enemy, especially to Philip. Fixing my thoughts instead on Wantonka and our unborn child, on our future and the peace we would enjoy, I settled at last into a deep sleep that was broken only when my cousin roused me to the dawn.

"It's time," he whispered.

Gathering our fighters once more, Church dispatched two Sakonnet warriors forward to scout the entrance to the swamp. In minutes, they returned, running and hollering, sending our troop into an abrupt but practiced envelopment maneuver. Leaving a handful of men at the swamp's entrance, Church and Nompash quickly led half our force to the right while I led the others to the left. Positioning our men as we'd done before at marked intervals along the periphery of the swamp, we were soon able to surround the enemy camp.

No sooner were the last of our fighters in place, however, and Church and I rejoined than an enormous party of the enemy appeared before us. Scores of shirtless, painted braves, some with shaved heads, others with elaborately braided hair, swarmed into the open ground before my cousin and me. Seeing our force was outnumbered at least six to one, I was about to issue the command to take cover when Nompash stepped boldly forward and shouted to the enemy ahead. He stood tall, seeming to taunt the Pokanoket with his pluck. Not understanding his native tongue, I glanced to my cousin.

"He's telling them to surrender," Church whispered with a wink. "He says they are outnumbered and surrounded, that if they don't put down their weapons they will all be shot dead."

For several seconds none of the armed warriors moved. Sensing their apparent confusion, Nompash took another brisk stride forward, this time barking an angry command. And at once, the enemy did as he'd ordered. Fearing Bradford's murderous force was waiting in hiding for them, more than a hundred enemy gave up their arms to an army barely large enough to take them. So unexpected was our victory that I dared not take a breath until the last Pokanoket brave was stripped of his musket and war club.

Bringing the rest of our men forward from their hiding places, we carefully gathered our prize, counting one hundred seventy three prisoners. It wasn't until they were collected in a small hollow with our armed troop standing along its rim that they realized their folly. Staring past our menacing guns, their eyes wide with disbelief, they searched the surrounding trees for the larger English army they still believed was there.

For many minutes, we scanned the astonished faces of our prisoners looking for their king. When several of the captives lowered their heads or turned away, Nompash sprang into the hollow among them. After pulling each of the sulking Indians to his feet, our Salkonet war captain then shook his head.

"Metacom is not among them," he sighed.

"Be certain," Church cautioned.

As Nompash walked among the squatting prisoners one final time, my cousin and I circled the rim of the hollow, studying their up-turned faces.

"Philip sent these others forward when he saw our scouts," Church at last decided. "Then he ran as he always does."

"There," Nompash pointed to a patch of dry ground leading to a cluster of trees that covered several dozen acres at the swamp's center.

Now we had a difficult decision. With only a handful of men to spare from guarding our prisoners, did we dare enter the trees in pursuit of Philip and the desperate men he'd chosen to make his final stand with? For Benjamin, it was an easy choice.

"Daniel," he called me to him. "Help me gather the captured weapons."

Choosing a dozen of our English volunteers, Church and I distributed loaded muskets among them laying three or four at the feet of each man standing at the rim of the hollow.

"If any of them moves," Church shouted loudly enough to be heard by everyone, "kill them all."

Having Nompash repeat the order in his Wampanoag tongue, my cousin then dispatched two more of the Plymouth men to the far side of the trees.

"Be alert," he instructed them. "Position yourselves so that when Philip runs again you can kill him too."

After allowing sufficient time for the volunteers to take up their positions on the far side of the swamp, Church then ordered us ahead. In seconds, I was panting. So densely clustered were the trees before me they could easily conceal a hundred ambushers. If the Pokanoket captives we'd left behind rose up now against the few men guarding them, we could find ourselves trapped between two large enemy war parties.

But as that black thought flashed through my mind we were suddenly confronted by our quarry. Not more than sixty yards before us, Philip himself appeared. This time I recognized the Pokanoket prince. Despite his close cropped hair, there was no mistaking the pinched and swarthy face. He was in the company of a dozen of his warriors. And when he spotted us, he quickly turned and ran, just as Church had predicted.

"Stand and fire," my cousin ordered.

Immediately, the braves on either side of us emptied their muskets and several of the enemy fell. As two of the remaining turned to flee, our Sakonnets swept forward and captured the rest.

"Daniel," Church shouted. "Leave our brothers with these prisoners and come with me."

Quickly, I was at his side, racing through the trees, the low hanging branches slapping my face and shirt. Suddenly, all anxiety was gone. I was so caught up in the action now, I hardly felt a pang of fear. Our enemy was on the run. Distant musket shots indicated the Plymouth volunteers might well have shot down Philip by now. My cousin and I had only these two more to catch.

We raced for at least a quarter mile, tramping through the tall grass, splashing through the muddy slime. The trees ahead were thinning and I was straining for a glimpse of the men we were chasing when I nearly cried out in terror. Appearing no more than twenty yards before me one of the two men we chased, a burly warrior no older than me, suddenly stood from hiding in the grass, his musket pointed squarely at my chest. And in the instant before my enemy killed me, my eyes fixed absurdly on the bright red rag which secured an enormous knot of hair atop his head.

I watched the comely swath of red dip once as the Indian took aim. I listened for the lock to strike the flint, waiting for the muzzle flash and the searing shaft of pain that would end my life. I heard the click of iron. And then I saw the swath of red twist sharply to the right as the Indian threw down his musket and ran.

"His gun misfired!" Church shouted.

That was when I realized I was still running. Without my feeling them, my legs had continued carrying me toward my assassin. In seconds, I overtook him, threw him to the ground, and struck him unconscious with the butt end of my weapon.

"Daniel!" my cousin shouted again.

Looking up, I saw the second warrior lunge from hiding with his musket pointed at me. This time there was no misfire. This time the air exploded. But instead of killing me, the speeding ball whispered past my ears and struck the attacking Indian with a sickening thunk in the middle of his forehead. It had been Church who fired first, killing my attacker, tumbling him to the earth beside me, sparing my life for the second time in less than a minute.

"Are you all right?" my cousin asked.

Glancing to the left and then to the right, I looked from one of the fallen Indians to the other, struggling to slow my racing heart.

"Were you hit?" he took my arm.

Still unable to draw a breath to speak, I stared dumbly as he inspected my unblemished shirtfront.

"We must keep after Philip," he told me.

But my feet were rooted to the ground between my two attackers.

"I heard shots ahead," he said. "We must go to help the others."

At last my breathing slowed.

"You nearly killed me," I managed. "Your ball came inches from my head."

My cousin grinned.

"At least a foot," he joked. "Come."

And he led me by the arm, hurrying from our fallen enemy toward the far end of the woods. But the scene we encountered there was more troubling than any of the narrow escapes we'd had. The two volunteers Church had sent ahead to block Philip's escape lay dead, shot through the head. The enemy king had gotten away. Despite our success, our victory was a hollow one. The risks we'd taken to end the war were not to be our last.

XXIX

By August, Church and I and our swift moving band of Sakonnet and English fighters had removed nearly half of Philip's army from the war. Together with the two to three hundred Pokanoket and Narragansett killed and captured by Bradford, Moseley and Talcott, less than three hundred of the enemy remained. Only a few dozen of these were thought to be standing with Philip. The rest were scattered in hiding places throughout the swamps surrounding Mount Hope Bay.

Within a week of our arrival at Plymouth with our army of prisoners, after another congratulatory visit from Governor Winslow, we received word from the west that Weetamoo had been killed. Fleeing a group of Taunton militia, the last of her Pocasset braves shot down around her, the gray haired sachem attempted to swim to safety across the Taunton River. Caught in rapids, however, perhaps wounded herself from the gunfire she was attempting to escape, my wife's mother had drowned.

Finding her remains the next day tangled in reeds that bordered the river embankment below the town, several English soldiers mutilated her body, cut off her head and carried it to Plymouth. With them, they brought news of the death of another of Philip's captains, Totonson, and the capture of Quinipian and Sagamore Sam. Great rejoicing greeted them. And as their terrible, bloody trophy was spiked and raised for display above the stockade walls, Winslow gave the order for the Plymouth army to disband and the men to return to their farms and families.

Without a fighting force to lead, Philip was reduced to the status of an outlaw murderer, to be shot on sight by any man, red or white. A bounty was placed on his head, and the colony returned to its business content the Almighty would provide them justice.

For Church, however, the fight was hardly ended.

"Return with me to Alice and Wantonka," he told me. "We will visit there awhile and then set out to finish this."

Anxious to accompany my cousin home, I said nothing about his plan to keep tracking Philip. Although several of our fighters, mostly Sakonnet, volunteered to join Benjamin in continuing the hunt, I kept quiet. Concerned foremost about my wife, I withheld my decision until I saw her. I bore heavy word of the death of Wantonka's mother. In her delicate condition, the news might lay her so low that I might have to remain by her side until our child was born.

The week before, we'd received word that our women had moved closer to Plymouth, to Newport, where they were being lodged in the home of Peleg Sanford, a merchant friend of Church's. Crossing that day to Aquidneck Island, my cousin, I and six others secured horses for ourselves at Portsmouth and rode together south to the busy port. There we found the women helping dry fishing nets on the crowded beach.

Seeing our group thunder toward them from the forest, workers and bathers stood to watch. Shielding their eyes against the bright sun, they were struggling to identify us when one of the women in the group cried out and fainted. It was Alice. So shocked and relieved was she at the sight of her husband returned safely to her that the poor woman collapsed into the arms of my pregnant wife.

At once, Church sprang from his mount. Sweeping his wife into his arms, he revived her with a shower of kisses. Reining my own mount, I dismounted into the trembling arms of my wife. News of our successes must certainly have reached Newport. But Wantonka was experienced enough in the ways of the war to know that any victory came at great risk. We'd been separated but a few weeks. There was no need for words, no need to speak of my close encounters with Philip and with death. There was need only for the warming hug we'd feared we'd never enjoy again.

With Oneka by our sides, we then walked together to a quiet section of the beach. There my cousin, my young red brother and I stripped off our shirts and plunged into the churning surf. In minutes, we were children again, catching one another, plunging together into the cooling water. On shore, our wives laughed and shouted at our frolic. Beyond them, on the apron of beach we'd just left, several more of the town's people had gathered to stare. Though we behaved like children, their quiet eyes told us we were welcome among them. No matter what we did this day, we'd be treated as heroes.

After chasing one another at last from the ocean to the beach, we sat side by side in the soft sand watching a distant sloop tack toward us.

"It's Captain Goulding," I said. "I recognize his bark from the pea field fight."

"Still carrying the scars of our escape, I'd reckon," Church grinned.

Carefree in the company of our wives, we watched the sloop draw closer, growing larger and larger until we could make out our friend and rescuer standing in the stern.

"He's signaling to us," I told my cousin.

Jumping to our feet, we returned to the surf, wading out to greet the daring seaman who had saved our lives the year before.

"Cast a bow line," Church shouted to him. "Pull up your keel and we'll tow you to shore."

Goulding gestured wildly, his face bright red from the effort to be heard over the rolling waves. Church and I were standing in water above our waists, straining to hear him.

"Return to shore," my cousin suddenly barked. "Something is wrong."

As I turned back, I heard the first of Goulding's shouts.

"Philip has returned!" he hollered.

"We know this," my cousin answered him. "We've been tracking him for weeks."

"No!" Goulding's voice grew louder as he closed on shore. "He's here. At Mount Hope. I've found an Indian who will lead you."

"Gather the men!" Church roared. "Tell them to leave the horses and come at once."

My clearest recollection of that moment was the look on Alice's face when I splashed from the surf again. Gone was the girlish spark that had greeted our earlier frolicking. Now my cousin's wife was hurt by what she'd heard, her face a crushed flower. With a glance at Wantonka, seeing reassuring quiet in her eyes, I wordlessly hurried past them to the place where our men had retired with their horses.

Seeing me race across the sand toward them as my cousin worked to land the Goulding sloop was all the indication our Sakonnet needed that the news was urgent. Gathering their muskets, they ran to us at once.

"The tide is with us," was all Goulding had to say.

Without a word of question, the Sakonnet followed Church and me over the sides and onto the narrow deck of the sloop. As my cousin had predicted, the hefty oak mast still held the marks of the Pokanoket muskets fired on us during our narrow escape from their territory the previous year.

We were green then, unaware of the terrible consequences our people, red and white, would suffer after that day. Now we would return to the same Pokanoket Peninsula where it all began, borne by the same craft, steered by the same skipper who had saved us from annihilation. How fitting it would be, I thought, if we who had survived the desperate day that marked the start of war would now ride the same chariot to its conclusion.

"Captain Goulding has found a man who will lead us to Philip," Church told Nompash.

The Indian captain quickly translated to the delight of his men. It was yet another irony, I realized, that many of these Sakonnet braves had been among those firing on my cousin and me at the pea field that day. Perhaps one of these fighters had even left his mark on Goulding's sloop. Perhaps it was the leaden ball of one of these warriors, intended for me, that had lodged in the intrepid sea captain's tall mast.

Now these same men who once had stood with the rebel king suddenly delighted in his capture. What twisted alliances had marked the past fourteen months. The war that had begun as red against white had turned into brother against brother.

"The man is Pokanoket," Goulding shouted above the waves rushing past. "Philip killed his brother for suggesting they sue for peace."

Not only had the great Indian alliance fractured, the Nipmuc, Narragansett, Sakonnet and others deserting Philip. Now the Pokanoket king had even lost control of his own tribe.

"It took all morning for me to reach Newport," the captain told us. "But with the wind and tide running with us, it should take no more than two hours to return."

Nightfall, I calculated, the perfect time for us to surprise our enemy.

With our Sakonnet brothers grouped before us in the bow, I imagined we were warriors from an ancient time. Armed with spears and bows, their faces painted and their hair tied up in elaborate knots, our allies could well have been sailing for Troy or Carthage. The summer sun set slowly, baking the crowded deck. Only the occasional rolling swell cooled us, breaking over the bow, sending the Sakonnet shouting with boyish glee at every sudden shower of ocean water.

Slowly, steadily, the tide and breeze drew us closer to the rocky tip of the peninsula. Soon we could see land and several figures watching for our arrival. With Goulding's weathered hands feathering the rudder and my cousin's strong arms drawing at the sail lines, we came swiftly to rest fifty yards from shore.

As Church and I had done at Newport that morning, two of the figures on shore waded into the gentle surf to gather our bow line. With the two men drawing on the taut rope, and two of the Sakonnet pulling on the sloop's oars, we closed the final distance, leaping over the sides and gathering around the lone Pokanoket who had volunteered to guide us.

Surrounded by his enemies, the man stood tall. He was not young, perhaps a dozen years older than my cousin. Though unarmed, but with arms and legs twice the size of mine, he seemed more than a match for any of us. And after warily eying the Sakonnet, he turned and, recognizing Church, he spoke at once.

"Metacom is camped on high ground by a swamp, there." He pointed to the base of Mount Hope, a mile distant.

"How many warriors does he have with him?" my cousin asked.

Again the man turned his wary eyes on our Sakonnet.

"More than this," he said. "By a few."

With our guide in the lead, we spread our force as always and followed at a slow and stealthy pace to maintain surprise. There was no need to hurry. Midnight was still hours away. By then, if we avoided detection, we should find Philip and his men asleep.

The surrounding woods were deathly quiet. But in the quiet, I was certain I could hear whispers of the spirits of the Pokanoket who had lived and died here. This was Massasoit's land, his capital, where the great king of the Wampanoag confederation first retreated to consider the arrival of the English. Then, the whispering spirits who resided among these sweet pines had counseled the Indian leader to befriend the white intruders, to join them in settling the land emptied by plague. What message did they have now, I wondered? With English coming to kill the son of Massasoit, would the ancient spirits cease to haunt this land, or would they forever torment our intrusion?

By nightfall our guide gathered us in a shallow indentation he reported to be no more than half a mile from Philip's camp. Reluctant to make a fire, we used the last of the dying light of day for him to draw a map and help us form a plan. Employing the same tactics Nompash had taught us the month before, we divided our force. Goulding, who had insisted on leaving his sloop to join us, would command the front for our attack.

Creeping on their stomachs, the sea captain and a dozen of our Sakonnet would follow our guide forward to the enemy camp. As they inched to within firing distance, Church and I would move the rest of our force to the flanks, Benjamin to the left, me to the right, arranging our men in a tight encirclement to prevent another escape by Philip. Once in position, once my cousin and I were rejoined at the far side of the swamp, we would wait for dawn for Goulding to give the signal to attack.

At my side stood a man named Alderman, a Pocasset who had renounced Weetamoo and returned east weeks before her death . He was new to our force, joining us on our most recent return to Newport from Plymouth. I had spoken little to him and noticed he had kept his distance from the Sakonnet he now fought with. As the first breezes of night began to cool my sweat soaked skin, he touched my arm.

"I will come with you this night," he whispered.

He was a small man, at least a head shorter than me, but with the scars of many battles on his arms and chest.

"My musket will serve you well," he promised.

Though he held his antique flintlock up for me, it had become too dark to see more than its clumsy outline.

"Trust me, English," he insisted. "Though my gun is old, my powder will be dry and quick when the morning fog slows these others."

In addition to the vagaries of powder and dampness, however, there was another reason I chose to keep Alderman with me. He was newly arrived, unknown to my cousin and me, and watchful of the Sakonnet. Because of that, I wasn't certain I could trust him, especially on a mission where stealth was required. If it was his plan to warn Philip of our approach, I wanted to stay near so I could silence him when necessary.

With Alderman at my side, I gave a final salute to Church and Goulding before leading my small force into the swamp to my right. As on our earlier assaults, I was again astonished at the calm that settled over my Indian allies once our march began. Having no idea how I must appear to them, feeling my heart pound as though it wanted to pierce my chest, I marveled at the quiet faces aligned behind me. Perhaps they were as anxious as I. Perhaps their stoic masks were practiced to conceal whatever fear they might be feeling. But as long as I'd fought beside these warriors, I'd drawn courage from them and was glad I no longer had to face them in battle.

It took much of the remaining hours of darkness to move ourselves into position surrounding the Pokanoket camp. As we closed the circle and the first sliver of gray light appeared through the trees ahead, I spied my cousin, crouched and waiting. After a quick search of the ground around us, I placed Alderman beside me at the crest of a rocky ledge within a hundred yards of Church's position. There we waited in concealment as the dawning light slowly illuminated the ground before us.

One by one, the wigwams of our enemy were revealed, appearing through the blanket of swamp mist that had settled over us during the night. There were nearly ten, arrayed before us as our guide had promised. Straining my eyes through the dense curtain of fog, I was looking for signs of Goulding's force in hiding on the far side when I saw three enemy braves stumble sleepily from one of the nearest lodges. Behind them appeared the rebel king himself.

As I watched, more Pokanoket men staggered forward through the fog. Among them was Anawan, his musket in his hands, standing a head taller than the rest. Counting nearly fifty, realizing we were outnumbered nearly four to one, I was preparing myself for the signal that would begin the fight when I saw one of the Pokanoket suddenly separate himself from the others. Loosening the leather string that held his breeches, the lone Indian was just entering the trees on the far side of the camp to relieve himself when the air before him exploded and he fell dead.

Immediately, Goulding and the rest of his men stood and fired. Several more Pokanoket fell as they rushed to the muskets they'd stacked in the center of the camp. Some held their ground and were shot down as soon as Goulding's force reloaded. A larger group led by Anawan raced to our right in an attempt to break through my cousin's flank. One Indian separated himself from the others. Ducking low to avoid the hail of shot, he grabbed his powder horn and musket and raced directly toward my hiding place.

It was Philip, stooped and worn, far older looking at this panicked moment than I'd reckoned. Still clinging to the damp earth, I counted the seconds until he came into range, calculating how I would stand and make my shot. At fifty yards, I continued to hold my ground. At forty yards, I heard Alderman bark at me. And at thirty yards, I made my move.

At once I was on my feet, my musket raised, my finger on the trigger, my barrel aimed at the fleeing sachem's chest. I squeezed, waited for the spark to light the powder in my pan, for the sudden flash and then explosion of the charge. Time had stopped. Philip froze before me, his eyes locked on mine. Then, as my musket wavered in my trembling hands, as I realized my powder had failed to ignite, Alderman's antique roared, Philip's chest tore open and the Pokanoket king fell hard to the ground at my feet.

I was too stunned to breathe. My heart raced. My hands ached from the tight hold they still had on my musket. But though gunfire and battle shrieks continued to fill the air around me, I couldn't remove my eyes from Philip's lifeless form. Seconds earlier, the savage spirit that filled this twisted, broken shape had menaced an entire land. Now it was gone, snuffed out the instant its living eyes touched mine.

We lost five killed among our Sakonnet brothers that day. Of the Pokanoket that stood with Philip, nearly thirty lay dead beside their leader. As echoes of the fighting dimmed, clouds of smoke from our muskets slowly lifted in the sultry air. It had been little more than four hundred days since the rebellion began. Now it was ended, for Philip at least, in the place where it had begun.

Though Anawan managed to escape, breaking through our lines with nearly two dozen braves, the rejoicing among the survivors of us was undiminished. Philip's body was dragged to the center of his camp where my cousin gave the orders for its disposal. Standing on still trembling legs, I watched him restrain the Sakonnet from desecrating the body until he finished speaking.

"For his crimes against God and man," Church announced, "Metacom is to remain unburied, to be fed on by the beasts of the forest."

It was at that moment I turned away. I knew the Sakonnet could not be held for long from taking bloody trophies of their victory. I wanted nothing to do with their savage ceremony. Catching Goulding's eye, I walked with him from the clearing, deep into the forest.

"It was nearly you who was the hero this day," the older man said to me.

But even in victory, I felt mournful for the losses suffered.

"I'm glad it wasn't me," I answered him.

Goulding knew as I did what sacrileges were being committed behind us. Church would be powerless to keep the Sakonnet from dismembering Philip's body. Afterward, he would be forced to grant some trophy, a severed hand perhaps, to the man who'd killed the Pokanoket sachem. Then he would be compelled by his duty to Governor Winslow and the other vengeful Pilgrim elders to deliver Philip's head to Plymouth.

"I want only to be away from here," I told the captain. "If you will take me with you, I would be obliged to return to my wife in Newport."

Goulding agreed at once. And we walked together in silence along the path of attack we'd followed the day before. Last summer, my world had changed in just a flash, I was thinking. And now, with a second unexpected flash, was it supposed to change back to what it had been? I was a builder of homes who had become a soldier. How was it possible that, at a stroke, the soldier was expected to drop his musket and resume life with his hammer and chisel? To illuminate once more the shadowed places this war had filled me with seemed so unlikely.

Leaving Church and the others to go by land to Plymouth with their hideous trophies, Goulding and I put out together onto the wide bay. Incredibly, the sun had barely risen in the morning sky. So much had happened since dawn, it seemed as if a full day had been consumed rather than just a few hours.

Taking turns at the tiller, the captain and I caught some needed rest among the canvases in the bow. We'd traveled all day the day before, spent the night creeping through the fog shrouded trees of the peninsula and fought a terrible battle without stopping once for sleep. But with the tide running against us and a light summer head wind slowing our progress, we were able to steal a few hours to recover ourselves.

After sleeping for the first hour, allowing the captain to perform the necessary maneuvering to get our craft into the main channel, I'd just relieved him at the stern, when I was struck by an unexpected calm. Unlike my cousin who was as comfortable on sea as land, I'd never much taken to the water. But now, far removed from the shadowed forest, exposed to the cleansing light of the sun, I felt such peace.

It had been my destiny, I realized, to be transformed by war. Yet when I arrived with Goulding in Newport, when I greeted the eager English there with news of Philip's death, I shared none of their enthusiasm. I felt numbed instead, not by what we'd accomplished, but by how far removed I felt from it. One boat trip, one bay passage had done more to heal my spirit than I ever could have imagined. And rather than the bloodied soldier I'd been, I returned to Wantonka a builder once again.

XXX

Though it lasted just a few days, my peaceful interlude with Wantonka and Oneka was a most pleasant time. Perhaps, as I'd considered on my return from Mount Hope, war had sharpened my appreciation for peace and quiet. For hours, we did nothing but sit together, Wantonka's hand in mine, watching the boy fish and swim, staring across the sunlit bay to nowhere. An occasional friend would pass by. He might wave or stop to say hello. Most times, however, the people of Newport simply nodded their greetings, hesitating long enough to draw some comfort from the image of the English hero and his wife, the daughter of the fallen rebel queen.

But with the passing of each precious day, I felt increased certainty that Church would call me back. We were not yet done. Anawan was in the forests. And though I had no desire to hunt the warrior captain, I found myself feeling increased obligation to act in his behalf.

Anawan must be captured. His presence in the Rhode Island swamps must be ended, his role in the rebellion punished. But someone needed to speak for him, to tell of his help in freeing the Rowlandson children. Otherwise, he would be killed and mutilated as Philip had been, his legacy lost with the fabled story belt of his people.

By now I knew Wantonka could read in me whatever I was thinking and in her silence I was certain she supported me. Still, out of consideration for her, I decided at last to speak to her of Philip's captain. It was evening, three days after my return from Mount Hope. We were sitting together in the dying light of our cooking fire, marveling that the colors in the glowing embers so perfectly matched the vivid oranges and reds in the sunset sky. My hand was on Wantonka's belly, feeling yet another exuberant kick of life beneath my fingers from our child inside her.

"Benjamin will ask me to go with him again," I whispered. "In search of Anawan."

My wife said nothing, her shallow breaths barely heard above the lapping water.

"Then it will be ended," I promised her.

"No," she said. "For Benjamin, it will never end. He has a fever for this fight."

"But his wife," I tried. "His child."

"That is you," she told me. "You are the one with the woman and, soon, the child. That is not enough for him. He burns for war."

I thought I knew my cousin. We'd worked so many years together building our home and the homes of our neighbors. We'd planned our lives together, the women we would wed and all the children we would have.

"He and Anawan are well matched," Wantonka pronounced.

We were alone. Oneka had left us to spend the night with Goulding. Together they had taken a cargo of fish, canvas and powder to the garrison at Mattapoisett, planning to spend the night before returning in the morning.

"The Sakonnet say the war has spread to the Abenaki in the north," Wantonka told me.

"Yes." My cousin had spoken of it.

"They say the white *francais* of Canada will also fight the English," she went on.

I knew what she was hinting at. Benjamin would leap at an opportunity to take a commission from the Puritan governor of Boston.

"I will not fight in northern Massachusetts," I promised her.

We were lying together now, our heads resting side by side in the cooling sand. Above us, the light had retreated before an advancing army of stars.

"And when he asks you?" Wantonka murmured.

"I will tell him no," I said.

"Because of me?"

"Because of you? No." Again, I laid my hand against her stomach. "Because of us."

In the morning, Church arrived as we'd expected, eager for another attempt into the swamps. With him, he brought six of the Sakonnet who had stood with us against Philip.

"Anawan has been seen near Taunton," he beamed.

Behind him, among the Sakonnet, I spotted Nompash's scowling face.

"Daniel," the Indian captain hailed me at once. "Speak to your cousin. Ask him why he wishes to throw away his life on this new fight."

Church laughed.

"Tell him he has already seen many great victories," Nompash pleaded. "Tell him Anawan will not be taken alive, that the braves who fight with him have nowhere left to run. They will die together as brothers and spill our blood with theirs."

Church's response was predictable.

"I place my faith and my destiny in the hands of the Almighty," he told the wary Indian. "He has seen fit to guide and protect me this far."

In the distance, I saw Alice linger near the entrance to her temporary home, reluctant to come closer, hanging back well out of earshot to avoid the hurt her husband's bravado caused her.

"When do you intend to march?" I asked, my eyes still fixed on my cousin's wife.

"Now," he answered at once. "Anawan is camped in Squannakonk. North of here is a man who will lead us."

"Certainly, you can linger one more day," I tried.

Church shook his head.

"Our enemy is far too clever," he said. "He is said to change his camp daily. If we don't go now, he will be gone."

Looking one final time, I saw that Alice was gone. She knew her husband as well as I. No one could change him once his mind was set.

"Gather your musket, powder and shot," my cousin barked. "With luck we'll return by morning."

I knew what Church was thinking. Squannakonk was less than ten miles distant. If we left now, we'd arrive in time for another night attack. With Wantonka's hand in mine, I led her from the others.

"He is a foolish man," I told her. "To leave his wife so soon again like this."

"It is his strength," she answered. "He springs like a cat. First in one place. Then another."

I knew what she meant. Bold and unpredictable, my cousin must have appeared to our enemy to be everywhere.

"You must go," Wantonka told me. "I will wait with Alice."

With a last squeeze of my hand, she turned and left me. Already, the others were moving at a trot, disappearing into the trees, following the northern path to Portsmouth. The corn was high, concealing all but the last Sakonnet warrior in line behind my cousin. Still, it took me nearly two miles to catch them. Never had I seen my cousin so determined. With his head down, ignoring any threat we might encounter, he drove us forward, not stopping until we reached the Taunton River. There, in a brush covered hollow dug into the embankment, we found an old Indian who, as Church had promised, agreed to lead us to Anawan's camp.

"He's seen it for himself," Nompash translated the old man's toothless garble. "He came from there this day."

With the old man now in the lead, my cousin grew restless.

"We have only a few hours more," he confided to me. "If we don't arrive before dark, I won't be able to scout the ground for our attack."

Soon, however, it became clear that the old man's lack of speed was more than compensated for by his keen knowledge of the land. In far less time than I would have expected, he stopped us at the edge of the Squannakonk swamp. Pointing to a stand of willow approximately half a mile ahead, he spoke once again to Nompash. This time, however, my cousin didn't bother waiting for the Sakonnet to translate. Instead, he nodded for me to accompany him forward.

Leaving the others behind, Church and I crept deeper into the swamp. Passing carefully among the willows, we spied a distant rock formation, so rugged and out of place in the gently contoured land, it appeared to have risen directly from the center of the earth. Standing roughly fifty feet high and several hundred feet in circumference, the formidable elevation confronted us with a face of shear granite that extended from its base nearly to its summit.

"That is where Anawan has built his camp," Church pointed to the foot of the towering wall of stone. "I'm certain he has chosen to keep that formidable precipice at his back."

As if to confirm my cousin's guess, smoke from the first of our enemy's cooking fires suddenly rose among the trees that clustered at the base of the steep rock face.

"If trouble comes," he whispered, "he will expect it from here."

He indicated the open ground that lay between us and the distant fires.

"That's why I will attack from there." Again he gestured toward the enormous granite face. "Where he will least expect it."

"But that cliff is impassable," I tried.

"I'm sure that's how it appears to Anawan," he answered.

And he turned and crept back to the rear without another look at the imposing rock obstacle he'd chosen to climb. His mind was made up. Daring the impossible had become commonplace for Church. Returning in silence to the others, he sketched the rock formation and the location of the Pokanoket camp.

"Anawan has been running and hiding for months," he told Nompash. "His men are weary. Their guard will be down."

Pointing to the shapes he'd drawn in the ground at the feet of the Sakonnet, my cousin next indicated the path we would follow to the rear of the granite escarpment.

"We will ascend to the summit," he instructed, "wait until they sleep, and then use rope and tree branches to lower ourselves into their camp."

Whether Church was brilliant or mad, none would dare question him now, not with the successes he'd had, not with his fierce eyes inflamed by the dying sun. Using the last of the daylight, my cousin quickly discovered a means to execute the first part of his plan. Behind the granite elevation, well out of hearing of the Pokanoket, Church located a foot path that would lead us comfortably to the top.

After gathering what rope we had, cutting stout willow branches, long and strong enough to bear a man's weight, we slipped quietly up the path. The September evening was cool. Our breath left silver clouds that glowed in the bright, three quarter moon. We'd done this before, I was thinking, many times. Yet I couldn't help wondering if experience would work to our advantage this time, as it had in the past. Or had Church and I used all the luck chance had granted us?

It didn't take long for us to reach the top. Once there, we fanned out along the rim of the wide granite cliff and gazed down on our enemy dozens of feet below. To my right were my cousin and three Sakonnet braves. To my left, Nompash lay beside four other Indian warriors. Below, I counted perhaps three or four dozen enemy gathered around the flames of a half dozen cooking fires.

Now we would wait, marking the minutes in heartbeats, any one of which might be our last. As my eyes adjusted to the uneven firelight, I was able to distinguish the features of the men grouped closest to us at the foot of the steep drop. Letting my glance drift from one to another, I caught my breath when I saw Anawan's craggy profile. Touching my cousin's arm, I quickly pointed out the Pokanoket captain.

"He's with his youngest son," Church whispered after looking where I'd indicated. "His last. And see there?"

My cousin then nodded toward the shadows further to the right of the fire where the Indians had stacked their muskets.

"They've separated themselves from their weapons," he panted.

Suddenly, the air shook with the thunder of fallen rock. At first I thought one of us had dislodged a stone and had my finger on my trigger at once.

"They pound corn for their meal," Church told me.

Again and again, the air around us echoed with the heavy thuds of the native mortar. Now my cousin was on his knees signaling Nompash and the others.

"We must strike now," he whispered breathlessly. "Their pounding will cover the sounds of our descent."

My heart raced faster than ever.

"If Daniel and I can drop on them before they reach their muskets," Church said, "we can finish this."

In an instant, his plan was formed. With our hatchets clamped firmly in one hand and a rope in the other, my cousin and I were soon lowered over the brink of the cliff, dropping toward the Indian fires as though into the mouth of Hell. When the two Sakonnet who were holding us reached the end of their ropes, they tied the remaining slack around their waists. Taking hold of the ends of the stout willow branches we'd brought with us from the base, each man was then lowered by another Sakonnet. In this way, two by two, with adjacent drop lines, our small army descended.

Except for the coarse rope tearing into my hand, the crackling fires below and the suffocating fear of falling, nothing else existed. I forgot my cousin, my enemy and the fierce grip I had on the war hatchet with which I intended to slay him.

I calculated we were within fifteen or twenty feet of the gravel piled at the foot of the cliff. A night breeze rose, disturbing the smoke cloud from Anawan's fire. Soon sparks filled the air around me, stinging my face and chest. Still, I dropped lower, feeling the heel of my moccasin strike ground at last.

I fought for my balance as small stones slid beneath me on the uneven slope. Then I saw Church rush past, the glinting blade of his war hatchet cutting the air. Ahead, a dark shape trembled, a crouched figure cowering under a blanket before the flickering fire. Suddenly, the hidden figure cried out. Anawan leapt from the shadows, tall as tree, directly before me.

"Stand fast," Church growled, "or I will kill your son."

At his feet, the cowering shape cried once again. Then folds of dark fabric parted and the face of a terrified young brave appeared from under the blanket. And in the instant that followed, our Sakkonet friends dropped from the sky, their muskets aimed smartly at Anawan and the others.

"It is Anawan we want," Church shouted to the stunned Pokanoket warriors. "Surrender and you go free. But if any resists, we kill all of you."

Once more, my cousin had landed us in a delicate position. With perhaps fifty men standing before us, there was no chance we could do as he'd boasted. To my right, the Indians' muskets were stacked and waiting. If they made a rush for their weapons, some would die, but not all.

"Do you wish to see your son slain?" Church asked, his raised hatchet ready to fall.

In the firelight, I saw the eyes of our enemy shift from Church to their weapons and back again, waiting, calculating. None moved. None seemed to even draw breath when I stepped to the pile of enemy weapons and, lowering my musket, gathered them in my arms. At that dangerous instant, I knew any one of them could fall on me and kill me with his knife. But somehow I continued moving, returning carefully to my cousin's side, depositing my precious load of weapons, two by two, at the feet of each of our Sakonnet. Only then did I dare draw a breath.

"Well done," Church whispered. "Now we have them."

With our enemy's weapons safely in hand, Church lowered his hatchet at last.

"What then is for supper?" he quipped.

And reaching a finger into a steaming stew pot, he took a taste.

"Taubut." Anawan flashed an unexpected grin. "It is good."

Producing a handful of salt from his pouch, Church sprinkled some into the beef and corn mixture. And then he and Anawan sat to eat, a signal to the others that our action was ended. Both sides breathed as one with relief. And soon Sakonnet mingled with Pokanoket. With warm greetings and even some laughter, enmity vanished and old friends became happily reacquainted.

"Your word is good, Benjamin," the old warrior spoke quietly, regarding the others joined in small groups around us. "My braves have been hopeful it would be you who would find us."

Even though Bradford and Moseley had disbanded their forces, memories of their vicious tactics lingered.

"I can offer them freedom," my cousin answered. "But I can make no such promise to you. The governor in Plymouth must decide your fate."

Nodding his great, shaggy head, Anawan then glanced across the fire at me.

"Daniel," he said. "When the others sleep, I will return those things I have promised to you."

Throughout the war, his father's brightly adorned story belt had traveled the same troubled paths as we.

"I can't take it from you," I told him. "It is for you and your son."

"My son is too young to carry it," the Indian answered. "And my head will soon be raised above the castle of the Plymouth governor."

"No," Church's voice boomed. "Winslow will spare you when I ask him to. You are a great warrior. I need you to help me in the north against the Abenaki."

I watched Anawan scoop more salted meat from the pot, marveling at the calmness with which he considered his own death. His arms bore the marks of many great battles. Some of his scars were older than me, I knew, earned in the service of Philip's father.

"I will give Daniel the belt of my family," he said with firmness. "And I will trust my spirit to the God who rules all."

Though I had no intention of keeping his story belt for myself, I chose to say nothing more to Anawan about his treasure. If he brought the belt forward, I would take it from him and carry it proudly to Plymouth, returning it to the Pokanoket captain when Church and I successfully gained his pardon. For now, I let the quiet of the night settle around us.

The moon had advanced high in the sky, illuminating the other Indians clustered in the shadows before me. Why didn't they run, I wondered? We were so few and they were many. Surely, they could overpower us in the dark if they chose. But these Pokanoket seemed as pleased as I that the war had ended between us. Perhaps this was all they'd desired, for the fighting to stop. And soon their voices had quieted so that only the crackling of the dying cooking fires could be heard. Then, one by one, they fell peacefully into their blankets and slept.

Even Church succumbed at last, slumping wordlessly forward over his folded arms, his musket forgotten, his breaths coming deep and long. Only Anawan and I remained awake, each too weary to speak, too wary to close his eyes. Slowly, painfully, the night passed. As the moon completed its climb and began its descent among the ocean of stars overhead, my eyes grew heavy, my breathing shallow, my mind numbed to every thought but that of keeping watch on my formidable prisoner.

In repose, however, Anawan seemed nothing like the great warrior who had stood beside Philip, scorching the frontier. Though his fierce eyes still glinted bright in the firelight, he sat with his large hands folded before him, still, resolved, like any father watching over his son. His shoulders were set, his head high, his focus on me. But he seemed as much at peace in surrender as the rest of his slumbering army.

I was thinking of the first time I'd seen the famous warrior. I realized now that I'd been just a boy, newly arrived with my cousin in Sakonnet when I'd seen this same man pass by me, large and silent, a hunter moving through the forests with the swiftness and stealth of any of its wildest creatures. Later, when the Pokanoket captain was fighting with Philip and rumored to be in every corner of the colony, hiding behind every tree, present at every battle, the image of the larger-than-life hunter, gliding swiftly through the forests, was the one that fixed in my mind. Now he was still, unmoving as the night air around us.

"Where is he?" Church suddenly barked, shaking me hard by the arm. "Anawan? Did you see him?"

I'd fallen asleep. Our fire had died. The moon had vanished behind a wall of clouds. And, in the place where Anawan had been, the emptiness was undisturbed.

XXXI

With little choice, Church and I waited, praying our prisoner would return. I had no idea how long I'd slept and hoped Anawan had only gone into the trees to relieve himself. With Benjamin at my side, I watched and listened. At every rustling of leaves or cracking of twigs I tightened my grip on my musket. But the darkness was impenetrable.

"There," my cousin whispered.

I looked where he pointed and saw nothing.

"He comes," Church breathed.

I blinked to clear my eyes. Then I heard a sound, the padding of feet on soft ground. And suddenly, the moon slid from its hiding place in the sky and Anawan was again standing before me.

From the big Indian's shoulder hung the treasured story belt, its shimmering wampum beads alive in the light of the moon. In his hands, he carried a basket of woven reeds. Kneeling before us, he removed the belt from his shoulder and handed it to me.

"Great captain," he then addressed Church. "You have killed Metacom and defeated his army. Now these belong to you."

The first item he pulled from the basket was a great red blanket embroidered with the shapes of the animals of the forests. Standing, he opened the blanket and laid it across my cousin's shoulders. Then he turned and produced two more elaborate wampum belts. Unfolded, each stretched nearly to the ground. Like the red blanket on Church's shoulders, each was adorned with images of the birds and beasts, the rivers and lakes, the stars and mountains that filled our lives.

"You don't have to do this," Church told him. "You surrendered honorably. You should keep your peoples' treasures."

I'd been thinking the same, that Anawan could have put up a terrible battle, perhaps killed us all. Instead he'd chosen to finish his fight peacefully. For that we owed him far more than these simple trinkets.

"It is the end of my people," he told us. "After this night, the Pokanoket have lost their right to these things. It is for the English to keep them now."

After delivering the last of his treasures to Church, the weary Indian sat once more. And in the silence that closed around us again, I felt the war's many dead, thousands of them, red and white, assemble to witness this.

"I fought great battles in the time of Massasoit," Anawan sighed. "Many times, against many tribes, the Pokanoket raised their war clubs in victory."

"But my heart was never in this fight with the English," he avowed. "It was the young braves who forced it. They were like dried sticks heaped on the fires of Metacom's anger. In time, there was no voice that could be heard above their shouts for war."

"Now they're all dead," he whispered. "Except for these few."

He waved his arm toward the sleeping prisoners gathered near us.

"But they are like me," he said. "Their time has passed."

Until dawn, he talked, about the times he'd seen. Some of the stories I'd heard. Many were new. All filled me, even in my weariness, with wonder at a people who once had been.

Then, at first light, we roused our sleeping troop and marched our prisoners to Taunton. From there, word was sent on to Plymouth requesting their pardon. While the Pokanoket were placed together in a blockhouse under the guard of the militia, Church and I at last were able to sleep.

Finding shelter in the meeting house, we fell into our blankets and didn't wake until the following day when the messenger returned from Governor Winslow. With him the rider carried pardon for all but Anawan. As Church had promised, our captives were free to return to Mount Hope while he and I escorted Anawan to his fate in Plymouth.

Though peace reigned, we traveled with caution. Even Anawan, cast wary eyes from side to side, saying nothing, expecting ambush even though there were no enemy left to trouble either of us. As we got closer to Plymouth, however, the silence of the empty forest was shattered by the joyous shouts and cries of the farmers and families who awaited us. Philip was dead. Anawan surrendered. For the first time in more than a year, the living could stop mourning their dead and celebrate survival.

Though a few dark looks were cast on the tall Indian who accompanied us, most of the English we encountered seemed too relieved to scorn their former neighbor. Many simply stared in stunned silence at the sight of the humbled warrior who had terrorized their nights and days since the outbreak of the war.

After delivering our prisoner to the custody of the sentries at the town's outermost stockade, Church and I withdrew to the quiet of the forest again.

"I must go at once to Boston," my cousin told me. "I will leave this matter of our prisoner for you to resolve with the governor while I secure a commission to march north."

I touched the story belt knotted beneath my shirt, considering my promise to keep its owner safe.

"Winslow is a hard man," I reminded Church. "He did much to start this war. Now that it's ended, he'll be reluctant to leave any man alive who might remember that."

Church stroked the stubble on his chin.

"It's a heavy business, I agree," he answered. "There are many here, besides the governor, who wish to see Anawan's head on a pike."

"Stay here, then," I pleaded. "The Plymouth elders might listen to you, but they will never heed me."

"If I don't go directly to Boston, I'll lose my commission," he insisted.

"And if you do go," I answered, "there will be none but me to speak for Anawan."

But I could see my cousin already had one foot forward, already started north.

"Anawan is far more valuable alive than dead," he said. "They will see that. Make them see that." And then he was gone, vanished into the cool pine shadows so suddenly and silently it was as if he'd never been with me at all.

Returning to the Plymouth meeting house, I took it as a bad omen that the first person I saw among the gathered court attendees was Samuel Moseley. Not one to miss a chance to draw more Indian blood, the hateful former commander was among the handful of Winslow's staff who would decide my prisoner's fate. I could tell from his disdainful look that he intended to argue forcefully against me.

"And your cousin?" the governor asked when I stood before him with the others.

"Gone to Boston," I answered firmly.

After so many months in the forests, the air in the crowded meeting house was suffocating, a fitting image, Anawan might have told me, for the stifling English presence in his land.

"Now that we have delivered Anawan to you," I told them, "the frontier is clear of all enemy."

As always, Winslow refused to relax the stern look with which he masked his boyish face.

"With your permission," I continued, "Benjamin will take Anawan with him to hunt the last of the rebels who have taken refuge with the Abenaki of the north."

"Indeed, not!" Moseley bellowed, his voice echoing in the smoke blackened rafters. "I will see to it myself that his head will sit upon the highest palisade before this day is done."

Next to the coarse pirate, Major Bradford shuffled his heavy boots.

"It will set a dangerous precedent," the old officer spoke, "to let any of the rebel leaders live. Anawan has the blood of many brothers and sisters of our colony on his hands. To let him go unpunished will desecrate the memory of those poor souls."

"You wouldn't speak like this if my cousin were here," I argued.

"If your cousin felt as strongly as you say he does," Winslow answered, "he would have appeared before this court himself."

"He cannot, sir," I tried. "I've explained this to you already."

"Let me ask this man a question." Moseley bared his tobacco stained teeth at me. "Where were you this past winter when we were defending the frontier against the likes of Anawan?"

"You know my story." I spoke directly to Winslow, not wishing to acknowledge the pirate commander. "I was a prisoner of the Nipmuc at Menemesset and Wachusetts."

"Yet you return here among us now," Moseley barked, "bringing an Indian squaw as your wife, speaking for a savage who should be your enemy."

Suddenly, I was overwhelmed with fatigue. I had all I could do to remain standing and at last settled heavily onto one of the meeting house benches. I wanted to argue. But even if I had the energy to confront them all, I knew in my heart they were right. Anawan had the blood of many English on his hands. He'd brought this on himself.

"Enough," Winslow said. "We all know Daniel's story. He recovered Mary Rowlandson and her children from captivity. He tracked and captured Canonchet, killed Philip himself. He may have better perspective than any of us."

Stepping close, the governor placed his hand on my shoulder. I wasn't used to such solicitousness from any of them and briefly shivered at his touch.

"You've seen both sides of this fight," the governor said. "You know what Anawan has done, both good and bad. Forget your cousin's needs. Forget your Christian sympathies. Given what you've seen these past months, what do you believe our enemy deserves?"

Behind me, I felt the presence of others crowding into the meeting house to hear the court's judgment. The air grew even more stifling as I struggled to reckon with Winslow's request. It was a heavier choice than I'd thought. As Anawan's advocate and champion, my role had been straightforward. I wanted no one else to die, on either side. Enough of my own and my enemy had been slain already.

But by making me my prisoner's judge, Winslow had complicated my task immeasurably. Rather than the propriety of taking another life, I had now to consider the appropriate punishment for a man who had taken many lives himself. I considered my missive from Church, the good Anawan had done and his value to my cousin's future campaigns. Then I disregarded all factors but one.

"The appropriate punishment for what he's done?" I stopped to take a stuttering breath.

Moseley was about to intercede. He'd turned his scowling face to Winslow when my mind blanked to all but a solitary image from the very first day of the war. In a single clear and terrifying flash of recollection, I saw those scalped and severed heads impaled on spiked poles along the river south of Swansea.

"For what he's done," I repeated, the wide eyes of those horror stricken dead souls as vivid in my mind as the day I'd first seen them. "His punishment should be death."

These weren't my words, not exclusively, but the judgment of the fallen. With a stern faced nod from each of the others, Anawan's fate was decided. In a stroke, the last, most storied of Philip's outlaw warriors was condemned. And because of my role in the judgment, I was condemned also, to carry his family's belt and its history as reminder of what I'd done.

I chose not to remain in Plymouth any longer that day. My cousin would discover Anawan's fate when he returned. He'd see the Indian's bloodied head fixed to a sharpened stake atop the palisades of the foremost Plymouth garrison and learn of my role in his execution. Guessing from my departure that I'd had no interest in joining him north, he'd not follow me home. Instead, he'd leave Wantonka and me to comfort his wife and child while he followed war's drama to its newest theater.

I didn't hurry on my return home. Instead, I took my time to taste the air and breathe the fragrance of the new peace. Despite the difficult choice I'd made, perhaps because of it, I felt light and free. And with each step my mind slowly emptied itself of the dark visions of the war until, for the first time in more than a year, the promise of my future presented itself in images more vivid than any of the horrors of my past.